Murder Among Us

Books by Jonnie Jacobs

The Kate Austen Mysteries

Murder Among Neighbors
Murder Among Friends
Murder Among Us

The Kali O'Brien Mysteries

Shadow of Doubt
Evidence of Guilt

Published by Kensington Books

Murder Among Us

A Kate Austen Mystery

JONNIE JACOBS

KENSINGTON BOOKS
http://www.kensingtonbooks.com

KENSINGTON BOOKS are published by

Kensington Publishing Corp.
850 Third Avenue
New York, NY 10022

Library of Congress Card Catalog Number: 97-073786
ISBN 1-57566-276-0

First Kensington Hardcover Printing: April, 1998
10 9 8 7 6 5 4 3 2 1

Printed in the United States of America

For Laura and Vincent Jacobs,
the nicest in-laws I could ask for.

Prologue

*O*rphaned.

The girl rolled the word around in her mind. It sounded like something out of a Dickens novel. Like she was some poor, rag-bedecked child of the slums, not the daughter of a prominent network newscaster.

But here she was, fifteen years old, raw with grieving over her mother's death—and utterly alone. She'd been spared the orphanage at least, but she was afraid the alternative would prove just as bad.

The girl glanced at the lawyer. He sat sideways in his chair, fingers steepled at his chin.

"Are you listening to me, Julie? Do you understand what's been decided?" His voice was as flat and dry as summer asphalt.

Julie nodded. She kept her shoulders square, her spine erect, her chin firm. Inside, the pain and loneliness churned.

"Your mother's sister and her husband live in California, near San Francisco. They've agreed to take you in."

"Half sister," Julie said.

The lawyer frowned, removed his reading glasses, and cleaned them with his handkerchief. He wasn't interested in splitting hairs. "As far as I've been able to determine, there isn't anyone else."

Aunt Patricia and Uncle Walt. Julie had only the faintest recollection of them. A stern man. A woman whose face wore the look of immutable disapproval and was otherwise lifeless as straw.

"I assume this arrangement is acceptable to you," the lawyer said. It wasn't a question.

His voice droned on but Julie had stopped listening. She was thinking about her plan. Her secret.

A quest conceived one rainy afternoon late last winter. It had begun with a simple "*what if?*," and then lodged immediately in her breast like a ray of warm sunshine.

And now it had taken on new importance.

1

I could have said no. In fact, I should have said no. I knew that the moment I found myself agreeing to her visit. But it's not easy to refuse your mother-in-law, especially when she plays the grandchild card.

"I haven't seen Anna since last Christmas," she'd wailed, bellowing into the phone as though to propel her voice, by volume alone, all the way from Florida to California. "I tried to get you to come here over the summer, remember. Only you couldn't find the time, so now I'm coming to you. You're not going to deny your daughter a chance to know her own grandmother, are you?"

I assured her that wasn't my intention, but I did point out she might be more comfortable in a hotel than with us.

"Nonsense," Faye said. "I'll be perfectly fine staying with you. No need to go to any trouble, I can make myself at home almost anywhere."

That was partially what worried me.

It wasn't that Faye Austen was particularly difficult, as mothers-in-law go. And she doted on Anna. But the house was tight and cramped, even for the four of us who regularly inhabited it—a population, I reminded her, that currently included a man other than her son Andy. This was a detail that seemed to elude her. Or maybe she simply chose to ignore it.

Now, as I pulled the comforter up close under my chin, warding off the brisk October morning, I kicked myself once again for not having stood firm. I'd managed to get through the first night of her visit with the help of several glasses of zinfindel. An occurrence that Faye had noted with raised brows and starchy silence. Would I make it through the remaining nine? Certainly not without help, I decided. I made a mental note to stop by the store and pick up more wine. Maybe even a bottle of good champagne to share with Michael when Faye departed.

Michael. That was the hardest part. My right foot drifted to the empty space in the bed beside me. The space occupied for the last five months by Michael's lovely, warm body.

His moving out for the week made no sense to me at all, but Michael had been adamant. "I'd be uncomfortable," he said.

"But this is your home now."

"The last thing I want is to be stumbling around the kitchen in my pajamas making small talk to Andy's mother."

Since Michael doesn't wear pajamas, his argument was flawed from the start, but he had made up his mind. Nothing I said (and I said plenty) persuaded him to change it.

I rolled onto my side and punched the pillow in frustration. If only I'd stood my ground with Faye, insisted that she stay in a hotel. It seemed so easy in retrospect.

The story of my life.

At the other end of the house, the water pipes thunked, signaling the end of Libby's shower. That was another situation that seemed clearer with the benefit of hindsight.

It had started as a temporary arrangement early last spring, a favor to a friend. But temporary is a relative concept, and it now looked as though Libby would be with me until she finished high school. Although I was genuinely fond of Libby and had come to think of her as family, I hadn't, at the time, given due regard to the repercussions of living with a teenager. Particularly as they affected an impressionable six-year-old.

Finally, the bathroom door creaked open and Libby padded down the hall to Anna's room, which the two of them were sharing during Faye's visit. I hugged the comforter for a moment longer, then forced myself out of bed. No time this morning to wait for the steam to clear and the hot water tank to refill. Friday was one of my teaching days.

Not that much teaching went on in beginning high school art, dubbed by the students *Art for the Artistically Challenged.* The class was required for those who chose not to take the more rigorous course in drawing and design, but it was offered on a pass/fail basis with the understanding that attendance in a wakeful state practically guaranteed a pass.

From my perspective, this was a win/win arrangement. The students got class credit and I got a regular, though paltry, paycheck. My soon to be ex-husband, Andy, had certain virtues, but fiscal dependability was not one of them.

My shower was quick, my attempt at makeup even quicker. Fifteen minutes later I was pouring milk on Anna's cereal, trying to decide whether it would be wise to point out to her that orange and green pinstripe leggings were not usually paired with a purple print top.

"Where's Grandma?" she asked, kicking the table with her foot.

"In bed." Where I hoped she would remain until I was out of the house for the day.

"She promised me pancakes this morning."

"Grandma's tired after her long trip," I explained. "And she's still on East Coast time." As soon as I'd said it, I realized that I had things backwards. But Anna nodded wisely. She found the idea of time zones fascinating. I think she confused them with time travel.

"Tomorrow," I told her. "We'll all have breakfast together and we'll have pancakes."

"Even Daddy."

"I don't think Daddy will be here for breakfast."

Anna raised her chin. "Grandma said so."

"She did?"

My daughter nodded with authority.

"She gets things mixed up sometimes," I explained.

I was sure Faye saw Michael's absence as a promising sign, even though I'd taken care to point out that it was only temporary, and had been occasioned by nothing other than our concern for her comfort. Faye still clung to the hope that Andy and I were simply going through "a rough phase" that would eventually pass.

As I was pouring my own bowl of cereal, Libby made a pass through the kitchen, picking up a Coke and a handful of pretzels on the way. "I'm going in early. There's a newspaper staff meeting before school. And don't count on me for dinner. I'll get something to eat at the football game."

"You'll be careful?"

"It's a football game, Kate. There'll be hundreds of people around."

"Just make sure you don't wander off anywhere alone. Remember, they haven't caught that guy yet."

Libby flashed me an exasperated smile, swung her backpack over her shoulder, then nodded at Anna's attire. "Rad-looking outfit," she said, giving Anna's nose an affectionate tweak.

In between mouthfuls of corn flakes, I put the milk back in the fridge and started on Anna's lunch.

"Can I have pretzels and a Coke?" she asked.

"For breakfast? No way."

"Lunch then."

"Sorry kiddo. That's hardly nutritious."

"But Libby—"

"Libby's sixteen and you're six. There's a big difference." Though not as big as I would have liked. Under Libby's tutelage, Anna was whittling away at those ten years with unsettling zeal.

By the time I turned around again, Anna had fed her cereal to Max, who was lapping the remaining drops of milk from the floor. Doggy heaven. I was glad Faye was still in bed.

"Anna Austen," my mother-in-law called sharply from the doorway. "We do not let animals eat from our dishes."

I turned abruptly. "I thought you were still asleep."

"I'm afraid not." Faye's thinning gray curls had flattened considerably since her arrival yesterday afternoon, giving her a somewhat moth-eaten appearance. "In fact, I hardly slept at all. I'm accustomed to a firmer mattress."

Her tone was matter-of-fact, but I felt a reprimand all the same. "Why don't you try my bed tonight, see if that's better."

Faye brushed the air with her plump hand. "Don't be silly. I can manage." Emphasis on the last word. She planted a kiss on Anna's head. "How's my grandbaby?"

"I'm not a baby."

"No, of course you're not. But a grandbaby's something different."

I handed her a cup of coffee. "Anna and I are going to have to run off. Help yourself to anything you want. Cereal's in the cupboard and there's bread for toast on the counter. Jam's in the fridge."

"Don't worry about me. I never eat much anyway."

This from a woman who'd eaten as much of last night's meatloaf as the rest of us combined.

When I arrived at my classroom, my star pupil, Julie Harmon, was leaning against the wall, waiting for me to open the door.

"Good morning," I said, sounding to my own ears so teacherly it brought me up short. I'd never been fond of school in my youth, but now that I was on the other side of the desk I found I was enjoying it.

Julie raised her eyes and gave me a smile that barely touched the corners of her mouth. She was a tall girl with cornflower-blue eyes and straight blond hair that brushed her shoulders. She had a kind of regal bearing and grace that most of us never achieve, even in maturity. Her classmates found her standoffish. A number of the teachers agreed. For myself, I was inclined to see Julie's reserve as a sign of uneasiness rather than disdain.

"I thought there was a meeting of the newspaper staff this morning," I said.

"There was." Her voice was soft and without inflection.

"It's over?"

She shrugged. "I didn't go."

I unlocked the door and we moved inside.

Julie stood for a moment near the front of the room looking uncertain. Finally, she turned in my direction. "Can I work more on that charcoal drawing we did the other day?"

"Sure. You know where the unfinished pieces are, in the right-hand closet at the back."

Julie was the only one of my students with any real talent. She actually belonged in the advanced course, but since she'd enrolled in school after the deadline, her class schedule had been determined as much by available space as suitable placement.

She glanced toward the back of the room but showed no inclination of retrieving the sketch. Instead, she hovered around my desk, fingering the strap of her backpack. Twice, she cleared her throat as if to speak.

"You have a question?" I asked.

She tugged harder at the strap, clamped her lips together, and studied her feet.

From the look on her face, I thought it might be more than a question. "You want to talk?"

Julie's shoulders rose and then fell in an almost imperceptible shrug. I took a seat at one of the desks and motioned for her to join me. "What's on your mind? You seem bothered by something."

"You won't tell anyone, will you?"

"It depends. If you're in trouble—"

Just then Mario Sanchez appeared at the door, slouching against the frame as if he owned the place. "Mornin', Mizz Austen," he said, then crinked his neck in Julie's direction, beckoning her.

She chewed on her lower lip for a moment before heading for the door. "Guess I'll work on that drawing some other time," she told me. "Thanks, though."

"Anytime."

I'd have to ask Libby if Mario and Julie were an item. I hadn't seen them together before, but I'd learned that romantic pairings among teens were as ever-changing as the ocean. Still, it would be an odd match.

Five minutes later, on my way to the office, I passed Julie and Mario in the breezeway. Mario leaned against the gray stucco exterior, bracing his wiry frame with his elbow. His voice was low and intent, his jaw tight. Julie, who was several inches taller, stood facing him, arms crossed, face determined. If they saw me, they didn't acknowledge it.

I picked up my mail and the daily stack of announcements, grabbed a cup of coffee from the faculty lounge, and was headed back to my classroom when Yvonne Burton, who teaches biology, beckoned me into the science lab.

"You haven't forgotten the ten dollars, have you?"

"Ten ..."

"For Sarah's baby gift."

I offered an apologetic smile, set my coffee on the table, and reached into my purse for the money. "Sorry."

Sarah's unexpected maternity leave was the reason I was now employed at the high school. Two days into the fall semester, she'd received a phone call from the adoption agency. Twenty-four hours later, she was a mother—and her art students were without a teacher for the semester.

Yvonne stuck the two fives I gave her into an envelope and added my name to the list of contributors on the front. Like the rest of her, Yvonne's hands were small and delicate. With her olive complexion and cap of jet-black hair, she looked like an exotic, handcrafted doll.

"Any luck finding a painting for our front hallway?" she asked, sticking the envelope in her bottom desk drawer.

Art consultant was a career I'd stumbled into a year earlier when the gallery where I was working closed. Yvonne and her husband, Steve, were clients of mine, and well enough off that they could afford to select artwork based on what they liked rather than what fit their budget—a situation that was nice for both of us.

"The more I think about it," Yvonne continued, "the more I like your idea of something abstract. But subtle. We want our friends to know that it's *art*, not some class project Skye brought home." She smiled. "That's no reflection on your teaching, Kate. It's just that squares of black and red aren't what I have in mind for the hallway."

They weren't what I'd had in mind when I asked the class to sketch an everyday object, either. But when I told Skye I didn't want to see another horse, she'd settled on a checkerboard.

"I've got my eye on a couple of things," I told Yvonne, "but I'm not sure any of them are right."

"No rush. I don't want to settle for something that's a compromise."

I picked up my coffee and turned to leave, then stopped

in my tracks. A shiver worked its way down my spine. Harvey, the lab skeleton, was grinning at me from under a hooded black cape. A scythe had been wired to his right hand, a knife to his left.

"I see you've decked Harvey out for Halloween," I told her, stepping back.

"This wasn't my doing. If I had to guess, I'd bet it was someone from my senior physiology class. There are a couple of real pranksters in there."

"They've got a macabre sense of humor."

"That's what I thought, too. But then I figured maybe I was overreacting, letting what happened in the park get to me."

This was common shorthand for the murder of a twenty-year-old Berkeley coed whose body had been found two weeks earlier near the duck pond in Walnut Hills' Reservoir Park. With unspoken accord, we'd somehow adopted the manner of speaking obliquely, as if by avoiding the word "murder," we could avoid the fact itself.

Not that we'd talked of much else since it happened. Walnut Hills is a quiet, comfortable suburb whose residents are more at home talking golf handicaps and bond yields than crime. And while this wasn't the first homicide in the town's history, it was one of the most unsettling because it had the earmarks of big-city depravity. A young woman had been strangled to death, her body discarded with indifference, like the used tissues and bottle caps that littered the shore. Her blond hair had been shorn on one side, her toenails painted with blood-red polish.

"I think it's gotten to all of us," I told Yvonne.

"Except certain high school seniors." She gestured toward Harvey.

The notion of a madman loose on our streets had shaken the town in ways too numerous to name. It wasn't just that we looked over our shoulders as we left the grocery and jogged only with a friend, even in daylight. There was a subtler, more unnerving change as well, a sense of undefined menace that hovered continually somewhere in the back of our minds.

The killer shadowed us all.

I took another look at Harvey and met his ghoulish grin with one of my own. "Maybe the kids have the right approach, after all. Thumb your nose at the dark forces and ward off evil with a little humor."

"I'm not sure," Yvonne said, "that I consider this humor."

The warning bell rang and I headed back to my classroom. Julie was once again waiting by the door, along with half a dozen of her classmates. As the others settled into their seats, I took Julie aside.

"I have some time after class if you want to talk."

She shrugged. "It's nothing important."

"It doesn't have to be important."

Julie's hair fell across her face, obscuring her expression. But she nodded. "Thanks. I'd like that."

After I'd taken roll and read the morning's announcements, I started the class on their self-portraits. With back-to-school night approaching, I thought it would be fun for parents to pick out their own child. I'd stolen the idea from Anna's kindergarten teacher, I admit, but I thought it would work just as well for older students. It also tied in nicely with last week's exercise on facial drawing and representational portraits.

I saw a number of eyes glaze over while I gave instructions. Julie stared out the window, motionless as a statue.

Once I let them get to work, however, the energy level picked up. I'd learned, early on, that with teenagers, artistic expression is stymied unless accompanied by a certain level of verbal expression. As long as the conversations were good-natured and not too loud, I didn't mind.

While they worked, I walked around the room answering questions and offering help when needed. A couple of the female students took the assignment quite literally. They pulled out mirrors to study the planes of their faces, the width of their eyes and, I imagine, the state of their makeup. Others decided to have fun with the assignment. Grant depicted himself on a surfboard atop a giant wave, Michelle behind the wheel of her dream car, and Skye, predictably, shared the page with her horse.

Julie was back to staring out the window by the time I made it to her seat. Her sketch occupied only a small part of the page. She'd drawn the top half of her body, positioning it in the lower-right-hand corner so that her lower torso disappeared into space. Her front-button blouse, hoop earrings, and wispy, shoulder-length hair were drawn with close attention to detail. She'd begun the nose, but the face was otherwise featureless.

"Why don't you finish it," I suggested. "You've done a wonderful job so far."

Julie studied the picture a moment. "It is finished," she said, meeting my eyes with a look of defiance.

Just then Mr. Combs, the principal, stuck his head into the room.

"Mrs. Austen," he said without preamble. "I'd like a word with you after class."

"Sure."

"My office." He nodded, without looking at me, and was gone.

Skye made a face—pantomimed shock—but it was veiled in smugness. "Not to worry you or anything, but Mr. Combs must be pretty upset. He wouldn't come barging into class like that if he weren't."

"He didn't exactly come barging in," I replied, irked by her tone. Skye often used her mother's position on the faculty to intimate inside knowledge. In much the same way, she liked to flaunt her stepfather's status as judge. Usually, I ignored it. What bothered me this time was that I had the sinking feeling she just might be right.

2

"You wanted to see me?" I asked.

Combs looked up from his impressively neat desk and offered me the briefest of smiles. Not a good sign.

"Have a seat," he said solemnly.

None of the usual chitchat. That wasn't a good sign either.

Aaron Combs had once played professional football. I imagine he didn't play very often, or very well, which was why he had become a physical education teacher, a position he'd left only last year in order to take the helm at Walnut Hills High. He was not a tall man, but he was thickly built and surprisingly solid for a man nearing fifty.

He folded his hands on his desk, thumb pressing thumb. "I'm afraid I've received a complaint."

"About me?"

He nodded. "Well, not you so much as your teaching."

I swallowed a gulp of air. So much for the steady paycheck.

Combs did not look happy. He cleared his throat.

"Something about presenting pornography to the students."

"What?" My jaw dropped open in surprise. "Where'd you get *that* idea?"

"You deny it?"

"Of course I deny it. It's not true."

"No full-color slides of nude men and women?"

I shook my head in disbelief.

"No magazines filled with partially clad bodies?"

"Absolutely not."

Combs relaxed visibly. "Well, that's a relief. Not that I ever really thought there was any truth to the accusations. But these days, one never knows."

Apparently not. "What's this about, anyway?"

"I got a call from the family of one of your students. We have to take these things seriously, of course, but given the source, I must say I wasn't overly concerned."

There was, I noticed, no mention of my own sterling character and reputation as a mitigating force.

"They are opinionated, intolerant people," Combs continued. "Always disgruntled about something. Had a son who was a student here not too long ago. I thought we'd seen the end of them when he graduated."

"Which family is it?" I asked.

Combs leaned back in the chair, arms crossed behind his head. His customary affable mood was restored. "Their name is Shepherd. Julie Harmon is the girl. She's Mrs. Shepherd's niece. Julie's been living with them since last summer when her mother died."

I nodded. Julie's mother, well-known newscaster Leslie Harmon, had been killed in a boating accident last July. Julie had come to Walnut Hills to live with the Shepherds, her only blood relatives. According to Libby, it was not a good match.

"Why would they accuse me of something like that?" I asked. "I can't believe it came from Julie. She's a talented artist and she seems to enjoy the class."

Combs shrugged, clearly happy to have the crisis averted. "As I said, they're difficult people. The kind who are easily outraged. Who knows why they decided to vent their irritation on you?" He stood and smiled apologetically. "Anyway, I'm glad I can assure them you weren't corrupting our youth with pictures of bodies in the altogether."

I reached for my purse and stood, also. Then I had a horrible thought. "Wait a minute. Maybe I was."

Combs raised a bushy brow. The lines in his face deepened. "What do you mean, 'maybe I was'?"

"Not corrupting them, I don't mean that."

"What *do* you mean, then?"

"My art history lectures. On Wednesdays, instead of using the whole period for studio work, I give the class kind of a thumbnail survey of Western art."

I could tell from his puzzled expression that physical education majors didn't delve much into either history or art.

"Greek statues . . ." I explained. "Bosch, El Greco, Michelangelo." I pulled up names of artists I thought might have sparked the Shepherds' indignation. "The bodies are often unclothed."

Combs sank back into his chair. His face was glum. "So there are bared breasts and, uh . . . genitalia?"

"Sometimes. Other times it's fig leaves."

Not a flicker of a smile.

"It's not like that's all we deal with, though. And these are classic works of art we're talking about."

Combs gave me that look again, pressed his fingers to his temples. "Oh my."

"There's nothing degenerate or lewd about them. Macy's lingerie ads are more suggestive than any of the stuff I've shown."

"Why don't you bring me some examples so I can see what we're talking about. I suppose I'll have to have a conference with the Shepherds and explain." He sighed. "There are times I wish I'd never moved into administration."

I nodded sympathetically. I certainly knew about the clarity of hindsight.

As I left Combs's office, I almost collided with Marvin Melville, who was getting ready to knock on the door. Marvy Marvin, as he was sometimes referred to by the younger female members of the faculty, was the other teacher new to the school that year. He taught English and was advisor for the school newspaper.

Marvin looked at me in surprise. "Hi, Kate. What kind of mood is His Highness in?"

"Not the best. Why?"

He groaned, hunched his shoulders. Despite an athletic build and a disarming smile, Marvin often seemed unsure of himself. "I've got to check with Combs about this editorial the kids want to run. Condoms at school, of all things. Why can't they stick to the simple stuff like too much homework and lousy food service?"

"They're trying to put out a newspaper that's relevant."

He jangled the change in his pocket. "Relevant," he grumbled. "The word is not synonymous with controversial."

*   *   *

During passing period, I looked for Julie Harmon. In my panic at being summoned to Combs's office, I'd neglected to touch base with her after class. When I couldn't find her, I headed for the teachers' lounge. I'd offer my apologies tomorrow, and make sure we found time to talk.

Officially, I was free for the day. I would have gone home except for the fact that Faye was there. Instead, I called Michael.

He answered with unusual abruptness. "Lieutenant Stone here."

"Hi, it's me."

The tone softened, but his manner was still formal. "Hello, Kate." He was obviously not alone.

"Do you have time for lunch?"

He hesitated. "What did you have in mind, exactly?"

In the early stages of our togetherness, lunch often had less to do with food than passion. Those short midday breaks at Michael's apartment were too precious to be squandered on meals. Since Michael had moved in last spring, the need to carve out time wasn't as pressing. Still, we'd been known to sneak home in the middle of the day because it was the only time we could count on having the house to ourselves.

"Just food," I said with a twinge of regret. Faye's presence prevented anything else.

"Good. I'm kind of pressed for time."

"What a romantic response."

"You want romance, you shouldn't have invited your mother-in-law." But his tone was teasing. Altogether different than it had been when we'd first had this conversation.

"Thanks," I said softly.

"For what? Agreeing to have lunch with you?"

"For not staying mad."

I stopped by the deli to pick up soft drinks and sandwiches, then drove to the station house. The early-morning chill had vanished, but the sky was still gray. A cool wind scattered the fallen leaves and whipped my hair into my eyes.

Michael was on the phone when I arrived at the station. I knocked on the open door and held up the deli bag. He nodded and gestured to the metal frame chair across from his desk. I slipped in and took a seat.

The sight of him still brought a tingle to my skin, just as it had the first time I laid eyes on him. His dark hair was a little grayer now, though still longer than regulation dictated. And while he claimed to have put on a few pounds, you couldn't tell it to look at him.

Michael frowned into the phone. "Hmm, I see." He spoke without a lot of enthusiasm. "And what is it, exactly, that you see in these visions?"

He listened with studied silence.

"A human figure, uh-huh. In the shadows. Something small and dark in his hand. I see. Anything more?"

Michael looked at me and smiled. "No, that won't be necessary. Yes, do let us know if more details come to you. And yes, I have your number."

He hung up and grabbed his coat. "Let's get out of here."

With his hand on the small of my back, he guided me through the tight maze of desks out front.

"What was that about?" I asked, once we were outside.

"A psychic, or so she says. The woman had a dream about the murder. Claims the dead sometimes reach out to her in her sleep, tell her things they want passed on to the world of the living."

"You're not a believer?"

Michael opened the door of his standard-issue Ford and tossed an empty McDonald's box into the back. "What she saw in this vision of hers was a shadowy male figure strangle a slender young blond woman and bury her body under a pile of leaves. Anyone who'd watched the news or read a paper in the last couple of weeks could have done as much."

We drove out to Reservoir Park and pulled into a spot overlooking the lake. Because of an early frost, the foliage had already begun to turn. Among the evergreen oaks and pines were clusters of yellow and scarlet, dotting the hillside like bonfires. To our right, in the reeds along the lake, a lone fisherman sat patiently waiting for a bite. A flock of geese flew overhead.

"Is this a working lunch?" I asked.

"Sorry. You want to go someplace else?"

I shook my head. "It's beautiful here. Especially this time of year. Before the murder, I started a sketch from that spot over there by the boathouse. But I haven't been back to finish it."

I wasn't the only one who'd stayed away. The place seemed oddly deserted, even for an overcast autumn day.

Michael unwrapped the sandwich I handed him, then gazed out over the smooth, dark surface of the water to the marsh on the western shore. "I keep thinking if I come here often enough maybe some key piece of the puzzle will fall into place, some small detail that I've overlooked. Every day that goes by, our chance of breaking this thing grows less."

"I take it there've been no new developments?"

"Nada. We know Cindy was killed here, not elsewhere. But whether she came with her killer or alone, or was brought here against her will, is anybody's guess. No sign of a struggle, though. According to Cindy's roommate she was cautious, especially at night. She doesn't think it likely Cindy came here alone."

"But her car was here."

He nodded. "The roommate says this wasn't a place Cindy frequented. In fact, she'd never heard Cindy mention the park."

I let him talk, even though I'd heard it all before. I liked the fact that Michael shared his work, let me listen in on his thoughts. There was an intimacy about these lopsided discussions I found touching.

"Cindy was last seen leaving the video store in Berkeley where she worked. That was about five-thirty. It wouldn't have been dark yet, but this time of year the sky is gray by then, the temperature chilly. And she didn't have a jacket with her. I don't think she was planning to spend much time outdoors."

Yet she'd wound up thirty miles away in a Walnut Hills park that was closed to cars after sunset. "Would she have offered a ride to a stranger?" I asked.

Michael shrugged. "Not according to her roommate. But they'd only known each other for a couple of months. Cindy was from Philadelphia, found her roommate through an ad in the paper. Philadelphia detectives have been talking to friends and family back there. Unfortunately, they haven't turned up much that's useful."

"Did you ever reach her boyfriend?"

"Yeah. He's an engineering student at Cal. Pulled an all-nighter with a couple of friends studying for an exam. I don't think he's involved."

"How about other friends?"

"Mostly from the drama and production department. That was her major. They say the same things as the roommate. Cindy Purcell was easy-going and well liked."

Michael finished off his sandwich and took a swig of Coke. I offered him the untouched half of my own turkey on whole wheat.

"You really don't want it?"

I shook my head. Murder-talk had untested potential as an appetite suppressant.

"It's the weird stuff, though," Michael said, "that makes me think there's got to be some angle we're missing."

The weird stuff. It gave Michael hope, the thread by which he might unravel the crime. It gave me the creeps.

The picture of Cindy Purcell that had run in the paper was her high school graduation photo. She was attractive, without being actually pretty. Square face, full cheeks, a thin, straight mouth that made her expression appear somewhat stiff, despite the smile.

The pictures from the crime scene were of a different nature. Cindy's face had been blackened with dirt. Her shoes had been removed, her toenails painted a garish blood-red, her feet encased in plastic wrap. And on one side of her head the blond, shoulder-length hair had been cropped close to her scalp. She lay in a bed of leaves, arms outstretched, feet together, like Jesus on the cross. A small, plastic skeleton was at her side.

"Of course, her purse was taken," Michael continued, "so robbery might have been the motive, and this other stuff just an afterthought."

"Seems like an awful lot of work for someone who could just as easily snatch a purse and run off."

Michael nodded. "That's my take on it, too." He crumpled the paper wrap from the sandwich and dropped it into the deli bag, then tossed the whole thing onto the backseat.

"How are you making out with the senior Mrs. Austen?" he asked, after a moment.

"It's just been last evening and this morning. How about you? Is Don's sofa as lumpy as he said it was?"

"Worse. My back feels as though I was tackled by the Incredible Hulk."

I reached for his hand and traced the lines of his palm with my finger. "It's not too late to change your mind and move back in. Faye won't bite. She even asked about you."

"I bet. And I can well imagine the unspoken agenda behind the words."

"She's going to get the wrong idea with your not being there at all."

Michael leaned across the gear shift and kissed me lightly. "I'll come by some evening to beat my chest and set the record straight."

"It would be easier to simply move back."

"No," he said grimly, "it would not."

3

I managed to delay my return home until after I'd picked up Anna from school. I figured there was strength in numbers, if only because Anna's presence seemed to diffuse the tension.

The drone of the television was audible as we came up the front walk. I couldn't make out the words, but the cadence of the dialogue made me think it was probably one of the afternoon soaps. Inside, the noise was almost deafening.

"Faye?"

No answer.

I headed for the nook off the kitchen where we kept the TV, and turned down the volume. The room was empty.

"Faye?" I yelled louder this time.

"Out here, dear. I'm just finishing up the ironing."

"What ironing?" I made a point never to buy anything that didn't come out of the dryer ready to wear.

"Just odds and ends."

I joined her on the laundry porch. "You didn't have to do that," I said, motioning to the stack of neatly pressed and folded items. I'd never known anyone to iron pillow cases and sweatshirts.

"I need to keep busy. I'm not one to sit around all day."

"You should at least have moved the ironing board into the den so you could watch your program at the same time."

She made a face of disgust. "Television. There's nothing worth watching anyway. It's all trash."

"It was on when I came in."

Her hand brushed the air, gesturing disdain. "I just listen in, you know, to keep my mind occupied."

I didn't understand how listening to the stuff without actually watching made it any more tolerable, but for Faye there was obviously a distinction.

She turned her attention to Anna. "How was your day, honeybun?"

"Good."

"I made brownies. Why don't you come into the kitchen and have some while you tell me what happened at school."

I made coffee for Faye and myself, and poured Anna a glass of milk. She chattered away about dodgeball and freeze tag while Faye tried her best to fend off Max, who wanted to be part of the festivities.

"This dog needs to go to obedience school," she muttered, pulling her cup away from Max's nose.

I laughed. "He's been."

She gave me a stern look. "Poor manners are never funny."

I bit my tongue, shoved Max out back, and shut the

door. "Be brave," I whispered in his ear, "she's only here for a week."

I could see that Faye had indeed kept busy during my absence. In addition to the laundry, she'd washed the kitchen floor, cleaned the cupboards, and had the table already set for dinner.

I thanked her. "Libby won't be here for dinner tonight," I said, noting she'd set the table for four.

Faye broke off a piece of brownie. "I know that. I've invited Andy."

I gulped. "You've what?"

"I thought it would be nice if we had an old-fashioned family meal."

"Don't you think you should have asked me first?"

Faye's forehead creased. Her lips compressed into a thin line. "I don't understand the problem. He *is* Anna's father."

I wasn't sure I understood either. Whatever bad feelings there were between us, neither Andy nor I wanted anything but the best for Anna. To that end, we had occasionally done the very thing Faye was now suggesting. Only this time I felt manipulated. And uncomfortable as well, thinking about Michael spending his nights sleeping on a buddy's sofa, catching his meals at deli counters and all-night diners. I bit my tongue, though, and reminded myself of the wisdom I'd offered Max. Only a week.

Handing Anna another brownie, Faye addressed me over her shoulder. "Oh, by the way, you had a couple of calls."

"Who were they?"

"One was a woman. Something about driving for a field trip. The other sounded like a girl. She asked for you first, and then Libby."

"Did you get the names?"

Faye shrugged. "You know me and names."

"Try, please."

She shook her head, then stopped. "The girl's name was Julia, or maybe Julie. I imagine they'll try again if it's important."

My poor tongue was going to be chewed to pieces if I bit it any more. "That's why I have an answering machine," I said, working hard to keep the irritation from showing. Why, in fact, I'd specifically told Faye to let the machine pick up my calls.

"I hate those things," Faye sniffed. "So impersonal."

As it turned out, Andy did not stay for dinner that night, after all. He showed up at the appointed hour, helped himself to a beer, gave his mother a kiss on the cheek, his daughter a mighty bear hug, and me one of his bright, self-satisfied grins.

"What do you mean 'you can't stay for dinner'?" Faye admonished. "I'm fixing fried pork chops and mashed potatoes with gravy. Your favorite meal."

Not that I'd ever heard.

Andy seemed unconcerned with the menu. "Mom, I told you I'd come by, but not to count on me for dinner. I'm meeting someone."

"Who?"

He rolled his eyes. "No one you'd know."

"A date?"

"Business."

"Maybe you can come by afterwards then, for dessert."

"I don't think so. We're apt to be late."

"Well, another night then." Fay picked up a pot and began scrubbing it with short, quick strokes. I could see that she was working hard not to let her disappointment show.

Later, as I walked Andy to the door, I took him aside. "You've got to spend some time with her," I said.

"I will." He pulled at the sleeves of his blue blazer.

"Maybe tomorrow. You could take your mom and Anna somewhere. They'd both like that."

Andy gave Anna's hair a playful tug. "Sure. Only not tomorrow, okay. I'm playing golf."

"Golf!" Anna and I spoke in unison.

"Since when can you afford to play golf?" I asked.

He glared at me. "It's a good way to make important contacts."

Anna tugged at his hand. "Are you going to the Fun Center? Can I go, too?"

"Tomorrow's for grown-ups. But we'll do miniature golf soon, Anna Banana."

He held out a palm. Anna giggled and slapped it.

"Can't your mom stay with you, Andy? I'll make sure she gets to see plenty of Anna. It would be easier if she weren't here all the time."

"Jesus, Kate, we've been over this. I've got a one-bedroom apartment."

"So give her the bed and sleep on the sofa."

He grimaced. "My back hurts just thinking about it."

Not as much as Michael's back, I thought angrily. I took a breath. "Don't you think it's about time you learn to think about someone besides yourself?"

Andy gave me a cocky grin. "Why?"

Saturday afternoon Libby went to the library to do research for a term paper and Faye took Anna to a movie. I kept my appointment with Steve and Yvonne Burton, whose spacious new home was in need of artwork for the walls. Meeting Yvonne had been an added bonus to the teaching job. It wasn't often that clients landed in my lap.

"Yvonne will be back in a minute," Steve said, greeting me at the door. "She had to run Skye over to the stables."

Steve Burton was a prominent local judge currently up for re-election. But you'd never guess that from meeting him. He was surprisingly soft-spoken and unassuming. A perfect complement to Yvonne's bubbly, and at times overly gregarious, disposition. I don't think he cared much one way or another what went on his walls, but he tried his best to feign interest for Yvonne's sake.

He led me to the kitchen. "Would you like some coffee?"

"That would be lovely."

"Cappuccino okay?"

"More than okay."

I took a seat at the marble-topped center island and watched as Steve's experienced hands worked the espresso maker. Whereas Yvonne was dark and petite, Steve was tall and broad-shouldered, with the faintest trace of freckles along his arms. His hair was silver at the temples, but thick and full.

"I swear that horse of Skye's takes more time and attention than a baby," he said. "Not to mention the cost. That girl spends every free minute she's got out there at the stables."

"She does seem devoted to him."

"Do you ride?"

I shook my head. "Do you?"

"Skye is after me to learn. I've tried it once or twice, but frankly, I don't understand the attraction. On the whole

I'd rather walk than ride. Better exercise and a whole lot more comfortable. If it was excitement I was after, I'd go with a motorcycle. I rode one of those for years.''

Steve filled a metal pitcher with milk and held it under the steam spout. "Maybe it's a gender thing. The guys seem to go for bikes, girls for horses. Bet there's some psychiatrist's got a theory about that.''

I laughed. "I'd hate to hear what he'd have to say about those of us who feel at home in an aging Volvo station wagon.''

Steve smiled. "It's certainly the safest of the three.'' He handed me a cup topped with thick foam and powdered chocolate. "We do worry about Skye when she's out on her horse alone. Especially now, after what happened at the park. It's a damn shame how one deranged individual can hold the rest of us hostage.''

I licked the foam and nodded in agreement.

"People in town are fearful in a way they weren't before,'' Steve said. "Things have changed, maybe forever.''

"I'm afraid you may be right. Especially if the guy is never caught.''

Steve's face clouded with misgiving. "Even if he is, they may have a hard time pinning it on him. I used to be with the DA's office. I saw it time and again. The police would zero in on a solid suspect, but without the evidence to back up an arrest. It's frustrating as hell.''

I'd heard Michael say much the same thing. It was why the closed cases and convictions were so dear to him. Why each new crime claimed some part of his soul.

"Yvonne's thrilled to have you helping her,'' Steve said, bringing the conversation back to the reason for my visit. "She's been talking about buying paintings ever since we got married.''

"Have you been married long?"

"Three years next month. Second time for both of us." He turned at the sound of the door. "Here's Yvonne now."

She dropped her purse on the counter and ran a hand through her hair. "Sorry I'm late. It was one of those mornings where nothing went according to schedule."

"No problem, I told her."

She took a sip of Steve's coffee, then draped an arm around his shoulder. Her gaze was flat, as though her mind were elsewhere. After a moment, she took a breath. "You ready to get started?"

I set down my cup and nodded. "I brought along a silkscreen I'm thinking of for the hallway. Also some slides of water colors that are possibilities for the dining room. I'd like to get your reaction to them. You want to start with the hallway?"

"Sure."

The Burtons' was a sprawling two-story house with high ceilings and a wall of glass along the back. The kind of house where a few well-chosen pieces of art would be shown to their best advantage.

Steve carried the framed print to the hallway and propped it against the wall where I indicated. "Looks good to me," he said, kissing Yvonne's cheek. "But it's up to you gals. I've got to run. Nice to see you again, Kate."

"Honestly," Yvonne said when he was out of earshot. "It's his money going into this, you'd think he'd care what we ended up with."

"What do you think of it?" I asked, stepping back to view the effect from the entry. The piece looked darker than it had in the gallery, the colors less true, but the size was good.

Yvonne considered it for a moment, came to stand by me, and shrugged. "It's okay."

"Just okay?"

Another shrug.

"If that's your reaction, then it isn't right. I'll keep looking."

"I'm sorry, maybe it's just my mood. I feel like there's a pall over everything."

"Why?"

She bit her lower lip. "You haven't heard then?"

"Heard what?"

"Julie Harmon is missing."

"What do you mean 'missing'?"

"She didn't come home last night. That's all I know. Skye talked with Mrs. Shepherd this morning. They're treating it as a runaway, but after what happened to that girl at the reservoir, I'm worried."

"What do the police think?"

Yvonne shook her head.

"They've reported it, haven't they?"

"I'm sure they must have." Yvonne's voice lacked conviction.

Anxiety settled in my stomach like lead. "Do you know much about the aunt and uncle?"

"Their son was in my class a few years back." Her face was pinched, as though she were squinting into the sun. "I can understand why Julie might not be happy there, but . . ." She hugged her arms across her chest. "I don't know, it doesn't feel right somehow."

Like Yvonne, I felt the tremor of alarm. It was possible Julie had run away. But there were other reasons why she might not have come home. And even if she had *left* of her own volition, it didn't mean she was safe.

4

On the way home, I stopped by the library to check on Libby.

I knew that Anna would be safe in her grandmother's company. I didn't think Libby was in actual danger either. But the news of Julie's disappearance brought into full bloom all those irrational, motherly fears that usually saved themselves for the dark, sleepless hours of night. The fact that Libby was not actually my daughter didn't change this in the least.

Libby had come to live with me last year after her mother, who was a friend of mine, had been killed. It had been a temporary arrangement initially, prompted by Libby's refusal to live with her father and, more importantly, his bimbo of a fiancée. Since the bimbo was now his wife and neither of them had much time for Libby, they'd offered me a monthly stipend for "keeping" her until she graduated. The money was useful but I'd have done it anyway. Libby may not have been my flesh and blood, but I couldn't have cared about her more if she were.

Pushing my way past the tissue-paper pumpkins and

black cats that adorned the library entrance, I scanned the room for Libby. When I didn't see her at the reference table or in the periodical section, I gave in to a moment of panic. Then I caught sight of her in the courtyard, deep in conversation with blue-eyed, silver-tongued Brian Walker—a young man renowned for being the only member of the senior class to have his own trust fund and his own apartment. From the expression on Libby's face, he might have had his own kingdom as well. This was not the sort of menace I'd been worried about, but it was a situation fraught with peril all the same.

I watched for a moment longer while Brian whispered something in her ear. When Libby looked up to laugh, I quickly pulled back behind the magazine shelves, then slipped out the door before she could see me.

After Brandon, with his punk piercings and metal-studded apparel, I'd thought anyone Libby dated would be an improvement. But I'd forgotten that old adage about the wolf in sheep's clothing.

The light on my answering machine was blinking when I got home. Three calls for Libby, one for Anna, and two for me—both from Michael. I ran through the list of numbers he'd left, and finally reached him in his car.

"What do you know about a high school student by the name of Julie Harmon?" he asked without preamble.

I bit my lip. "She's missing, isn't she?"

"How did you hear that already?"

"A woman I teach with. Her daughter spoke with Julie's aunt."

Michael's response was lost in a burst of static. From the accompanying sigh, however, it was likely his comment related to the speed at which news makes its way through town via the grapevine. It's a phenomenon Michael has come to accept, but one he sometimes has trouble understanding.

"Have you found her?" I asked.

"Not yet. We were only notified of her disappearance a couple of hours ago."

"A couple of hours ago? She's been missing since last night!"

"Don't yell at me, Kate. We got on it as soon as we heard."

"I wasn't yelling; I was just surprised." I took a breath and asked the question that I'd been avoiding in my own mind. "Do you think she was abducted?"

"Her aunt and uncle believe she ran away. I'm on my way to talk to them now. Since the girl is a student at the high school, I thought you might know something about her."

"She's in my class. The only one of my students with any real talent."

There was another burst of static. When I heard Michael's voice again, it sounded as though he were under water.

"I can hardly hear you," I shouted.

"I'm in the Caldecott Tunnel." If he was shouting in return, it didn't make much difference. But without the static, at least I could make out his words.

"How about you come with me when I talk to Julie's family," he said. "It would be a big help. I haven't had a chance to find out anything more about her than what the responding officer handed over, which wasn't much."

"I'm not the Shepherds' favorite person at the moment," I mumbled.

Some garbled words, and then ". . . find her soon."

"Michael, I can only hear half of what you're saying."

Finally, he must have emerged from the tunnel because

the connection was suddenly clearer. "You're my favorite person, too. I'll be by in about ten minutes."

"I said I'm *not* their favorite—" But Michael had already hung up.

Well, I'd tried. If they didn't want me there, they could say so. Besides, I was curious to meet them, and more importantly, to help locate Julie.

Michael made it home in half the anticipated time. "You must have been speeding," I said, climbing into the car.

He grinned. "Prerogative of the job. Now tell me what you can about Julie Harmon."

On the way to the Shepherds', I filled him in as best I could, both about Julie herself and her family situation.

"Do you think she's okay?" I asked finally. "I mean with what happened at the reservoir . . ." I took a breath. "I guess there's no shortage of ways she could be in trouble."

If I was looking for easy assurances, I wasn't going to get them from Michael. As a policeman, he knows better than I the countless terrible things that happen to people through no fault of their own.

He gave me a solemn look. "I expect we'll know more after we talk with the family."

The Shepherds lived near the high school, in one of the less prestigious parts of town. The neighborhood, although pleasant enough, was a tract development of small and undistinguished houses built in the early fifties. Over the years, owners had remodeled and added on, often replacing the original tar and gravel roof with shingle, or adding brick to the facade. As a result, the houses no longer appeared to be stamped out of the same mold, but the area was still short on charm.

The Shepherds' house was located on a corner, which gave them a somewhat larger yard than their neighbors. It was obvious that no one in the family enjoyed gardening. Juniper bushes and ivy, interlaced with weeds—that was the extent of the landscaping.

Michael rang the bell and introduced me as "someone from the school." He used my full name and I cringed, but I was clearly the only one listening. My classroom lectures on art history, however distressing to the Shepherds, were not uppermost in their minds right then. Rather, they seemed intent on enumerating their grievances with Julie's behavior.

"She's been nothing but trouble since the day we took her in," complained Walton Shepherd. The irritation in his voice was softened somewhat by a Texas drawl. "Evidently her mother let her run wild and do pretty much as she pleased. The girl's never had an ounce of discipline. Doesn't have the least respect for authority."

"Now, Walt. It's not quite that bad." Patricia Shepherd touched her husband's thickly muscled arm. "Julie was used to a different environment, is all. She's learning."

He glowered at her. Walton Shepherd was not a tall man, but he was solidly built with broad shoulders, short, thick arms, and almost no neck. His complexion was ruddy and his jowls loose. In both temperament and appearance, he reminded me of a bulldog.

"I know you don't like to speak ill of your sister," he said. "But facts are facts. Leslie Harmon was a libertine and profligate, more interested in her own conquests than the path of righteousness. If she'd raised that girl properly, we wouldn't have had any trouble."

Michael cleared his throat. "May we come in? I'd like to talk with you about your niece. The first hours after a child disappears are sometimes the most critical in terms of leads."

"We told everything to that other fellow," Shepherd said. "The one down at the police station." But he opened the door wider and stepped aside to allow us in.

He ushered us to a lace-draped table in the dining area off the kitchen. Patricia Shepherd followed wordlessly.

The interior was dim, and from what little I saw on my way to the table, dreary and dated. It smelled of a lifetime accumulation of cooking odors and stale air. I took short, shallow breaths to keep from choking.

Once we were seated, Michael took out a notebook and pen. "I appreciate how hard this must be for you," he said kindly, "and how difficult it must be to remember exactly what happened. But the more you can tell us, the better our chances of locating her."

Mrs. Shepherd nodded. Her husband crossed his arms. Behind them on the wall was a large painting of Jesus in a flowing, white robe, and on the table beneath, a photograph of a similarly clad Walton Shepherd.

"It's my understanding," Michael continued, "that Julie left here about six o'clock Friday evening on her way to the high school football game."

Mrs. Shepherd nodded again.

"And you've seen nor heard nothing from her since?"

"The way I see it," said Walton Shepherd, with a twitch of his shoulder, "those football games are nothing but an excuse for rowdy behavior. Our son had more sense than to involve himself with such stuff. We try to be fair, though. We allow Julie to attend the home games."

"We did put our foot down about the dance afterwards," his wife added. She directed the words to her thumbs, which were folded one over the other on the table in front of her.

Walton Shepherd frowned. "When Julie wasn't home by nine, we assumed she'd disobeyed us and gone to the dance anyway." He paused, then added with some bitterness, "Apparently, she did more than that."

"You think she disappeared of her own accord?"

"Wouldn't surprise me. The girl will find out soon enough how little life on the streets has to offer. Our rules won't seem so harsh to her then."

Michael scratched his chin. "What makes you so sure she's run away?"

Shepherd shrugged. "She never tried to hide her displeasure at living here."

"It was a change from what she was used to, Walton."

He snickered. "That's for sure."

"I take it you and your sister weren't close," Michael said.

"Julie's mother was my half-sister," Patricia Shepherd offered by way of explanation. Although she'd raised her gaze, her fingers were still tightly laced. "We shared the same father, but little else. And I used the word 'shared' only in the most basic sense. Leslie saw far more of him than I did."

"Leslie was the child of a second marriage?" I asked.

She nodded. "Leslie and I barely knew each other growing up, but after college we made an effort to get to know one another better." Mrs. Shepherd paused. "It was a disaster. We were very . . . different."

The furnace clicked on with a rumble, although the house was already quite warm.

"How did Julie end up here with you?" Michael asked.

"Leslie was killed in a boating accident last spring."

Walton Shepherd blew his nose on a large, stained handkerchief. "We're all the family she has. A matter of some significance—which the girl seems inclined to overlook."

"Her father's dead as well?"

Patricia Shepherd lifted her chin. "According to Leslie, he died before Julie was born. But she'd never said a word about him while he was alive, so I have my doubts."

Walton Shepherd laughed harshly. "I have no doubts about it at all, myself."

"How long has Julie been living with you?" Michael asked.

Shepherd ignored the question. His eyes narrowed. "It's women like Leslie Harmon who've brought moral decay to this fine country of ours. Women who think they can stand alone, who imagine they've no need for a man or God." This time Shepherd's Texas twang did nothing to soften his words. He spoke with such ferocity I half expected a bolt of lightning to follow.

"But we couldn't simply turn our backs on the child," Mrs. Shepherd protested. Her voice was as soft and tentative as her husband's was strong. "It's our duty to see that she's looked after properly."

"The sins of the mother are in her blood. She may be your kin, Patricia, but she's in the Devil's grasp all the same."

His words brought a chill to my heart, a spasm of foreboding that left me shaken. I was afraid he might well be right, but not in the sense he'd intended.

5

At Michael's request, Patricia Shepherd showed us Julie's bedroom, which was located near the front of the house. It was a small room with peeling paper and heavy green drapes. A single bed with a quilted tan spread was pushed against the far wall. A desk, a bookcase, and a five-drawer bureau lined the walls to either side. Hardly feminine or youthful, but surprisingly neat. Obviously Julie didn't share Libby's conviction that clutter spurred creativity.

Michael stepped inside. "We'd like to look around, if we might."

Patricia Shepherd nodded. "Of course."

"Have you removed anything since she's been gone?"

"No."

He opened the closet door and surveyed the contents. "Any of her clothing missing?"

"Not that I know of. But I'm not sure I'd know one way or another."

"How about money?"

She blinked. "Money?"

"Cash you and your husband might have had around the house. Is any of it missing?"

Patricia Shepherd drew in a breath. "I never thought to check my purse. I don't make a habit of carrying much cash, though."

"Did Julie have any money of her own?"

"Quite a bit. Everything that was her mother's, including the life insurance proceeds. But it's all in trust. We give her spending money when she needs it."

"There's no way she can access it on her own?"

"Not until she's eighteen."

Michael pulled a crumpled piece of paper out of the waste basket. "You the trustee?"

She nodded. "Although Walt handles the details. I've never understood much about investments and such."

He smoothed the paper, then tossed it back into the trash. "What day is your garbage service?"

"Friday."

"They came this morning?"

She nodded again.

"So any notes Julie tossed out last week would already have been picked up."

"I'm afraid so."

Michael sat down at Julie's desk, which looked to be vintage maple, circa 1950, and began sifting through the drawers. After a cursory check, he nodded in my direction.

"Why don't you have a look. Since you know Julie, you're more apt to recognize anything of significance."

While Michael inspected the rest of the room, I made a more careful check of the desk drawers. Pencils, papers, art supplies, school work, and chewing gum. No surprises.

And no indication of where Julie might have gone. In fact, with the exception of the drawing pencils and charcoals, there was nothing in the least personalized about the contents.

"Is this her mother?" Michael asked, picking up the silver-framed portrait from the dresser.

Patricia Shepherd nodded. "You might have seen her on television if you watch the news. She was quite successful, but that kind of life has its price." There was an edge to her voice that sounded like disapproval, although it might have been envy.

"Does Julie still have friends in New York?"

"I imagine so."

"Close friends?"

Patricia Shepherd smoothed her collar. "She got a few letters."

"How about calls?"

"We don't hold with squandering time on the telephone."

Michael sucked on his cheek, gave the room another sweep with his eyes. "What about a computer?" he asked.

"In our son's room. There wasn't space for it here."

"Your son lives at home?"

"No, not anymore. But he comes home for meals fairly often. And laundry."

I started to smile at the last comment, then realized that her voice held not the slightest trace of humor.

"Where's your son's room?" Michael asked.

"At the end of the hallway."

He slipped off to have a look at the computer. I didn't hold out much hope that he'd find anything useful. In truth, I didn't hold out much hope about any of it. If Julie wanted to run away, my guess would be that she'd have planned it carefully. And if she didn't want to be found, she wouldn't be.

But that possibility was better than the alternatives. What if she'd been accosted? Or been snared, unsuspecting, into some dangerous course of action? Julie was bright, well traveled, worldly beyond her years. And yet, she was only fifteen. Old enough to think she could handle anything; young enough that she couldn't. A prime candidate for tragedy.

"Any luck?" I asked when Michael returned.

He shook his head. "Looks like more school stuff. No modem, not much in the way of software at all."

Patricia Shepherd had vanished after showing Michael to the computer. We found her in the driveway talking to her husband, who was tinkering under the hood of a shiny new pickup.

She pulled at the sleeve of her sweater. "Maybe if you hadn't—"

"Don't you be lecturing me, woman. I've got no stomach for that rubbish."

"But Walt, if she—"

Their voices were low and serious. They stopped speaking and stepped apart as we approached.

"Did you find what you were looking for?" Walton Shepherd asked between clenched teeth.

"I wasn't looking for anything in particular. Just hoping to pick up on something that might give us a lead."

"And did you?"

Michael shook his head.

"If I were you, I wouldn't waste too much energy on this. Wouldn't create too much of a furor about it, either. It will only go to her head."

Patricia Shepherd looked uneasy. "She might be in trouble, Walt."

He grunted. *"Making* trouble, more likely."

Michael stepped forward. "Mr. Shepherd, your wife is right. You seem to think Julie ran away. But that's only one possibility. I don't want to frighten you unduly, but this may be more serious than you think."

Shepherd leveled his gaze at us. His mouth went through a series of twisting and chewing motions, as though he were practicing some new form of facial exercise. Finally, he went back to his tinkering.

"Have you checked with Julie's friends?" Michael asked.

Mrs. Shepherd drew her mouth tight. "She doesn't have time for a lot of friends."

"They're a worthless lot of hooligans, in any event." Walton Shepherd's voice drifted out from under the hood of the truck. "Like that spic kid who kept bothering us, what was his name?" Shepherd paused, pulled his head out, and looked at his wife, then answered the question himself. "Mario, that was it. Kid had an accent that sounded like he'd just crossed the border from taco land. Those people think they can come here and live off the rest of us."

Mario's father and his uncles operated a commercial cleaning service. I thought it unlikely they lived off anything but their own sweat and hard work. I would have said so except that it wouldn't have changed the man's thinking. Besides, I was more interested in learning about Mario's friendship with Julie, if that's what it was.

"What did you mean about Mario bothering you?" I asked.

"Dropping by, calling, offering Julie rides. She didn't

want to hurt his feelings so we had to put a stop to it ourselves.''

"Julie found him annoying?''

Mrs. Shepherd brushed the air with her hand. "He may be a nice enough boy," she replied crisply, "but he isn't the sort we want her mixing with.''

I thought back to Mario's appearance at my classroom door Friday morning. I tried to replay in my mind the unspoken exchange between the two of them. There was definitely a tension there, but I'd sensed a bond as well, or at least an understanding. Had I misread the situation?

"How about other friends?" Michael asked.

"Well, let's see, there's a girl in her history class. Julie borrowed her book once when she'd left her own at school.'' Patricia Shepherd looked to her husband for help, and got none. "Oh, and the girl who called here this morning. Her name is Skye, if you can believe it. When Julie first mentioned her, I thought she might be Indian, but Julie assured me she wasn't. Her mother is a teacher at the school.''

This last comment was directed to me, so I nodded. Apparently Skye had passed an acceptability test that Mario hadn't, which I thought spoke volumes about the stupidity of the whole approach.

"Was she going to meet anyone in particular at the football game?" I asked.

Mrs. Shepherd misunderstood the question. "Oh no," she said, pulling in a breath as she spoke. "We don't allow Julie to date.''

"I think Ms. Austen was speaking more generally," Michael explained. "We're going to want to talk to people who saw her Friday night. If you could give us names, it would save some time.''

"Austen?" Patricia Shepherd's eyes widened and her voice took on a guarded quality. "What did you say your connection to the school was?"

Suddenly, I wished I'd told Michael the full story. "I teach there."

"What subject?"

I swallowed. "Art."

"Oh, my." Mrs. Shepherd's hands fluttered for a moment and then settled on her chest. "Oh, my," she said again, looking in the direction of her husband.

Walton Shepherd emerged from under the hood just then, and I braced myself for a verbal assault. At least, I was hoping it would be only verbal. There is a decided advantage to having a heated discussion in the presence of a police officer.

"Art." He spat the word like a wad of chewing tobacco. "Thought your name sounded familiar, you're that teacher warping the kids' minds with smut."

I looked toward Michael then back at Shepherd. "You don't understand. I'm—"

Shepherd's steely gaze was no longer fixed on me, however, but on the vintage red Mustang that had pulled up in front of the house. A young man toting a white canvas bag got out of the driver's side and slogged up the walkway.

"That's our boy, Dennis," Mrs. Shepherd explained.

And his laundry, I added silently, eyeing the duffel. Like his father, Dennis was short and thick, with closely cropped hair and a fleshy face. Although he must have been in his early twenties, he still had the soft, downy skin of preadolescence.

"Sorry," he said, handing the bag to his mother. "I didn't think you'd have company."

Walton Shepherd wiped his hands on a rag. "They're not company. They're here on police business."

"Police?" The word squeaked out in two distinct syllables.

"It's about Julie," Patricia Shepherd said. "She's missing."

Dennis shifted his weight to the opposite foot, slipped his car key into his back pocket. "Missing? What do you mean?"

Mrs. Shepherd explained. Throughout her recital, the young man's expression remained flat, as though his mother were talking about nothing more stirring than her prize petunias.

"No kidding," Dennis said when she finished. He ran his hand through the feathery tufts of hair at his forehead. "She sure keeps things lively around here, doesn't she?"

"You know anything that might shed light on the situation?" Michael asked.

"Like what?" Dennis squared his shoulders, copying his father's posture.

"About her interests, her habits. Maybe she said something about her plans."

"Not to me she didn't. Julie's stuck on herself. Thinks she's all high and mighty, and so much better than everyone else. She hardly gives me the time of day."

"You didn't see much of her then?"

"Oh, I'd *see* her plenty. We just never talked."

Mrs. Shepherd cleared her throat. "We've tried hard to be understanding. The poor girl's been through a lot, after all. But . . . well, the effort seems to be largely one-sided. Julie likes to keep to herself."

"Except for the complaining," Walton Shepherd

grumbled. "She's plenty willing to tell us what she doesn't like."

Michael turned back to Dennis. "When was the last time you saw Julie?"

Dennis looked at his mother. "Must have been Thursday, right? Wasn't that the night I stopped by for dinner?"

"How did she seem?" Michael asked. "Anything unusual?"

Dennis shrugged. "Same old stuff. The kid is used to having her own way. Thinks she's a princess. Like I always used to tell her, 'Welcome to the real world, where not everybody's rich and famous. And nobody ever gets the gold star.' "

Michael stuck a hand in his pocket. "What do you do, Dennis? You in school?"

"I'm taking some courses at the community college, but I work, too. At Macy's."

"You live around here?"

"Berkeley."

Michael wrote down the address and phone number, then handed Dennis a card. "You think of anything, call me. Okay?"

Another shrug. "I can tell you right now, I don't know nothin'."

"They're a warm and friendly bunch, aren't they?" Michael said when we were back in the car.

I slumped down in the seat, too depressed to do more than nod. Julie was someone I genuinely liked. Maybe it was her artistic talent, or the fact that I understood what it was to feel like an outsider. Whatever the reason, I'd taken to her instinctively. And I knew from Libby that she wasn't happy living with the Shepherds. Yet, I'd made no overture to help. No attempt to discern what was really going on. In fact, I'd admired the maturity with which she seemed to be handling a difficult situation.

And now I felt the weight of my failure.

"You think she ran away?" Michael asked as he pulled the car into the street.

"I don't know. I can see why she might want to."

"Amen to that."

"She's never been in any trouble at school, though. Do kids who are responsible and conscientious suddenly just up and run away?"

Michael nodded. "Sometimes."

"I'd heard she wasn't thrilled living where she was, but she seemed so even-tempered. The only time I saw her upset was Friday." I told him about the featureless self-portrait. "And she came to class early. I think she wanted to speak to me."

"About what?"

"I don't know." I tried to recall what her reaction had been when Mario showed up at the door. Could they have gone away together? Or was he part of the problem? "She left with a friend before we had a chance to talk. It was that boy, Mario, that the Shepherds were so displeased with. We were going to talk after class, but then I had to, uh, run off."

Michael raised an eyebrow. "What's Mario like?"

"He's a nice kid, though not much of a student. Only shows up for classes when he feels like it. Kind of cocky, but good-natured. He doesn't hang with the troublemakers that I know of."

"Doesn't hang with . . ." Michael grinned. "You're picking up the lingo, Kate."

"When you're surrounded by teenagers, it's hard not to."

He scratched his chin. "So this Mario's not a bad kid, just something of a nuisance as far as Julie's concerned."

"I'm not sure what Julie's feelings are."

Michael pulled up in front of the house but didn't turn off the engine.

"What's the next step?" I asked. "Do you think we'll know anything soon?"

"We'll get Julie's name and description out there, talk with people who might have seen her Friday night. Hopefully get some television and press coverage." He touched my knee. "You wouldn't know it to listen to the news, but most teens who are reported missing turn out to have left on their own."

I crossed my fingers and said a silent prayer that Julie was one of them. That she didn't end up like Cindy Purcell, her body discarded in the underbrush of a nearby park.

6

Faye and Anna were already home by the time I returned. The remnants of chocolate ice cream dotting Anna's shirtfront attested to the success of the outing. Anna is a devout chocoholic.

"How was the movie?" I asked.

"Wonderful," Faye said, wiping her hands on her apron. "It's simply amazing what they do with special effects these days."

Anna was lying on the kitchen floor, scratching Max's ears. "It was okay," she mumbled, "for a *kid's* movie."

Faye smiled. "What do you mean, a kid's movie? I enjoyed it and I'm hardly a kid."

"It was rated *G*," Anna sniffed.

"G for good."

Anna gave her head a quick toss, a gesture she'd picked up from Libby. "G means no swearing and no sex. The couple in the movie were practically engaged and they didn't do anything but hold hands."

"I should hope not." Faye looked at me, no longer amused.

I ran my tongue over my bottom lip, and made a quick mental inventory of the movies Anna had watched recently. Certainly none had been aimed at adult audiences.

I glanced at Faye and shrugged. Her expression of disapproval didn't soften.

I nodded at Anna's shirt. "I see you had ice cream."

"And a whole carton of popcorn," Anna said. "With extra butter."

"Your grandmother is a soft touch."

"A box of red licorice, too."

I looked back at Faye, who gave me the same sort of helpless shrug I'd given her moments earlier. We both laughed.

The front door opened, then slammed shut. There was a second loud thunk as Libby dropped her backpack on the floor near the front hallway.

"I'm home," she yelled.

We'd have to have been deaf not to know.

She swept into the kitchen, where she made a beeline for the refrigerator, poured herself a Coke, and flopped into the nearest chair.

"Did you find what you needed at the library?" I asked.

"Sort of." She took another swallow of her drink and frowned. "Have you heard about Julie Harmon? She's disappeared."

Anna looked up. "Disappeared? You mean like vaporized?"

"Like lost," I explained, wondering how you related something like this to a six-year-old. "Her family doesn't know where she is."

"Kidnapped," Anna said knowingly. "By bad guys."

"Or killed," Libby added. "Like that girl in the park."

Faye cleared her throat.

"It's creepy," Libby continued, "thinking there might be a murderer out there walking the streets, just looking for his next victim."

Faye made a show of removing her apron and hanging it on the hook. "Anna, honey, why don't we go read a story."

By way of response, Anna gave an exaggerated snore, eliciting a like response from Max.

"Then how about we finish that game we were playing this morning." Faye reached for Anna's hand, not about to take *no* for an answer. With a sigh, she added, "You can invite Max to come along, too, if you'd like."

"Sorry," Libby said when they'd left. "I keep forgetting Anna has big ears."

"I think Faye may be overly protective. She doesn't realize how much kids are exposed to these days." But it was a question I grappled with often, especially given Michael's job. There was a fine line between innocence and ignorance.

"Anyway," I told her. "It might not be as bad as it sounds. Julie's family thinks she's run away."

"Nu-uh. No way." Libby's tone was adamant. "She wouldn't have done that, not now."

"Why not? You told me yourself that Julie didn't get along with her aunt and uncle."

"She didn't. But something big was going to happen in the next couple of weeks. Something that was going to make everything better."

"Better? How?"

Libby shook her head. "That's all I know. Julie

wouldn't tell me the details, but she said it looked like everything might be okay, after all.''

I was perplexed. ''When was all this?''

Libby sucked on an ice cube while she thought. ''She's been dropping hints for a while. Then last Wednesday she said it looked like she was saved.''

''Saved?''

''I don't think she meant in the religious sense.''

I got up and put the kettle on for tea. ''I got the impression Julie and her uncle had a fight last week.''

''So?'' One of the hundred most common words in a teenager's vocabulary.

''So that might be a reason she would run away.''

Libby's hand swept the air, brushing aside my logic. ''They were always fighting.''

''Maybe there was a different reason, then. Something about school, or boys, or friends . . .'' I tried to imagine the kinds of things that would drive a fifteen-year-old out on her own. ''Aside from the situation at home, was anything troubling her?''

Libby ran her finger up the side of the glass and around the rim. ''I think she was lonely. She didn't really fit in at school yet.''

I nodded. I'd seen that even in my classroom.

Libby kept her eyes on the glass. ''She missed her mother.'' The words came out softly, almost like puffs of breath on a winter's morning, and I knew that she was speaking not only to Julie's loss, but her own as well.

I wrapped an arm around Libby's shoulder and gave her a hug.

''Julie's aunt and uncle cut her off every time she tried to talk about her mother,'' Libby continued. ''And most of the kids at school . . . well, I mean, you talk too much about your mother and they think you're weird. Julie said I was the only one who understood."

I gave another nod. This was the reason the school had asked Libby to take Julie under her wing and help her learn her way around.

"I feel so bad, Kate. Half the time I tuned her out and didn't even listen."

"But the other half the time, you did. And you helped in other ways, too."

"Not as much as I should have. She's only a sophomore and I didn't like her always hanging around. Maybe if I'd been a better friend, this wouldn't have happened." The words sounded like a lament. She looked at me and tried for a smile that wouldn't come.

"We both know Julie," I said. "Maybe we can think of something that will help the police find her." I thought the effort might allay my own sense of guilt as well.

The kettle whistled. I took down a bag of black currant tea and made myself a cup. I'd never been much of a tea drinker until recently when my friend Sharon saw the *lite,* so to speak, and took up the cause of healthy living. In a burst of enthusiasm for spreading the word, she filled my cupboard with an assortment of odd-sounding and equally odd-tasting brews, most of which I tossed as soon as she stopped checking my supply. But in the process, I discovered the comfort of an occasional afternoon cup of tea. Of course, the teas I drank made no claims to promoting health beyond the fact that they were calorie-free. A benefit I reversed by adding a heavy dose of sugar.

"You want a cup?" I asked Libby.

"I think I'll stick to Coke." She poured herself a second glass and grabbed an open bag of potato chips.

"Who are Julie's closest friends?" I asked, taking a tentative sip of tea. It was so hot it burned my mouth.

"She didn't really have any. She gets along with people, but she keeps her distance, too. Like I said, she doesn't really fit in yet."

"What about clubs, activities, that sort of thing?"

"There's newspaper, but she doesn't contribute much. Only thing she seems to care about is the project she's working on. Mr. Melville is so impressed with the fact that her mother was a famous news reporter, he lets her get away with it."

I ignored Libby's pique. "Any other activities?"

"She was going to try out for the school play, but her aunt and uncle wouldn't let her. They're really strict. And kind of weird."

That was my take on the situation, as well. "What about boyfriends?"

Libby gave a sarcastic laugh. "You think they'd allow her to go out with boys?"

"But around school, does she . . ." I looked for the right word and settled for the only thing that came to mind. "Does she pair up with anyone in particular?"

"At first, because she was new, there were a lot of boys who were interested in her. But mostly they'd talk *about* her rather than *to* her." Libby paused and the tenor of her voice changed slightly. "The only one I know of who actually asked her out was Brian Walker."

The same young man Libby had been in deep conversation with at the library that afternoon. "She went out with him?" I asked.

"They went off campus for lunch a couple of times. Sophomores aren't supposed to leave without written permission from their parents, but nobody ever checks."

Libby covered her mouth with her hand. "You won't say anything, will you? I keep forgetting you're part of the faculty now."

"I won't say anything. Technically I'm not even part of the faculty." But I did tuck the information away to pass along to Michael. Brian had his own apartment, after all. In the eyes of a lonely and unhappy young woman, that might have considerable appeal.

"What about Mario Sanchez?" I asked.

"What about him?"

"Are he and Julie friendly?"

Libby laughed. "Mario is everybody's friend. He'd make a good politician."

"There's nothing special between the two of them, then?"

"Julie and I didn't talk about stuff like that."

"You knew about Brian, though."

Libby's face reddened, although she did her best to act nonchalant. "I guess I must have heard it somewhere."

Remembering the adoring look Libby had given Brian outside the library, I was willing to bet she'd been keeping fairly close tabs on his social life. Certainly closer than she kept on Mario's.

Libby finished her Coke. "Why'd you ask about Mario?"

"He and Julie were having what appeared to be a rather intense conversation Friday morning. I thought it might be important."

"It's funny you should mention that. I saw them arguing a couple of days ago. It's the first time I've ever seen Mario angry about anything. Usually, he's really laid back, and like 'Hey, whatever happens is cool.' "

I laughed. She did a good job of mimicking Mario's tone, which seemed always to be laced with droll geniality.

"I'll ask some of my friends," Libby said. "See if anyone knows if they were going around." She paused, shifted forward in her seat. "I'll ask about Friday night, too. Maybe I can find out who Julie sat with at the game." She stopped suddenly and rocked back. "Assuming she made it there."

By Monday, there was still no word on Julie's whereabouts. Fliers bearing her picture began appearing in store windows and on telephone poles. The local papers and television stations carried news of her disappearance. But despite the publicity, there were no leads, no sightings, no real developments of any sort.

"Do the police know anything more than what's in the papers?" Yvonne Burton asked, pouring herself a cup of what passes in the faculty lounge for coffee.

I shook my head. "They haven't found anyone who remembers seeing her at the game Friday evening. But that leaves open the question of whether her absence was voluntary or forced."

"Which do they consider more likely?"

"I don't know that the police have an opinion on that. Libby thinks she wouldn't have run away though."

"How come?"

"Julie was unhappy at home, but she was expecting some change. Libby says she was pretty excited about it."

"Change?" Yvonne asked. "Like what?"

"I don't know. Libby doesn't know either."

A furrow formed in her brow. "I didn't realize Libby and Julie were close."

"They're not really, but because Libby lost her own

mother last year, someone in the administration got the idea that the two of them would have a lot in common.''

Yvonne made a noise, somewhere between a laugh and a snort. ''Reminds me of one of the other transfers we had—a boy with a heavy speech impediment. They paired him with a kid who stuttered. To my mind it did nothing but underscore the problem. Not to mention the fact that one of the boys was an all-around athlete and the other a computer nerd. You wonder where the powers that be put their brains when they make these decisions.''

The bell rang. Yvonne picked up an armload of books and we headed for the door. ''Keep me posted, okay?''

There was an urgency in her voice that caught me by surprise. It must have surprised Yvonne, too, because she looked a little nonplussed. ''Sorry, I guess this whole thing has hit pretty close to home.''

Marvin Melville was coming in the door as we went out. He looked like his mind was elsewhere, but he raised a hand in greeting. Then added, ''By the way, Kate, condoms aren't a problem.''

Yvonne stifled a laugh. ''I've heard plenty of rumors about Marvin, but I'd never suspected that you were part of it.''

''I'm not,'' I told her as we parted ways, then wished I'd thought to ask what *it* was.

7

I was prepared to devote most, if not all, of my first-period class to venting students' concerns over Julie's disappearance. But there was surprisingly little interest. Friday night's football win over the favored rival and plans for the upcoming Halloween Masquerade were the topics of the hour, although there *was* some speculation in passing on the benefits of running off to live a life free of parents.

"It wouldn't be worth doing unless you had lots of money," said Miranda, who knew better than many of us the advantages of money.

"Sounds good in theory," added Charles. "But if you lived alone, you'd have to do your own shopping and laundry and crap."

"Presumably you'd do the last yourself, anyway," said a voice from the back of the room. The male half of the class practically fell out of their seats guffawing.

Skye waited until the noise died down, then she said, "You're all forgetting that something terrible might have happened. We've got a killer running loose in town, remember."

One of the boys grabbed his throat, slid down in his chair, and flailed about dramatically, the vaudeville picture of death.

The class tittered.

"Under the circumstances," I told him, "that's hardly funny."

He sat up, sheepish. "Sorry."

The rest of the class exchanged glances and fell into an awkward silence. I sighed and went back to my desk. So much for easing the strain.

After class, I gathered my things, including the art history books that had caused the Shepherds to blanch, and headed for the office. If a student editorial on condoms passed muster, how could Combs find fault with a Michelangelo nude?

As I rounded the corner, I passed Mario at his locker.

"Have you got a minute?" I asked, stepping free of the moving horde.

He closed the locker door quickly. "Hey, Ms. Austen." Mario had a marvelous smile, which looked for all the world to be genuine. It was one of the things that made him such a charmer despite his sometimes roguish behavior.

"Can we talk?"

"Hey, I know I ain't been to class the last couple of days, but I got an uncle who's real sick, see, and first-period class is hard—"

"That's not why I want to talk to you."

"It's not, huh?" The smile widened in relief. "I'm going to start coming regular though, just as soon as I can."

"I wanted to ask you about Julie Harmon."

He shifted position. "I heard about her being missing and all." His eyes darted along the stream of passing students. "Sure hope she turns up okay."

"You wouldn't happen to know if she was in some kind of trouble, would you? Or if she was worried about something?"

Mario ran a hand through his slicked-back hair. "Me? sorry, I don't know nothin'." He started to move away.

"I saw the two of you together Friday morning, in what looked like . . ." Like what? I probably wouldn't have noticed at all if Julie hadn't approached me earlier that morning, and if Mario hadn't beckoned her from my classroom just when we were about to have a private chat. "In what seemed to be kind of a tense discussion," I concluded.

"Tense?"

"Serious, maybe a little strained."

"Nah, we were just shooting the breeze."

"About what?"

He shrugged. "Stuff. Wasn't nothin' worth remembering."

"Were you at Friday's football game?"

He cocked his head, looked at me. "I worked that night. I work most Friday nights."

"Doing what?"

"I help my uncles clean office buildings."

"So you wouldn't know Julie's plans for the evening?"

" 'Fraid not." Mario raised his hand in greeting to a passing student.

Surely their conversation had been something more than an idle chat. I could read it in their expressions. "Are you sure Julie wasn't troubled about something?"

Mario rubbed the back of his neck with his hand. "Ms. Austen, do I look like a priest?" He snapped the latch on his locker. "Listen, I gotta go do my English homework. Grammar, it's a real bear."

I checked my watch. "You've only got a minute before class."

"That's why I've got to get to it." He gave me another smile and a quirky half-salute, then loped off in the direction of the parking lot, without so much as a book or paper in hand.

In the office, I checked Brian Walker's schedule and saw that he had Civics next with Mr. Tanner. I sighed. If I wanted to talk to Brian, I'd have to wait until the end of the period. Leonard Tanner ruled with an iron fist.

The office secretary, Ruth, looked up. "What's the matter?" she asked.

I explained, without saying why it was that I wanted to speak to Brian.

"He's absent today, anyway."

"He's sick?"

She smiled. "Of course he's sick. You think he'd call up and say he was skipping school because he felt like it? Once these kids turn eighteen, they like to flex their muscles a bit. They'll cut school, then call in an excused absence just for the joy of thumbing their noses at us."

I knew the drill. Because many Walnut Hills parents held off a year before enrolling their young sons in kindergarten, hoping to give them the competitive edge of relative maturity, we already had more than a few eighteen-year-old seniors.

"Of course Brian was an emancipated minor all of his junior year," she continued, "so it's not such new stuff to him. His attendance record is actually pretty good."

"Emancipated minor?" I knew the term, but that was about all. "What does it mean exactly?"

"I don't understand all the legal implications. As far as the school's concerned, it means the student can live on his own, assume responsibility for himself as though he were eighteen. We don't need a parent's signature for absences, permission slips, detention notices, that sort of thing."

"Sounds like every student's dream come true."

"In theory. The home situation has to be pretty bad, though, before the court will declare someone an emancipated minor."

A little light went on in my head, just like in the comics. Was *that* Julie's secret plan, to have herself declared an emancipated minor? "Is there a minimum age requirement?"

Ruth shook her head. "I don't know. In my experience the kids have all been juniors and seniors." She paused with an expression of concern. "Have you been having trouble with Libby?"

"No, Libby's not a problem. In fact, most of the time she's a real joy. I was thinking of Julie Harmon. From what I've gathered, she hasn't been happy living with the Shepherds."

"Can't say as I blame her," Ruth muttered.

"She told Libby she was expecting things to change soon, for the better. And she knows Brian. I'm thinking maybe she's been looking into the idea of having herself declared an emancipated minor."

"The family situation certainly fits." Ruth's brows furrowed in thought. "If she was expecting a court ruling, though, it hardly seems like she'd run away."

"Maybe there was a better solution."

That's what I was hoping would turn out to be the case at any rate. The other alternative was too frightening to dwell on. I took a piece of scratch paper from Ruth's desk and copied down Brian Walker's address and phone number. I could at least find out from him if he and Julie had talked about the subject.

"What's Brian like?" I asked, slipping the scrap of paper into my purse.

"Smooth," Ruth said. "He's always polite, does reasonably well in school, but I've never quite trusted him."

"How come?"

She thought for a moment, then shrugged. "No reason, really. Maybe I'm just jealous of boys who have longer lashes than I do."

"It does seem too bad to waste those eyes on a male."

Ruth clicked her pen. "By the way, you got a couple of calls. I stuck the message slips in your box."

I retrieved them. Michael and Sharon had both called. With a wave to Ruth, I headed for the faculty room and the only phone available to teachers.

Sharon answered on the first ring.

"Were you sitting by the phone?" I asked.

"Actually, I was washing it."

"Washing the phone?" That didn't sound like Sharon.

"It's kind of a necessity now that Kyle has started calling his friends. This time it was grape jam, but we've had chocolate syrup, peanut butter, purple ink, and Elmer's glue, all in the last week."

Kyle is Anna's age, but since he's a boy, our experiences are often quite different. I'd certainly never thought of washing the phone.

"I called to invite you for lunch today," Sharon said.

"Sounds wonderful."

"I've invited Faye, too."

"What?" My enthusiasm began to fade.

"I told her you'd pick her up around noon. I hope that works for you. If it doesn't, I'll run over and get her myself."

I groaned. "Why did you invite Faye?"

"I'm trying to be helpful, Kate. I know you're not thrilled about spending a lot of time alone with her—"

"I'm not thrilled about spending a lot of time with her, period."

"But you can't simply ignore her."

"Why not?"

Sharon wasn't interested in a protracted discussion. She brushed aside my question with a click of her tongue. "I know you don't mean that. And we'll have a chance to go over plans for the Fall Festival, as well."

"What plans?"

"That's what we have to decide. As you know, Mary Nell had agreed to chair the event. But her mother's sick and Mary Nell had to fly home to Kansas. I said we'd take over for her with the festival."

"We?" Sharon had a way of volunteering me for jobs I'd have run from if given the chance.

"I don't want to do it alone," she explained.

"You might have asked me first."

Sharon laughed. "You might have said no. See you a little after noon."

I tried Michael next, but he wasn't available. I left a message that I'd called and that I'd be at Sharon's. Then I took a deep breath and dialed Brian Walker's number. No answer. When the machine clicked on, I hung up.

8

Sharon isn't much of a housekeeper, but her home is airy and tastefully furnished so one tends to overlook the clutter and ever-present patina of dust. Where my house is *messy*, hers is simply imbued with casual elegance. Even Faye was taken with its charm.

"What a lovely home you have," she murmured, settling herself in a comfortable down-cushioned chair. She said nothing about the fact that she'd first had to remove a foam football and plastic bin of Legos. "It was so kind of you to invite me."

"My pleasure. Kate's been talking about your visit for weeks."

I cleared my throat, hoping to cut her off before she tried to elaborate. Although Sharon usually operates from the best of intentions, she often stumbles in the delivery.

She took the hint. "What can I get you to drink?" Sharon asked. "Coffee? Wine? I have gin and scotch, too, if you'd prefer something stronger."

"Coffee will be fine." Faye set her handbag on the floor next to the chair. She'd washed and curled her hair, and dressed in the turquoise pantsuit she saved for special occasions.

"What would you like, Kate?"

I debated for a moment, wondering if a glass of wine was worth Faye's disapproval. I opted for prudence. "The same," I said.

Sharon set out a platter of sandwiches—cucumber, avocado, and alfalfa sprouts on whole wheat. Faye eyed them suspiciously. Sharon returned to the kitchen for coffee, then poured herself a glass of wine, which she deems a health food.

"So, are you enjoying your trip to California?" she asked Faye as she took a seat.

"Goodness, yes. I hadn't seen Anna in over a year. She's become quite the little sophisticate."

Sharon nodded. "Of course, she has a live-in tutor in Libby."

"So I've noticed." Faye did not sound particularly pleased. She took a tentative bite of sandwich. "Interesting," she said through a stiff smile.

"Those are sprouts," I explained.

"I'm not a total simpleton, Kate."

But I could tell she'd been uncertain.

She took another nibble, still tentative. "Well, it's certainly not egg salad. Just wait until I tell the girls back home."

Sharon sipped her wine. "We ran into the Burtons last night," she said, looking in my direction. "Yvonne told me you're working for them now."

I nodded, then explained to Faye, "My art consultant business."

Sharon grinned. "The Burtons are well connected. Steve is respected professionally, and with this election coming up he's been out mingling with the powers that be. He knows a lot of important people. You work this right, you'll get some great referrals." She gave me the thumbs-up sign. "Movin' into the big time."

"Hardly that. Anyway, I have to wow the Burtons first. Yvonne's been less than thrilled with what I've shown her so far. And Steve, sweet as he is, doesn't really care one way or the other."

"Maybe not directly, but if Yvonne's happy, he will be too." Sharon turned to Faye. "Steve is a widower. He was sort of a lost soul before Yvonne and Skye came into his life."

"Skye?"

"Yvonne's daughter."

Faye lifted a brow. "Yvonne must have been a latter-day hippie to come up with a name like that."

"Skye chose it herself, actually," Sharon said.

This I hadn't known. "You mean it's not her real name?"

"It's real now. She had it changed legally."

"Surely her mother could have stopped her," Faye snipped.

Sharon shrugged. "If she'd wanted to. Yvonne's first husband ran off and left them when Skye was six. Couldn't handle the responsibility. Always looking out for number one, sort of like Andy—" Sharon had been in the midst of an empathetic nod in my direction when she remembered how Faye and I were related. She stopped mid-sentence with an expression of chagrin.

Faye pushed her plate to the side, sandwich largely

untouched. "Andy came back, however," she said in a tight voice. "There's a difference."

Not as big a difference as she thought, but I let it ride. Faye considered the divorce my fault. Her son had erred by leaving, certainly. She never implied that he was perfect. But I'd committed the greater sin in not forgiving him.

"Anyway," Sharon continued after a moment of heavy silence, "Skye took it pretty hard. She felt rejected, guilty, the whole trip. It's only been the last couple of years that she's gotten her act together. Changing her name was part of it."

Faye straightened. "Skye must have been an emotionally unstable child to begin with, if she reacted so poorly. Anna is doing just fine. I've never seen a happier, more well-adjusted child."

This was not the line I'd heard over the weekend when Faye had been concerned about Anna's language, her tastes in movies and music, her *worldliness,* to use Faye's term. But we'd been talking then about my loose standards and Michael's "outside" influence.

"Anna's a doll," Sharon concurred, and quickly stood to clear the table.

Faye folded her napkin, then excused herself to use the "powder room."

"Geez," Sharon said, slapping herself on the cheek. "Foot-in-mouth disease. I thought I was over that. And we'd been having such a nice time, too."

"Don't worry about it. You didn't say anything that wasn't true."

The phone rang and Sharon answered it. "For you," she said, handing me the receiver. In a whisper, she added, "It's Michael."

"What are you and Sharon up to?" he asked. "You concocting some wild scheme, or is this an afternoon of pure girlish pleasure?"

"Neither. Sharon was doing her civic duty by having me and Faye to lunch."

"Ah."

"Exactly."

Michael made a throaty sound that passed for sympathy. "I was hoping I could see you this afternoon," he said.

"What's up?"

"What's up? Maybe I just miss you."

I smiled into the phone. "I miss you, too. We all do, even Max."

A chuckle, and then a beat of silence. "There's also something I'd like you to look at."

"Will we need privacy?"

The chuckle erupted into a laugh. "Don't I wish. Unfortunately, it's work related. Patricia Shepherd found a list of names among the homework files on Julie's computer. I wanted to see if you recognized any of them."

"Couldn't you read them to me over the phone?"

"I could, but I'd prefer to have you look them over in person, sitting next to me. I wasn't making up the part about missing you."

"Neither was I."

"Can you do it?"

"I'll be by in about an hour, is that okay?"

"I'll be waiting."

Faye was napping on the living room couch when I left to see Michael. She'd dozed off five minutes into the afternoon soap opera she'd dubbed the "silliest thing on earth" when she turned it on. I hadn't asked why, in that case, she bothered to watch it.

I left a note explaining that I'd gone out. On impulse, I covered her with the heathery green afghan she'd knit for us when Anna was a baby. "Knit with love," she'd written on the card. "It will come in handy—for cool evenings and those dismal, droopy days when you wish the world would go away." I thought Faye might be feeling a little that way herself at the moment.

Michael was at his desk in the midst of a yawn when I knocked on his open door. He looked up, smiled, and yawned again.

"You really know how to make a girl feel welcome."

He closed the door and gave me a kiss that more than made up for the yawns. Then he yawned again.

"If Don's couch is that uncomfortable," I told him, "you might find Faye the lesser of two evils."

"The couch wasn't the problem." His tone was petulant. "I was up most of last night working on the Cindy Purcell murder."

"The girl at the reservoir?"

He nodded, ran a hand over his chin. "We got a lead yesterday on a witness who saw her talking with some guy outside the video shop the night she disappeared. Told us he was sure he'd recognize the guy if he saw him again. So we bring our witness in, have him look through mug shots. Nothing. Then we call in a sketch artist, one of the best in the area. And our witness turns out to be a total flake. Can't remember whether the hair was blond or black, long or short, whether his face was full or thin. Only thing he was sure of was that the person Cindy was talking to was male. He'd probably have caved on that as well if we'd pushed him."

"Come sit down," I told him. "I'll rub your back."

While I stood behind him, kneading the muscles of his neck and shoulders, Michael read me the list of names from Julie's computer. Seven names. Five definitely female, one male, and one that could be either. None of them sounded familiar.

"Have you checked the phone book?" I asked.

Michael sighed. "Your confidence in my abilities is astounding."

I ran my thumbs across his shoulders and then kissed the back of his neck. "I take it that's a yes."

"We also checked with the DMV. Several matches for a number of the names, none local. I was hoping they might ring a bell with you."

"Sorry." I peered over his shoulder at the list. "There's a boy at school by the last name of Walker, but I don't know a Claudia Walker. Maybe it's his mother or his sister."

"Walker isn't exactly an unusual last name."

As I continued to rub his shoulders, Michael's head bobbed forward and his breathing grew thicker. Even without the benefit of exhaustion, Michael is able to fall asleep at the drop of a hat, much like Max. It's a gift I envy.

Fortunately, he could wake just as quickly.

The phone rang and he reached for it as though he'd been expecting the call. "Detective division, Stone here." There was a pause. "Yeah, I got it." He scribbled something on a pad of paper, glanced my way, then sighed audibly. "Give me half an hour."

I could tell from the angle of his shoulders and the tension in his voice that the call hadn't brought welcome news. Michael turned and took my hands.

"That was the Berkeley PD. They've discovered the body of a young woman who fits Julie Harmon's description."

His words hung in the air. I heard them first, then felt them in the pit of my stomach. "Body. That means she's dead?"

"I'm afraid so." He pulled me close and cradled me against his chest. "They don't have a positive ID yet, so there's still a chance it's not her. They'll have the Shepherds go by the morgue once the body's been moved there."

I closed my eyes and focused my attention on the steady rhythm of Michael's heartbeat. "How was she killed?"

"Shot. A jogger found her body a couple of hours ago in the underbrush near the northern edge of Tilden Park. I'm heading there now."

"Do you want me to come with you? I can tell you whether or not it's Julie."

He rocked back. "You don't have to do that, Kate."

"But it would help, wouldn't it?"

I could sense his hesitation. "Are you sure you're up to it?"

"Just let me call Sharon and ask her to pick Anna up from school."

9

Tilden Park runs along the ridge line of the Berkeley hills. Hiking trails, both official and unofficial, criss-cross the area, interspersed with picnic areas, play fields, and lakes. The terrain is gentle in some places, steep and rugged in others.

We pulled in at a group barbecue site off the main road. The small parking area was jammed with official vehicles, including the coroner's car.

"You can still change your mind," Michael said.

I shook my head. "I want to know."

We headed across an open field and then followed a narrow dirt trail into the forested canyon to the west. About half a mile in we came to a flat glen and the buzz of human activity. I felt my stomach tighten.

"Why don't you wait here for a minute," Michael said. "I'll be right back."

He joined a group of three men, two of whom he apparently knew. They conversed for a few minutes, looking frequently at a spot of shrubbery some ten yards beyond.

After a moment, Michael motioned for me to join him. He introduced me to the detective in charge, Jim Gates.

"You ready to have a look?" Gates asked, squinting at me with steely gray eyes. His manner, though polite, was brusque and to the point.

I nodded

"The body's been covered with leaves, out in the elements for a couple of days, so be prepared. She's not going to look like her yearbook picture."

She didn't. At first glance, she barely looked human. Her entire body was mottled with leaves and grime. Her skin was purplish, her features swollen and distorted. But I was reasonably sure it was Julie.

I swallowed hard against the tightness in my throat when I recognized the pink sweater as the one she'd worn to school the day she disappeared. Only now it was blackened with dried blood. And something else that I identified too late as the movement of insects. I averted my eyes, took a deep breath, counted to ten. My legs felt like Jell-o and my body was seized by tremors. I looked back again when Michael swore under his breath.

Gates stepped closer. "What is it?"

My eyes moved from Julie's stained sweater to her face and then back down to her slacks. And that's when I understood what Michael had reacted to.

She was lying face up, hands spread at her sides like wings. Her clothing was fully intact but her feet were bare, and encased in plastic wrap. Her toenails were painted a deep blood-red. Just like Cindy Purcell.

"This looks a lot like the homicide we had out at the reservoir a couple of weeks ago," Michael explained.

"The pose, the feet, the fact that she was covered with leaves."

Gates rocked forward onto the balls of his feet. "The young woman who was strangled?"

Michael nodded. "Did you happen to find a plastic toy skeleton near the body?"

"About six inches from her left hand."

Michael stepped forward, kneeling near Julie's head. He pointed. "Looks like there's a chunk of hair that's been cut. That fits as well." He looked at me. "Can you tell, Kate? See where it's shorter there on the side. That wasn't the way she wore it, was it?"

I hadn't noticed at first, but now that I was looking, I could see where a handful of shoulder-length hair had been chopped off close to her face.

I shook my head "She . . . she had . . ." I brought my hands to the side of my neck to indicate length. I no longer trusted my voice.

Michael put a hand on my arm. "Why don't you go find a seat over there?" He nodded toward the breadth of a fallen log. "I'm going to be a bit longer, but I'll make it as quick as I can."

I nodded mutely, realizing that I suddenly felt light-headed. Gates called to one of the other officers, a black woman with a figure more befitting a fashion model than a policewoman.

"Can you see that Mrs. Austen finds a place to rest?" he said.

"I'll be fine," I mumbled, although I wasn't so sure.

The woman took my arm and guided me to the log. "It's never easy," she said softly. "And kids are the hardest. Even when you haven't known them personally."

"She was a student of mine," I mumbled. "A sweet, gentle kid."

"You want me to sit with you awhile?" the officer asked.

I shook my head. "Thanks, but that's not necessary."

"You sure?"

I inhaled deeply, cleansing my lungs from the stench of death. "I'm sure."

She hesitated before heading back to join the others. "My name's Tira, Celeste Tira. You holler if you want some company, okay?"

When the woman was gone, I closed my eyes and took another deep breath. The afternoon sun was warm against my back. A picture-perfect fall day, a day for joy and laughter and ice cream in a cone. I thought of Julie standing hesitantly by the corner of my desk, troubled and unsure, reaching out for help the only way she knew how.

Tears dampened my cheeks. Julie Harmon, no longer merely missing, but murdered. Although that possibility had been in the back of my mind all along, it hadn't prepared me for the harsh reality of knowing she was actually dead.

10

Julie's death didn't make the six o'clock news, but it rated a front page headline in the following morning's paper. The face in the accompanying photo, carefree and smiling, brought a lump to my throat. I scanned the story to see if it contained anything I didn't already know. It didn't.

I was still staring at the paper when Libby skittered into the kitchen. She glanced at the headline from across the table, then turned away and busied herself pouring a glass of orange juice.

"Are you okay, Libby?"

She mumbled acknowledgment without really answering.

I'd broken the news to her last night. She'd listened silently and then quickly retreated to her room. When I checked on her an hour later, I found her lying on the bed, staring at the ceiling. "I don't want to discuss it right now," she said. The message was the same when I knocked on the door a second time. I knew this was

Libby's way of coping, the way she'd dealt with the deaths of her mother and a friend the year before. But I thought that grief turned inward took its toll, especially in one so young.

"Do you feel like talking yet?" I asked.

Libby sat across from me and drank half the glass of juice. "What's there to talk about?"

"Sometimes it helps."

She shrugged.

"I know this is hard on you."

"I'll live."

I touched her hand. "Julie was a friend, honey. It's only natural that you'd be upset."

"Some friend I turned out to be." Her words were clipped, but her voice sounded on the edge of crumbling.

"What do you mean?"

"I don't want to talk about it." Libby stood, finished her juice, and hurried off, practically mowing down Faye on her way out of the kitchen.

Faye hugged her robe across her ample figure. She eyed the newspaper photo. "Is that the girl?"

I nodded.

"Such a young thing, and pretty, too. It's a frightening world we live in."

"It certainly is."

Faye poured herself some coffee. "How's Libby doing this morning?"

"I don't know. She's keeping it all inside."

Libby made another sweeping pass through the kitchen, grabbing a carton of yogurt and an apple on her way. "Gotta run."

"You'll be careful, won't you?"

"You think I'm stupid, Kate?" Libby's voice spiraled

in volume. "Of course I'll be careful. There's a murderer on the loose."

"It's just that I worry—"

"I'm fine, really. So stop breathing down my neck like I'm Anna's age." Her words were punctuated with the slam of the door.

Faye fanned her face with an open hand. "Goodness, such manners."

"She's upset," I explained. "And scared." What's more she wasn't the only one. I'd been awake half the night wending my way through the labyrinth of grief and apprehension.

I turned to Faye. "What would you like for breakfast?"

"Don't bother about me. I know how rushed your mornings are."

"Not today. My class doesn't meet until afternoon. I could scramble some eggs," I told her. "Or whip up an omelette if you'd prefer."

Faye folded her hands around her cup. "Don't go to any trouble. Cereal's fine."

Anna arrived just then and settled the matter. French toast with half a bottle of syrup. Faye had several pieces of French toast herself, and almost as much syrup.

When I returned from dropping Anna off at school, Faye had cleaned up the dishes, and was tackling the remainder of the kitchen.

"You don't always have to be cleaning," I told her. "This should be a vacation."

"I like to keep busy."

I took the bottle of cleanser from her hand. I couldn't tell if I was feeling guilty or simply irritated, but I wanted her out of my kitchen. "I don't have to be at school until

one o'clock today," I said. "Is there anywhere you'd like
to go?"

"I'm fine."

"Shopping?"

"I can shop at home."

"San Francisco?"

"I've been to San Francisco."

Seen one tree, seen them all. "Why don't you come
with me then while I take Max for a walk. We can go into
town and stop off for a cappuccino or something."

"I'm not much on walking, and I've already had
coffee."

I sighed. "I don't suppose you'd like to borrow a
book?"

"Thanks, but I think not. Most of the stuff that's written
these days doesn't hold my interest."

"I've got a copy of *David Copperfield.*"

She shook her head. "I heard him on *Oprah* last
month."

I started to set her straight, then wondered what purpose it would serve. Instead, I grabbed Max's leash. He
was at my feet in an instant, alternately sitting at attention
and then hopping about with unequivocal joy. The jangle
of the leash, like the opening of the refrigerator door
and the click of the can opener, never failed to catch
Max's attention.

The day was crisp and clear. Max trotted along happily,
sniffing every tree and post along the way. I tried to clear
my head, to think of nothing but the vibrant palette of
autumn's reds and golds all around me. Instead, the
darkness of Julie's death was everywhere.

When we returned, Faye was still in the kitchen, lining
shelves. I went into the bedroom and called Andy.

"Are you doing anything for lunch?" I asked.

"Well, this is a surprise."

"Are you?"

His voice dropped a level. "I know it's not my birthday. Must be the pleasure of my company that's the big draw, right?"

"You might say that."

Andy chuckled. "I knew someday you'd come to appreciate my finer qualities."

His finer qualities had never been at issue. It was just that they were so heavily outweighed by the others. "You still haven't answered my question. Do you have lunch plans, or not?"

"Nothing I wouldn't be happy to cancel."

"Good, you're taking your mother to lunch."

"What?" The warmth in his voice had evaporated.

"Someplace nice. You'd better make reservations ahead of time. I'll bring her by your office a little before noon."

"You never give up, do you? Always meddling, always trying to run my life for me." The words were infused with the resentment of countless prior arguments.

"I'll see you in a couple of hours," I told him.

Andy sighed. "Just how I want to spend my lunch hour. What in the hell will we even find to talk about?"

I grinned. "Your favorite subject. Yourself."

Back in the kitchen I found Faye alphabetizing my spices.

"I just talked to Andy," I told her. "He wants to take you to lunch. I said yes. I hope that's okay."

"Lunch?"

"You didn't have plans, did you?"

"No, not really." She looked at my cupboards almost

wistfully. "I know how busy he is, though. I hate to be a bother."

"He's looking forward to it."

"Well, in that case . . ." Her hands drifted from the array of spices to her hair. "I guess I'd better think about getting ready."

"You've got plenty of time."

She frowned. "I don't suppose there's anywhere I could get my hair done on such short notice?"

"Let me check on it." The trendy salons were usually booked weeks in advance. And I didn't think the cut-rate, drop-in place Anna and I frequented offered the rollers-under-the-dryer kind of styling Faye was after. Then I remembered Marlene's, a tiny storefront salon near the pet supply shop. I called and got an appointment for later that morning.

I dropped Faye off in front, went to catch up on errands, and arrived back at the shop just as she was getting combed out and lacquered. Her hair certainly looked as though it had been *done,* although I couldn't say that it was necessarily an improvement. Nonetheless Faye was pleased, and that was what counted.

"Now I feel presentable again," she said as we headed for the car. "When I do it myself, it never looks as good."

My own experience was usually the opposite. I couldn't wait to wash out what the stylist had so painstakingly sculptured.

Faye checked her reflection in the car window before opening the door. "Beauty shop gossip is always so interesting, too."

Again, our experience differed.

"Of course, today everyone was talking about that girl

who died. Marlene, the woman who owns the shop, knows her. Or I guess I should say, knew her.''

"Knew her, how?''

"She lives across the street. Marlene hadn't heard about the girl's running away, so when she opened the paper this morning and saw the headline, it was a real shock.''

"I can imagine.''

"We read about tragedy in the papers all the time, but when you know someone who's involved it's a different thing entirely.''

I leaned over to help Faye, who was struggling with her seat belt.

"Marlene feels like she's partially responsible,'' Faye continued after I'd managed to secure the buckle. "That makes it even worse.''

I straightened into my own seat. "She feels responsible, how?''

"Because she didn't say anything.''

"Anything about what?''

"Sometimes when Marlene's little granddaughter came to visit, Julie would go over and play with her. The little girl is only four and she thought Julie was just the cat's meow. You know how kids are at that age. Marlene liked Julie, too. She says the same thing you do about the Shepherds being strict.''

"What does this have to—''

"That's why she didn't say anything.''

"Anything about what, Faye?'' It drives me crazy when the point of the story gets lost in the telling.

Faye gave me a stern look. "I'll get there if you'll give me the chance.''

"Sorry.''

"It seems that Julie didn't always obey the Shepherds' rules. Marlene saw her sneak out on several occasions, and she once saw her riding on BART in the middle of a school day. There may be some other things, too. Now she's kicking herself for not speaking up. If she had, the girl would have gotten in trouble, but maybe she would have stayed out of trouble, too. Bigger trouble, I mean."

I nodded. "She's not the only one wishing she'd done things differently. Julie tried to talk to me the morning she was killed, but the conversation got put off. I keep thinking that if we'd had a chance to talk, it might have made a difference. In retrospect, it was clear she was worried about something."

"Life is never tidy, is it?" Faye said, and then after a moment's pause added, "Marlene also told me about her daughter."

I practically drove off the road. "Julie's daughter?"

"Goodness, no. Marlene's daughter."

My breathing returned to normal.

"She and her husband were having some problems, but they saw a marriage counselor here in town. He's apparently very good." She paused. "They were on the verge of separating but now they're back together and quite happy. It all boiled down to the fact that they weren't communicating clearly."

We were stopped at a red light so I took the time to give her a solid look. "Andy and I are beyond the phase of 'having some problems.' We're in the final stages of divorce."

"But to throw away all that's good between you, just because of some . . ." She made a helpless gesture with her hand. "Just because of some temporary lapse in judgment."

"It's something that had been building for a long time, Faye."

"There's Anna to consider as well."

"We have."

"It wouldn't hurt to talk to a counselor, would it?" Her voice was as pinched as her expression.

"There'd be no point."

"Andy may not be perfect, but you could do a whole lot worse."

"You're right. But that's no reason to stay married." I took a breath. "Andy and I have worked this out, Faye. We're not bitter or angry, we just don't want to be married anymore."

She folded her arms and stared straight ahead.

"Besides, you're forgetting about Michael."

"The policeman?" Faye's expression soured. "He's the reason you've turned your back on Andy, isn't he?"

"Andy walked out on us before I ever met Michael."

She eyed me steadily. "In my day, we rode out the ups and downs of a bumpy marriage."

Even if it cost a lifetime of happiness, I added silently, remembering Andy's father. Besides, I'd tried riding out the bumps. All it got me was saddle sores.

I parked the car near the front of the building and we took the elevator to the third-floor offices of Sterling Enterprises.

"We're here to see Andy Austen," I told the receptionist, another new face in a series of many.

"Fancy office," Faye observed, impressed no doubt by the mahogany paneling and expansive glass-walled conference room. "Andy must be doing quite well for himself."

I didn't have the heart to tell her that Andy's office was a tiny, unpaneled nook with only a small interior window. On the other hand, given Andy's history, he *was* doing well. In a little over six months, he'd moved from an open cubicle to a closed office, and from administrative assistant to leasing agent. For a man who'd heretofore changed jobs as often as shoes, this was something of an accomplishment.

I saw him emerge from his office at the end of the hallway, accompanied by a shorter, stockier man in a flashy, mustard-and-black plaid jacket. Andy walked the man to another door closer to the reception area and ushered him through. It was when the man turned to shake Andy's hand that I recognized him.

"Wasn't that Walton Shepherd?" I asked after Andy had joined us.

He nodded. "You know him?"

"I've met him. What's he doing here?"

"The same thing all our customers are doing," Andy said, with only a hint of sarcasm. "He's conducting business."

"Shepherd's a customer? I thought he was an appliance repairman." Sterling Enterprises had its finger in many pies but most of it was rooted in real estate and development. I couldn't imagine what interest Walton Shepherd would have in commercial property.

"Was a repairman," Andy corrected. "He retired from that job a couple of weeks ago. He's taking space in that new shopping center we're putting in out by the hospital."

"Space for what?"

"A rod and gun shop. Shepherd's a hunter and fisherman himself. It's been a lifelong dream of his to open a store catering to others with the same interests. It's a damn good idea, too. Most of these mega-sports stores focus on skiing, biking, camping, that kind of thing. You want a good fishing rod or hunting rifle, they're not easy to find. And it's even harder to find a salesperson who knows what he's talking about.''

''That must be fairly expensive space.''

''It isn't cheap. 'Course, he's not going to have one of the prime locations.''

''But how can he afford it at all?''

''We wouldn't be leasing to him if he didn't have the money.'' Andy's tone was patronizing. ''We don't simply take people's word for it, you know.''

He leaned across the narrow counter and left instructions with the receptionist. ''I'll probably be a couple of hours,'' he told her. Then he turned to his mother. ''I hope you're hungry. We're going to one of the best restaurants in town.''

''Well, you know me, I'm not really a big eater.''

From behind her back, Andy winked at me, and for a moment we were back in the easy camaraderie that marked the early stages of our marriage. Although I would never admit it to Faye, there *were* moments when I missed him. Well, maybe not missed him so much as felt the sweep of nostalgia for the man I'd once thought he was.

The three of us walked to the elevator.

''It's Shepherd's niece who was found murdered in the Berkeley hills,'' I said.

Andy nodded. ''He told me.''

''It seems a little odd that he'd be going about his business as though nothing had happened.''

"I think it shook him up all right. He looked like he hadn't slept all night."

"Sometimes," Faye said, "carrying on with life is the best therapy."

I concurred, but I thought that Walton Shepherd might be pushing it a bit. Of course, he hadn't been any too happy with Julie's presence in his life in the first place.

It was the middle of the lunch hour when I pulled into the school parking lot, which meant that I had to jostle my way through clusters of screeching students en route to my classroom. As I was rounding the corner by the library, I spotted Mario Sanchez standing alone, tracing a crack in the cement with his foot. When I approached, he looked up with an uneasy expression and started off in the opposite direction. I called after him, but he either didn't hear me or chose to ignore my greeting.

"Mario giving you trouble?" Marvin Melville asked, falling into step beside me.

I shook my head. "There was just something I wanted to ask him."

"Looks like he wasn't any too eager to hear it."

"You're right. Funny though, we've always gotten along fairly well."

Marvin shrugged philosophically. "You get used to stuff like that when you're a teacher. The trick is not to take it personally."

I bit my lip. I wasn't so much hurt as perplexed.

"If you ask me," Marvin said, "there's more to that kid than he lets on."

"In what way?"

"I don't know exactly. But I suspect his laid-back, easygoing attitude is more armor than anything else. Whatever his real feelings are, he plays them close to the chest."

I thought the same could be said of Marvin, and wondered again what Yvonne had meant when she'd mentioned rumors about him. "Is Mario in one of your classes?" I asked.

"Two of them. English and journalism."

Maybe that was the connection I'd missed before. "Julie Harmon was in your journalism class as well," I commented.

At the mention of Julie's name, Marvin's expression darkened. "It's terrible what happened to her," he said, pulling at an earlobe. "I'd heard that she was missing, but I just assumed she'd had an argument at home or something, and run off."

"That's what most of us thought."

Marvin was silent a moment. "According to the papers, there are similarities between this case and the other dead girl out by the reservoir." His voice held the same strain of disbelief that had characterized every other conversation I'd had on the subject.

I nodded. Although we were loath to speak them aloud, the questions were there in our minds. How could such a thing happen in Walnut Hills? Did we really have a serial killer on the loose? Was this only the beginning of what might prove to be a long reign of terror?

Marvin ran a finger under his collar. "Two murders, one right after the other. It's eerie."

We came to my classroom door and stopped. "Libby mentioned something about a project Julie was working on for the school paper."

"The term assignment?"

"I guess so. Is it far enough along to be published? I was thinking it might be nice to run the piece in memory of her."

"Unfortunately, I know very little about it."

"Did she keep notes?"

"If she did, I haven't seen them. Julie was tight-lipped about the whole thing." Melville checked his watch just as the warning bell rang. "Oops, I'd better get going. Combs is already on my case for letting students use the classroom when I'm not there."

My own class poured into the room minutes before the final bell. Their mood was subdued.

It had been my initial intention to spend the week working on visual perspective, but given all that had happened, I didn't feel up to introducing a new subject. And I suspected that the students were in no mood to listen, either. The way I saw it, Julie's death had provided a lesson in perspective of a different sort. We all needed time to absorb it.

Instead of lecturing, I let the class work quietly, finishing up loose ends or working on sketches for their portfolios. I did the same, spending most of the hour on a charcoal still life made up of the odds and ends on my desk. The process was soothing, the final result a disaster.

As soon as the dismissal bell rang, Brian Walker poked his head through the door.

"I hear you're looking for me," he said, brushing a shock of straight blond hair from his eyes. Brian towered over me and I had to look up to meet his gaze.

I nodded. "Word travels fast."

He sat on the edge of the nearest art table and folded his arms. "It's about Libby, I bet."

"Libby?" My voice sounded like the croak of a frog. Did Brian know something I didn't? Something, maybe, that I *ought* to know.

"I saw you in the library last weekend, trying to pretend you weren't watching us." Brian grinned, pleased to have the upper hand.

"I wasn't really watching, just trying to locate Libby."

"Sure." His tone was amused. "Whatever you say."

Even among senior boys, who ran the gamut of shapes and sizes, Brian Walker was an anomaly. Tall, broad-shouldered, and as self-possessed as a movie idol. In fact, he looked more like Hollywood's casting choice for lead student than an in-the-flesh young man barely out of adolescence.

I gave him an icy glare. "What made you think I might want to talk to you about Libby?"

He gave his shoulders a casual shrug. "Seems like a lot of mothers do. 'Course, I understand you're not Libby's mother." He gave me a playful look. "You're much too young for that."

"You can cut the flattery," I told him curtly. "I'm not impressed."

Although at some level I was, but not in the way he expected. What I found fascinating was the fluid poise he managed to exude. It was no wonder Libby was smitten. I wondered if anyone at sixteen, or even eighteen, would be immune to his charm.

Brian laughed. "So, what's on your mind, then?"

"Julie Harmon."

His expression sobered. "I think she's on everyone's mind today."

"Did you know her well?" I gathered my belongings and moved toward the door.

"Hardly at all."

"I got the impression you did."

He shrugged.

"I was hoping you might be able to help me."

Brian held the door as we left the classroom. "I'm on my way into town to grab a cup of coffee. You want to come along?"

"Don't you have a sixth-period class?"

"Just Spanish." Brian matched his pace to mine. "I'm so far behind it's not even worth going to class anymore."

"That's hardly the way to catch up."

"Right, but there's no chance I'm going to catch up no matter how you slice it. And Miss Lathrop drives me loony." He paused. "So you coming?".

I wondered briefly if there was a rule against aiding and abetting student truancy. "Can't we talk on campus?"

"Not if I'm your designated conversationalist," he said with a trace of a smirk. "I'm outta here."

Well, I reasoned, I wasn't really helping him cut class; he was going to do that anyway. And Brian *was* an adult. I nodded, and followed him to the parking lot, feeling all the while as though I were attempting to slip over the wall at San Quentin.

Brian slid into the driver's seat of a red Mazda convertible. Despite the increasing cloud cover and cool temperature, he kept the top down. We pulled out of the parking

lot with a squeal of tires and a cloud of dust. I held my
hair with a hand to keep it from whipping into my eyes.

"I thought we were going to McDonald's," I said when
we bypassed the golden arches and swung onto the
freeway.

"That's not my style."

"But you had lunch there a couple of times with Julie."

He raised an eyebrow. "Where'd you hear that?"

"You mean it isn't true?"

He shrugged. "We may have stopped there once. Generally, we went back to my place."

I turned abruptly. "Why?"

A grin spread across Brian's face. "Why not?"

I could understand how mothers of the girls he dated
might be concerned.

Brian made a sweeping U-turn in the middle of town
and pulled into a spot in front of Josh's Noshes, one of
several new coffeehouses that had recently sprung up
around town. Brian was apparently a regular customer.
The woman behind the counter not only knew his name
but his usual order of a double espresso and a croissant.
If this was the way he routinely approached Spanish class,
it was no wonder he was behind in the subject.

I had a straight decaf and willed myself to stop drooling
over the croissants.

Brian leaned forward, elbows on the table. "So Kate—
it's okay if I call you Kate, isn't it? Since we're no longer
at school, there's no reason we should be constrained by
formality." He smiled and, without waiting for an answer,
continued. "What is it you wanted to know?"

I scooted my chair backwards a few inches. "Did you
and Julie see a lot of each other?"

"Not really."

"But . . ." I shifted uncomfortably. Despite the first-name business, I felt unaccountably old. "But you said the two of you spent time at your place."

He looked at me over the rim of his cup, enjoyed a moment of amusement at my expense, then sighed. "It wasn't anything like what you're thinking. Friends come by my house all the time."

"Did she ever talk to you about being an emancipated minor?"

Brian shook his head. "I'm not sure she even knew about it. I've been eighteen since August, before I met her." He paused for a sip of coffee. "It would make sense though that she'd want to get away from those yahoos she was living with."

"You know them?"

"Only by reputation. Their son Dennis is a couple of years older than me. We took swimming lessons together when we were kids, and we were both part of the school band my freshman year."

"I didn't know you played in the band." Somehow, Brian didn't seem the type.

"I don't anymore."

I rocked back and caught the look on his face. For just a moment it darkened, like the sun dimmed by a passing cloud.

"How come you stopped?"

He shrugged, examined his hands. "It was boring."

"Were you and Dennis friends?"

"Not likely." A grimace pulled his expression tight.

"I take it you didn't like him much."

"Mostly we were just different." Brian paused, downed a gulp of coffee. "He had a rough time in high school, but from what I've heard, he came through okay."

"Rough time?"

"Emotional problems. In and out of school for a while, spent time in some treatment center up north."

"Was there trouble with the law, as well?"

"Not that I know of."

I fiddled with the packets of sweetener. "Did Julie talk much about the Shepherds?"

Brian lifted his right shoulder in a semi-shrug. "I told you, I hardly knew her. They wouldn't let Julie date, so we got together a couple of times during the day. End of story, no big deal." He squinted at me. "What are you after here, anyway?"

"I'm not sure. I guess I'm trying to make sense of what happened."

"There's a lot of shit happens that doesn't make any sense. People just make themselves crazy thinking that it should." Brian broke off a piece of croissant and offered it to me. "You want some?"

I shook my head. "What was your impression of Julie?"

He blinked. "My impression?"

"Right."

He shrugged. "I guess mostly it's that she wasn't what I first thought. She had this kind of been-there manner about her, you know? But turns out she was just a kid underneath. And a lot more serious about things than I expected."

"Pretty insightful, for someone who 'hardly knew her.' "

He gave me a quirky smile. "I'm an insightful kind of guy."

"You aren't by any chance related to a Claudia Walker, are you?" It was the only name I'd recognized from the

list Patricia Shepherd had found in Julie's computer files.
I'd meant to ask about it before this.

"Afraid not," Brian replied.

Two well-built women in biking shorts walked by our
table, and Brian's eyes followed them.

"Funny you should ask, though," he said, finally dragging his attention back to the conversation at hand. "Julie
asked me about her, too."

I sat forward. "Did she say why?"

"At first, I assumed it was a friend of hers, but there
was something she said later that made me think this
Claudia person was someone Julie wanted to meet."

"Someone local?"

"I have no idea."

I tucked the information away for Michael, although
I wasn't sure that the names on the list mattered anymore.
The police were no longer looking for Julie, they were
looking for her killer.

We finished our coffee and arrived back at school just
as classes were getting out for the day. A pretty girl I
didn't know waved at Brian. He beckoned her over.

"Hi, gorgeous, want a ride?"

She flashed him a smile that was meant to dazzle.
"Sure, if there's room." The look she gave me was something altogether different.

"I'm getting out," I told her. Then I turned to Brian
and said, *"Gracias."*

He looked at me blankly.

"It's Spanish," I explained. "Your sixth-period class."

He grinned. "I thought it sounded familiar."

"You shouldn't give up on the class, you know. It's
only October."

There was a sardonic glint in his eyes. "Thanks, I

appreciate the advice." His fingers drummed the steering wheel. "If you want to know about Julie, you should be talking to Mario Sanchez, not me."

"They were good friends?"

Brian's laugh was quick and harsh. "I don't know what you'd call it exactly."

Gorgeous stood by the door tapping her foot. She gave me a pointed look. "I thought you were getting out."

"I am," I told her. Although if I could have found a way to do so, I'd have liked to stay and question Brian further. I had the distinct feeling he knew Julie better than he was letting on.

12

Anna was in a funk when I picked her up after school. "I'm starved," she announced, folding her arms indignantly across her chest.

"How come? I packed you a good-sized lunch."

"I had to throw it away because it was full of ants."

"Ants?"

"They got into all the lunches in the bottom cubbies. Mrs. Brown asked the rest of the class to share." She paused while she punched the buttons on the radio. "Kyle gave me his celery," she said.

"That's nice." Although hardly substantial nourishment.

"He should have given me his whole lunch. He's the one who dropped the stupid ant farm."

So that explained it. I mouthed the necessary words of sympathy. "How about I heat up a pizza for you when we get home?"

"Potato chips, too?"

"Well, I don't know about that."

"Please. I was *so* hungry all day long, my stomach hurt."
Anna did her best to sound pitiful.

"Okay, a few chips too."

"With a Coke?"

Anna is a master at this game, but with Julie's death still fresh in my mind, I decided there were worse things than junk food.

"With a Coke," I told her.

She smiled, and I had a sudden vision of Anna single-handedly plotting new ways to transport ants to school.

The phone was ringing as we walked in the door and Anna raced to answer it. I could tell from her end of the conversation that it was Michael. When I'd poured her soda, we traded.

"How are you doing?" he asked.

"All right, under the circumstances. Anything new on Julie's death?"

"Looks like she never made it to the game Friday night, but that's about the only piece of the puzzle that's solidly in place. Of course none of the lab reports are back yet so something may turn up."

"No suspects, I take it."

"Not that I'm aware of. But Gates isn't going to tell me any more than he has to. He wants the credit and the glory channeled his way." Michael must have leaned back in his chair; I could hear it squeak. "He's been angling for a management position, and something like this might just cinch it for him."

"A girl is dead and he's looking at it as a rung in his career ladder? That's sick."

"It's the way things work, Kate. And Gates is no fool. Whatever his motivation, he'll bust his butt to get the guy who did it."

"Even if it means elbowing you out of the way?"

"There's nothing personal in it. Besides, it *is* Berkeley's case."

"But shouldn't they work with you? You were involved in looking for Julie when she was missing."

"The two departments are cooperating." Michael paused. "I want to see the guy caught, and I don't really care which of us does it." But I could tell he was peeved. Turf wars are particularly irksome when you're the little guy. It was a fact of life that Michael hadn't counted on when he'd moved from San Francisco to the smaller department in Walnut Hills.

"Her murder is similar to Cindy Purcell's," I pointed out. "And you're working that one."

He sighed. "Gates sees it as similar, that's for sure."

There was a pensive quality to his voice I'd heard before. "You sound skeptical."

"Do I? Maybe I am."

"About what?"

The chair squeaked again. "Well, there are similarities, no denying that. The toy skeleton, the shorn hair, the bare feet encased in plastic. But there's stuff that's different, too."

"Such as?"

"The means of death, for one thing. Cindy was strangled; Julie was shot. Other than that, it's mostly little stuff. The differences may or may not be important. But once you've convinced yourself you're looking for a single killer, the strategy of the investigation changes. It's all a question of what assumptions you make up front."

"I thought you said Gates was good."

"He is. Even teaches a criminology course at Cal."

This last was delivered with a trace of envy. Michael had been trying for the last year to land a similar position.

I switched the phone to the other ear and checked on Anna's pizza. "Remember the name 'Claudia Walker' from that list in Julie's computer files? I asked the boy at school with the same last name if he was related. He isn't, but he said Julie had asked him the same thing. He got the impression that she wasn't someone Julie knew."

"Thanks for checking."

"I also found out that Dennis Shepherd has had some emotional problems."

"What kind?"

"I'm not sure." I told him about my conversation with Brian Walker. "It warrants looking into, don't you think? I mean, in light of his attitude toward Julie."

"It's not my call, but I'll pass the information along to the powers that be."

The front door opened, and I heard Faye call out, "Yoo-hoo, anyone home?"

"Is that Dragon Mother I hear in the background?" Michael asked.

"She's not *that* bad."

He laughed. "Probably not. I gotta go anyway. Love you, Kate."

"Love you, too."

"Oh," Faye said, wandering into the kitchen. "You are home after all." She glared critically at the phone in my hand.

"Bye." I hung up and smiled at Faye. "How was lunch?"

"Scrumptious. I'm so full I won't be able to eat for a week. I think I'll skip dinner tonight if you don't mind." She gave Anna a kiss. "And how are you, sweet pea?"

Anna wiped the spot on her cheek where Faye's lips had touched. "Starving," she replied pointedly.

I took the pizza out of the microwave and set it in front of her. "Careful, it's hot."

The front door opened again, and this time slammed shut, announcing Libby's arrival. A moment later she shuffled into the kitchen, followed by Skye.

Libby opened the fridge and grabbed two Cokes. "Is it okay if I have dinner at Skye's tonight?"

"Fine by me if it's all right with the Burtons." I was a bit surprised at the request, however, since Libby had, on previous occasions, referred to Skye as "the most self-absorbed creature on earth."

"My parents are going out tonight," Skye said. "But they don't mind if I have a friend over." She ran her tongue over her braces. "Libby and I are both real upset over what happened with Julie. We thought we'd write a memorandum for the newspaper."

"In memoriam," Libby huffed. "It's different than a memo."

Skye tossed her head. "Whatever."

I handed Anna a second napkin, which she badly needed. She had pizza sauce from her forehead to her chin. "How involved is Mario Sanchez with the newspaper?" I asked. "I know he's on the staff, but does he contribute much?"

"Some," Libby said. "But not a lot. He's a whiz at the computer, though. I don't think we'd ever get the layout right without him."

"Mostly he slinks around ogling the girls." Skye's nose wrinkled with contempt.

"He does not," Libby retorted.

"Yes, he does. I don't know where he got the idea that anyone in Walnut Hills would be interested in *him.*"

"What's wrong with Mario?"

Skye shook her hair from her face. She wore it in a style that was long and bushy, and not particularly becoming. "He's just, you know . . . different."

Libby crossed her arms. "Hispanic, you mean?"

"That too."

The doorbell rang and I went to answer it so I never got to hear how the discussion came out, but I thought Libby had probably hit close to the truth. It was my impression that Skye didn't have much use for people who weren't an easy fit in the stratum of society she imaged for herself.

I reached the door just as the bell sounded a second time. Susie Sullivan Lambert stood on my doorstep in a raw silk blouse, perfectly pressed wool slacks and blazer, and enough gold and diamonds to open her own jewelry shop.

"I hope I'm not disturbing anything," she said in a voice as honeyed as her hair. "I was wondering if I could talk to you about the murders."

Since her third and most recent divorce, Susie has decided to devote herself to her career. To that end, she now fancies herself a news reporter rather than local gossip columnist, despite ample evidence that her talents are better suited to the latter.

"Me?" I was genuinely taken aback. "I don't know anything."

She smiled. "You were there when they found the body. Besides, you must know something about the girl— she was a student at the high school." Susie stepped forward. "May I come in? This wind stirs up my allergies."

Susie had burned me once last year by misquoting my words in connection with another murder, so I was wary. But she was also a friend of sorts, and just as likely to make up what she didn't get in the way of solid information. Besides, I could hardly slam the door in her face.

I led her into the kitchen, where Skye and Libby were picking at the remnants of Anna's pizza. Faye and Anna were nowhere to be seen.

"What is it you want to know?" I asked Susie.

"Everything. In as much detail as possible. We've never had a serial killer in Walnut Hills before."

I winced at her tone, which sounded almost jubilant. "What makes you think we have one now?"

"That's what the radio said. I mean, they didn't come right out and say it, but that was the implication. The Berkeley police have given him a name even—The Parkside Killer." She crossed her legs and rolled the airborne ankle in a semicircle. "A Berkeley girl murdered in Walnut Hills, and a Walnut Hills girl murdered in Berkeley. There's a kind of symmetry to that, isn't there? I wonder if it means anything."

"What it means," I said with distaste, "is that two innocent young women are dead."

Susie looked at me. "Yes, that's the whole point."

It was obvious she'd missed mine.

Still swiveling her ankle, Susie turned to address Libby. "The Harmon girl was only a year behind you. Did you know her?"

"Yeah, a little." Libby scooted her chair back from the table, preparing to leave.

"So did I," Skye added, leaning forward.

"Wonderful. Tell me about her."

"She was just an everyday person," Libby said with a

shrug. "Not real outgoing, but then she'd been through a lot recently."

"Withdrawn? Gloomy?"

Libby shook her head. "Quiet, but friendly."

Skye crimped a lock of wiry hair with her finger. "It was kind of a surface friendly, though."

"I see." Susie undid the clasp of her purse and pulled out a leather-bound notebook. "People who knew the girl from Berkeley said the same thing about her—nice, quiet, no bad habits to speak of. Both victims were blond, too." Her tone was pensive.

Skye seemed intrigued. "I've heard that serial killers often choose the same type of victim over and over again."

"Actually," I said, interrupting before Susie could set the thesis of her story in stone, "Michael thinks the two deaths may not even be related. There are some serious discrepancies between the cases."

"Really? Like what?"

I pulled back. "He didn't tell me the details."

"I was hoping I could interview him. Do you think he'd have time to talk to me?"

"You'd have to ask Michael."

"It might be better if you asked him for me." Susie reached into her purse again and hastily freshened her lipstick, something I've never been able to do without a mirror. "In Berkeley they have a special office within the police department to handle questions from the press. There's been someone there every time I've phoned. Here in Walnut Hills, where I pay taxes I might add, it's hard to get anyone to return my calls."

I sighed. "I'll see if he's interested, but no promises."

She flashed me a smile. "Thanks, Kate." Then she

turned back to the girls. "What's it like knowing there's someone out there killing young women? Are you nervous?"

Skye nodded solemnly, with a touch of drama I found unnecessary. "Who knows where he'll strike next."

"It's awful to lose a friend," Libby said. "That's what I've been thinking about mostly."

Susie scratched a few additional notes, then tucked her pen and notebook back into her purse. "Don't forget to ask Michael. You can let me know tomorrow at the meeting."

"What meeting?"

"For the Fall Festival. Didn't Sharon call you? She said she'd reached everyone."

I harbored the hope, however slim, that Sharon had forgotten she'd involved me in the undertaking. My hopes were dashed when I checked the answering machine. There was a rather lengthy message from Sharon about the meeting and all that we, as co-chairs, needed to attend to. She did, however, close by suggesting dinner, her treat.

"I don't suppose you're free tonight," she said over the machine, "what with a house full of people and all. But after that disastrous lunch yesterday, I feel I owe you. If you've got time, we can even go shopping afterwards."

Normally, I wouldn't have gone. But with Faye not eating dinner and Libby out at Skye's, I figured my presence wouldn't be missed. And Faye had, after all, made this visit in order to spend time with Anna. An evening alone with her only granddaughter ought to be something she would relish.

13

Most of the time Sharon dresses the way I do—comfortable, casual and cheap. Unlike me, however, she also has an extensive wardrobe of sophisticated clothing, and perhaps more important, occasions suitable for putting it to use. When we shop together, it's usually Sharon who leads the way while I tag along like a kid in the candy aisle. Which is the way we spent an hour and a half working our way down the mall from Nordstrom to Macy's.

Not that I minded. My heart wasn't into shopping. The news of Julie's death had settled over me like a damp gray fog. I was grateful for Sharon's company and the semblance of activity. But I didn't much care what direction it took.

"How'd you manage to free yourself from mother-in-law duty tonight?" Sharon asked, pausing to hold a mauve and black print silk scarf against her skin. "What do you think? Are the tones right for my coloring, or do they make me look washed out?"

"It's good."

She picked up the same print in emerald green and draped it over my shoulder. "Take a look in the mirror, Kate. This is you. It looks terrific with your eyes."

I love the way scarves look on other women, but I can never wear them myself without feeling like I've been gift-wrapped. Nonetheless, Sharon was right about the color. And the material was luxurious—lightweight and soft. I checked the price tag and gagged.

"This is definitely *not* me," I told her.

"You have to pamper yourself sometimes, validate your own worth."

"You could pamper a starving village for what that scarf costs."

Sharon sighed. "You're hopeless."

"Just impoverished."

She held up the mauve scarf again and frowned. "So tell me how come you're not home cooking something for Faye to turn up her nose at?"

"She wasn't hungry. I shamed Andy into taking her out to lunch today."

Sharon returned the scarf to its hanger. "That's an oxymoron. Andy's beyond shaming."

"In any case, he took her to lunch. Did it up royally, from what Faye said."

"Well, the last part doesn't surprise me. Was Andy always such a no-account?"

"Probably, but it took me a while to see past his good looks and charm." And I still wasn't entirely immune to them. Not that I had any regrets about divorcing Andy. But I sometimes thought separating from him would have been easier if he'd been a bit more of a scoundrel. Bottom line is, Andy's a decent person—as long as it doesn't put him out any.

Sharon glanced at her watch. "Are you up for a quick stop at the shoe department? I need a pair of comfortable heels in something other than black."

"Comfortable heels. Talk about an oxymoron."

We made our way past purses and jewelry to women's shoes, where the merchandise most prominently displayed looked anything but comfortable. I nodded to a rack of platform sling-backs with thick, block-like heels. They reminded me of the shoes Miss Grundy wore back when I read Archie comics as a kid.

"How about these?" I asked.

Sharon snorted. Instead, she picked up a stylish gray suede pump and was immediately approached by a smiling salesman.

"I'd like to try this on," Sharon said. "Seven and a half, narrow."

As soon as the man was out of earshot, I leaned closer. "That was Dennis Shepherd," I whispered.

"Who?"

"The girl who was murdered, Julie Harmon? He's the son of the couple she was living with."

"The one who brings his laundry home for Mom?"

I nodded, remembering that Dennis had said he worked at Macy's. Nonetheless, the women's shoe department was a surprise.

Dennis returned with a stack of boxes. "We don't have that particular shoe in your size," he explained. "I brought an eight in the shoe you liked, and if it's close, I can always add a wedge in the back to make it a little snugger. I've also brought out some similar styles that we do have in your size."

He set the boxes at Sharon's feet and gave me an odd look. There was a flicker of recognition in his eyes, coupled with uncertainty. "You look familiar," he said after a moment. "Have I waited on you before?"

I hesitated, then shook my head. "I don't think so."

Dennis frowned. "I never forget feet, but I'm not so good with faces." He flexed his knees and squatted at Sharon's feet. "I could swear I've seen you before though."

Sharon cleared her throat, bidding for his attention. "Let me try the suede pump first."

He obliged by slipping off her loafer and delicately positioning her foot in the pump. He took his time, adjusting the fit. "There, how's that feel?" he asked, pulling himself upright.

She stood. "A little loose."

"It's the wrong shoe for you anyway," Dennis said, straightening his tie. His white shirt was no longer crisp. It pulled at the shoulders and across his middle, and was damp under the arms. "You have a classic foot. Slender, high arches, long toes. Not bony, not too full. Let me show you a shoe that will give you a better fit."

Sharon sat down again and Dennis bent over her foot like Prince Charming with the glass slipper. "There, give that a try." He looked up at me. "You sure I didn't sell you that pair of patent-leathers with an ankle strap?"

I shook my head. "I haven't worn patent leather since grade school."

Sharon took a few steps in the shoe he suggested, then slipped on another pair. Dennis was polite and helpful, an ardent sales representative without being pushy. And he certainly knew shoes. But his manner made me uncomfortable.

When he trotted off to fetch a different size, Sharon whispered in my ear. "Aren't you going to talk to him about the murder?"

"What's there to talk about?"

"The guy's a little weird, don't you think?"

"Exactly."

"So don't you want to get his reaction?"

"I can't just bring it up, out of the blue."

Dennis returned with another stack of boxes. He cradled Sharon's ankle, lifted her foot to his knee, and slipped off the too-tight shoe. Sharon leaned forward, then made a production of reading his name tag.

"Dennis Shepherd," she said slowly. "Now talk about familiar. I know I've heard that name recently. You didn't just win some big sales award, did you?"

Dennis looked bewildered. "No."

Sharon scrunched her nose and brows in thought. "Shepherd . . . Shepherd." She paused and then her hand flew to her mouth. "Oh my God, how crass of me. It was in connection with that poor girl who was murdered. It's not the same family, I hope."

Bewilderment gave way to embarrassment. "My parents. She lived with them."

"Oh, I'm so sorry. My mouth just goes off before I think."

"That's okay. She wasn't really part of the family or anything."

"I seem to remember that she was a relative."

"What I meant was, we hardly knew her before she moved here." He scratched his neck. "She was a nice kid though. I'm going to miss her."

Nice kid? Miss her? This wasn't the picture he'd painted last week.

Sharon murmured sounds of sympathy. "Do you think they'll find her killer?"

"Who knows? Me, I'm not holding my breath." Dennis smoothed his fingers against the toe of the shoe and then across the instep. His face was flushed. "How do these feel?"

"Great," Sharon announced. "I think I'll take them."

Once we were outside, she turned to me. "Well, I'll say one thing for your friend Dennis, he knows how to fit shoes."

"He's not my friend."

She clucked her tongue. "Figure of speech, Kate."

"Just don't want you to get the wrong idea."

Sharon ignored me. "You do have to wonder, though, about a guy who sells women's shoes for a living." She paused to grin. "Maybe it's a Freudian thing—straddling those shoe department benches, women's feet pointed at your crotch all day. Talk about job satisfaction."

"Only *you* would come up with an observation like that!"

"You have to agree that Dennis is into feet. He even said so himself. Wasn't so good with faces but never forgot a pair of feet."

From the depths of my subconscious came the ghost of a thought. Muted and only half-formed, it squiggled slowly to the surface. Feet. Women's shoes. A history of emotional problems. Perhaps Dennis was simply devoted to his job, but maybe there was more to it.

"Julie Harmon's shoes were missing," I told Sharon.

"What do you mean, missing?"

"When she was murdered. She was fully clothed but her shoes were missing. Her toenails were painted and her feet were encased in plastic wrap. The same with

Cindy Purcell. There's been speculation that the killer has a foot fetish.''

Sharon's expression was grim, as though I'd just pointed out a worm in her apple. "Are you suggesting that the man who just spent half an hour fondling my foot might be a . . . a murderer?"

"I'm not suggesting anything, simply making an observation. And I'll make another one as well. When Michael and I talked to Dennis less than a week ago, he told us that Julie was a stuck-up brat. Today he says she was a nice kid.''

"Terrific," Sharon said. "I finally find a pair of shoes that feel like they were made for me, and now I'm going to feel the shadow of death every time I wear the damn things.''

I tried reaching Michael when I got home, but he wasn't at work and he wasn't at Don's apartment. I grumbled under my breath. Bad enough that I missed the pleasure of his company, I was discovering that having him live elsewhere was also a major inconvenience. It struck me how easily I'd grown accustomed to the routine of our life together. What I didn't know was whether that was a mark of true love or merely testimony to the fact that I'm a creature of habit.

Anna and Faye were in the living room playing Chutes and Ladders, a game that severely taxes my patience. Max had been relegated to the laundry room; Libby had chosen to retreat to her bedroom. I decided to take advantage of the quiet, and curl up in bed with a book.

I stopped by Libby's room on the way there. She pulled the headphones from her ears and looked up.

"Did you and Skye have a nice dinner?" I asked.

She wrinkled her nose. "Lobster thermidor. From freezer to microwave to table in under fifteen minutes. It tasted like that gluey macaroni and cheese that Anna loves so much."

"How'd it go with the piece on Julie the two of you were going to write?"

"We got through a rough draft, sort of." Libby hit the pause button on her disk player. "Skye isn't much of a writer. It would have been easier to do the whole thing myself."

"I didn't know that she and Julie were friends."

"They weren't. Not close friends, I mean. But the last couple of weeks they started to kind of pal around together. It didn't make a lot of sense since they're so different. They didn't even have any classes together." Libby paused, looking grim. "All I know is that at the time I was happy to see Julie latch on to someone besides me."

This last was said with remorse that pained me. I took a seat on the bed next to her. "You are not responsible for what happened to Julie. You were asked to show her around, to be there in the beginning as a familiar face. Nobody expected you to be her constant buddy."

"Maybe if I'd asked her to come to the game with us, though, this wouldn't have happened. I knew she didn't have any real friends of her own."

"There are always 'what ifs,' honey. It doesn't take much to have twenty-twenty hindsight."

Libby rocked back against the wall and circled her knees with her arms. "I don't understand how it could have happened. A person couldn't just drive up and snatch her away. It would have been light still, and there are always people on that stretch of road. Julie wouldn't have taken a ride with a stranger, either. She was probably more cautious than most of us."

I'd found myself bothered by the same thought. Yet it had happened to other women; women older and more experienced than Julie. "Sometimes all it takes is a moment of letting your guard down," I told her.

"That's what Skye says. That things change in a flash, in ways you least expect."

"Or maybe Julie really did decide to leave home, and she ran into trouble later, somewhere else." Or maybe, I added silently, she'd taken a ride with someone she trusted. "Did Julie ever mention the Shepherds' son, Dennis?"

Libby thought for a moment, frowned. "The name's familiar so I guess she did. But I don't remember what she said. It must have been one of the zillion times I tuned her out."

There was only so much I could do to talk Libby out of the hair shirt. This time I passed. "Do you remember the general context of the conversation? Like whether Julie was complaining about Dennis or sounding friendly towards him?"

Libby shook her head. "More like he was just there. I mean, he wasn't really. He lives in Berkeley. But I got the feeling he was around a lot. Why?"

"Sharon and I ran into him tonight when we were shopping. He's a shoe salesman at Macy's."

"Yeah, now I remember. We saw him once at the mall. Julie pointed him out to me."

"And?"

She looked at me blankly. "And he was selling shoes. What did you expect?"

It was apparently a rhetorical question because Libby seemed satisfied with my noncommittal shrug.

I left Libby to her homework and her music, and settled in with my book. Half an hour later Anna came to say goodnight, and Faye trundled off to bed not long after.

Even though I felt exhausted, I was awake long after the house was quiet. And when I did finally drift away, it was to a world steeped in the shapeless illogic of dreams.

Julie had the lead role. The images flashed, one after the other. Sometimes distinct, sometimes blending layer upon layer.

Julie's lifeless remains transmuted before my eyes into a black-cloaked skeleton. Julie and Mario with heads bent, speaking in a foreign tongue. Julie alone, slouching before me, her blue eyes serious and somber.

She gives me a painting of herself, a work of remarkable insight and talent. A modern-day Mona Lisa that seems to vibrate with enchantment. And then, like melting paraffin, the eyes and nose and mouth lose their shape and blur to nothingness. The featureless face slides from the page. Finally, all that remains is a single hand, reaching into the blank sheet of paper, like a hapless soul drowning at sea. From behind me, Libby calls out, "Help her, Kate. Grab her hand and pull her back." I turn to search for Libby, who is nowhere to be seen. When I look back at the painting, the hand is gone as well.

And then Julie is beside my bed, a shadow without form. "Can I talk to you, Ms. Austen?"

"Maybe later," I tell her, although my mouth does not move. "I'm busy, can't you see."

The shadow ignores my response and climbs into bed anyway.

The stirring of warm breath on my neck pulled me from slumber. Although the sky was still black, the birds had begun to sound the coming day. I awoke to envelop my daughter as she snuggled against me.

14

Michael returned my call later that morning. I was in the kitchen making Anna's lunch and caught the phone on the second ring before it could wake Faye.

"Did you speak to Gates yet?" I asked, shooing Max away from the slice of jam-slathered bread he'd been eyeing. "About Dennis Shepherd, I mean."

"How about a 'Good morning, honey, did you have a nice evening'?"

"Did you?"

"No. An old girlfriend of Don's was in town, so I tried to make myself scarce. Sat through three dreadful movies, then crept home in the dark and practically broke my leg tripping over the coffee table they'd moved."

"I don't suppose you ever thought of coming home for the night?"

"In retrospect," Michael grumbled, "it might have been the better choice."

Max circled the table and approached the bread from the other direction. I gave him a stern look and a rap on the snout. "About Dennis," I said to Michael, "have the Berkeley police questioned him yet?"

"I left a message for Gates yesterday, right after you talked to me. I doubt he's had time to do much about it. And to be honest, I don't know where he'll go with it. A history of emotional problems, alleged emotional problems in fact, hardly qualifies as evidence."

"There's more," I told him. "Sharon and I were at Macy's last night. And who do you think waited on us?"

Michael sighed. "Dennis? He told us he worked there, remember?"

"Yes, but you'll never guess which department." I paused for emphasis. "Dennis works in women's shoes."

"You were shopping for shoes?"

"Sharon was, but that's not the point."

Michael hesitated. "Guess I'm missing something here."

He certainly was. I pulled myself up straight. "Don't you think it's a strange coincidence that we have two recent murder victims with their shoes missing, and the cousin of the most recent victim is a shoe salesman with a history of emotional problems?"

"It's a coincidence, all right," Michael conceded. "But you're making an awfully big leap in logic."

"If you could have seen the way he talked about shoes, the way he handled Sharon's feet. Dennis Shepherd is definitely not your average, apathetic salesman."

"Maybe he's simply good at his job. Look, Kate, I know you're trying to help. And I'm grateful, honestly. But if I call Jim Gates with this, he's going to be pissed. I already told him about Dennis's background. I'm sure he'll look into it."

"You seem to have more faith in Gates than you did yesterday."

"I never said I didn't have faith, only that we don't always see eye to eye."

I sighed. Arguing the point would get me nowhere. I knew that if Michael actually thought the connection was significant, he'd have been willing to incur the wrath of Gates and anyone else who needed convincing.

Michael was silent a moment, then he said, "Looks like we may have a new development in the Cindy Purcell homicide."

"Great." I twisted the lid off the jar of peanut butter. "What is it?"

"Ever hear of cybersex?"

"What-sex?"

"Electronic sex."

I wasn't sure I'd heard correctly. "Electronic?"

"As in via computer, not the plug-in variety."

I knew very little about computers except that they cost a hunk of money, demanded more and more in the way of software, and turned ordinary, literate folk into Pod People who conversed in a language as alien to me as Martian. We had two computers at home, Libby's and Michael's. So far, I'd studiously avoided having anything to do with either of them. If sex figured into the picture, however, I might have to reconsider.

"How do you have sex with the computer?" I asked.

"You don't, at least not in the customary sense. It's conversational. Or more accurately, textual, although I understand that with some servers you can have graphical interface, too. First point of contact is usually a chat room, bulletin board, or USENET newsgroup, but as bonds develop, people often move to one-on-one e-mail exchanges.''

One-on-one. Finally, a term I understood. ''How does this relate to Cindy Purcell's death?''

''I'm not sure. But she apparently participated in this stuff. It can get pretty lurid, since theoretically the whole thing is anonymous. People live out their fantasies, talk in ways they might not in real life. Most participants are out for a little fun, like Cindy. But these places attract some real oddballs, too.''

''I can imagine.''

''Anyway, we're going to follow up on it. She might at some point have given out her real name and address, or even agreed to meet one of these guys.''

''That's asking for trouble, isn't it?''

Michael's response was the verbal equivalent of a shrug. ''She wouldn't have been the first,'' he said after a moment. ''I suppose on some level it's no different than building a relationship with a pen pal.''

A pen pal you'd met through Sex Is Us, maybe.

''I gather there are some heartwarming case histories. Couple connects over the Internet, hits it off, meets face to face, and falls in love. Next thing you know it's wedding bells and pure bliss. Of course, for every one of those stories, there are probably ten of the other kind. The world is crawling with sadists, pedophiles, perverts of all types ready to prey on people's loneliness and insecurities.''

''What does this do to the tie-in between the two murders? As I recall, Julie's computer didn't even have a modem.''

''Like I said the other day, I'm not convinced it was the same guy. But it could be. That doesn't mean that he had to have met both girls the same way, however. There are a lot of permutations to this thing." There was a voice in the background, muffled conversation. "I gotta run, Kate. Talk to you later."

I went back to making Anna's lunch, but my mind was on murder and mayhem rather than peanut butter and jelly. A lot of permutations, Michael had said. But when you got down to basics. there were really only three options.

Julie could have been a random victim, her death a tragic consequence of being in the wrong place at the wrong time. But it might also have been more methodical than that. Suppose the killer had been after Julie in particular. Some guy she'd communicated with perhaps, if not through cyberspace then maybe someone who'd seen her around town, someone who'd befriended her in some way, even.

Or it might not have been a stranger at all.

Maybe it was the overlay of my dreams from the previous night, or maybe the weight of regret at not having done more when I could. Or maybe just the unsettled feeling I had that there was something unusual going on in Julie's life.

In any case, I couldn't shake the image of Dennis Shepherd from my mind.

As soon as I was finished teaching for the day, I drove through the Caldecott Tunnel and into Berkeley, a city of geographic as well as every other kind of diversity. At its eastern edge are the contours of forested hills and large, well-maintained homes. As you move west, toward the bay, the terrain flattens. The houses there are smaller, the neighborhoods less prosperous. Dennis Shepherd lived in the flatlands, far enough from the university that rundown conditions were no longer deemed colorful.

I found the address, then parked across the street and down a couple of houses. Ahead of me, there was a gas station on one corner, a liquor store on the other. Dennis's place was a pink stucco bungalow with a front yard of glittering white rock and several large cacti. The drapes were pulled and the house was still. It was impossible to tell if anyone was home.

I wasn't sure how to proceed, in any case. My curiosity about Dennis Shepherd had brought me this far, but without any hint about what came next. As I was mentally shuffling through the possibilities, I caught a flicker of movement in the rearview mirror. Turning, I saw a woman with shoulder-length red hair come down the front path from Dennis's house. She was about my height and probably forty pounds heavier. I saw her face briefly as she crossed the street, but it was impossible to judge her age.

Without thinking, I climbed out of the car and followed. At the second cross street, she turned right. Her stride was quick and determined, if not particularly graceful. I followed her for another block, working up my nerve to approach. Near the corner, she paused to glance over her shoulder in my direction. The stoplight was green and the woman crossed. I picked up my pace in the hopes of reaching the intersection before the light changed, but I missed by about thirty seconds.

By the time the traffic had cleared, the woman was halfway down the next block, moving at a quick clip. With another glance over her shoulder, she suddenly veered to the curb and boarded the AC Transit bus that had pulled to a stop moments earlier. The bus took off again before I had a chance to react.

Had the woman been headed for the bus all along, or had she deliberately tried to elude me? And what if she had, I chided myself. Who wouldn't be nervous at being followed by a stranger?

Exasperated, I turned and marched back the way I'd come. But now I was almost as curious about the woman as about Dennis.

As I neared the house again, I saw a man in a wheelchair coming down the driveway next door. He was in his late thirties or early forties, with broad shoulders and well-muscled arms. He reached the sidewalk just as I was passing by.

"Did she lead you where you thought she would?" he asked, with a gleam to his eye.

"Did she . . . ?" My face reddened as his meaning became clear. "What makes you think I was following her?"

He grinned. "Just a guess. Which you've now pretty much confirmed. You might simply have been trying to catch up with her, of course. But it didn't look that way. More like you were keeping your distance. And you didn't get out of the car until you saw her leave."

Being a nosy neighbor myself, I shouldn't have been surprised to discover that someone had been watching. Still, I hadn't considered the possibility. "Do you know her?" I asked.

"Not by name. I've seen her around, though."

"Does she live in the place next door?"

He shook his head. "There's a guy lives there. He has a couple of women friends. She's one of them. The gals all make themselves right at home, seems like. I've been waiting for the day when two of them show up at once. Somehow Denny doesn't seem like the type to juggle more than one."

Dennis Shepherd a ladies' man? This was a side to him I'd never imagined. "How many women friends does he have?"

The man looked at me and his grin faded. "Shit, you're not one of them, are you? Hey, I'm sorry if I let the cat out of the bag. You're the best-looking by far, and that's the gods' truth."

I could feel myself redden again, from a different sort of embarrassment. "I barely know Dennis, and there's nothing romantic in the least about my interest." Even giving voice to the thought caused an involuntary shudder.

The man grinned again. "I'm glad to hear it." He held out a hand. "Luke Martin," he said.

"I'm Kate." His hands were strong and callused across the palms, but surprisingly smooth elsewhere.

"So, why were you following that gal?"

"To tell you the truth, I don't know. I guess I thought she might be able to tell me about your neighbor."

Luke raised an eyebrow.

"It's a long and complicated story," I told him.

"If you're willing to tag along for a couple of blocks, I'll buy you a cup of coffee. Sounds like the story might be a good one."

I was tempted, but I had one more stop before I picked up Anna. "Maybe another time."

He nodded. "Didn't figure you'd say yes, but it never hurts to ask, right?"

I smiled, oddly flattered that he had. "Did you ever

see your neighbor with a much younger woman? A girl really, about fifteen. Tall, with straight blond hair?''

Luke Martin started to shake his head, then stopped. ''Now that you mention it, I might have. The other women he's with are all of a type, you know. But the girl was different. She wasn't a regular there, either. I think I only saw her maybe once or twice.''

''Do you remember when that was?''

He chewed on his bottom lip a minute. ''Not really.''

So what that Julie had come to visit Dennis. He was family, after all. ''Do you recall how long she stayed, whether the visit was friendly, that sort of thing?''

Martin didn't answer. He looked at me for a moment, then spun his chair in a quick 360-degree turn. Just as quickly, he spun in the other direction and pulled the chair backward, like a kid doing wheelies. ''I've become so proficient with this thing, I no longer think much about the fact that my legs don't work. I can probably out swim you and out ski you. And believe it or not, I can hold my own on the tennis court.''

His voice was even and controlled. ''I'm no shiftless cripple who sits by the window all day living vicariously through his neighbors. I've got better things to do with my days.''

For the third time in less than ten minutes, I felt my face grow warm. ''I wasn't implying that you were.''

He nodded and fixed his eyes on mine. ''I just wanted to make sure you understood. I'm a writer. I work at home and my computer's by the window so I see a lot of what goes on. And being a writer, I'm curious about people. But a lot of it's idle observation. It doesn't really register until there's a need. I hardly know this guy Denny, in case you're interested.''

"But you've met him?"

"I had him over for pizza once."

"What do you think of him?"

Martin chuckled, turned his chair again so that he was headed down the sidewalk. "Look me up, I'm in the book. The coffee offer's good any day of the week but Thursday evening."

"What's Thursday?"

"My AA meeting," he said, propelling himself easily up the incline in the direction I'd come.

Luke Martin. I repeated the name silently to myself, and wondered if I dared take him up on his offer.

15

Dennis Shepherd struck me as a peculiar young man. My opinion was not, however, shared by Jim Gates of the Berkeley Homicide Division.

"I appreciate your concern," he said, frowning at me over a thick stack of message slips. "But you could have saved yourself the trouble of coming in. Your friend Michael Stone faxed me a note about Shepherd the other day."

I nodded. "But that was before I'd learned that he's a shoe salesman."

Gates had gone back to sorting through his stack of papers and didn't respond. He was not a big man, but the thinning, closely cropped hair coupled with the steely gaze and perpetual scowl made him an imposing figure.

I shifted uncomfortably in my chair. "You heard what I said about Dennis and feet, didn't you?"

He lifted his gaze. "You made your point quite clearly."

"And coupled with the history of emotional problems," I continued. "Or the possibility of a history of emotional problems . . ."

His attention remained elsewhere.

"I thought it was something you might want to look into," I concluded, pulling myself straighter.

Gates shot a look in my direction.

"You know, so that you've covered all the bases."

"No offense, Mrs. Austen, but this is what we do for a living. Day in and day out. We have a pretty good idea how to proceed."

"It's just that I wasn't sure you knew about these *particular* pieces of information."

His lips moved. I couldn't tell if it was meant as a smile or a snarl. In either case, it signaled the end of our conversation, such as it had been. I stood, thanked him for his time, and found my own way out.

As I emerged into the cool, gray afternoon, a slender black woman approached, accompanied by a German shepherd on a short leash.

"Feeling better than you did the other day?" the woman asked, slowing her pace.

It took a moment before I recognized her. Celeste Tira, the policewoman from the afternoon at Tilden when I'd identified Julie's body. "My stomach has settled down, if that's what you mean. But I'm not sure the rest of me has."

Without thinking, I reached out a hand to pet the dog. Officer Tira yanked on his leash with a fierce "No!" It wasn't clear whether she was talking to me or the dog, but I pulled in my arm and stepped back.

"Sorry," she said with an apologetic wave of her free hand. "I didn't mean to startle you. But you really don't want to go sticking your hand in the face of a police dog. It's those quick, unexpected motions they're trained to watch for."

With a mumbled thanks, I brought my arm slowly from behind my back and slid it into my pocket.

"So what brings you here?" Tira asked.

"I stopped by to see Detective Gates."

"Something to do with the Harmon case?"

I nodded and told her about my encounter with Dennis Shepherd in the shoe department of Macy's. Somehow, with each retelling, the episode seemed less suspicious.

"It's not that I think you folks need help," I said lamely.

"But you want to make sure nothing slips by."

"Something like that."

"Makes sense to me." Her words were accompanied by the hint of a smile.

"Gates wasn't exactly overjoyed about my input."

She smiled again, more broadly. "He wouldn't let you know it, even if he was. Superficial evidence to the contrary, however, Jim Gates is a decent guy and a good cop. He runs a thorough investigation."

I eased my hand out of my pocket to a more comfortable position at my side. "I guess patience isn't my strong suit. I want the killer identified and behind bars."

"We all do. But you have to remember, it's only been a couple of days."

"It feels much longer. Maybe because Julie was missing first. And then there's the other murder out by the reservoir. It's like there's a dark fog that's settled in and won't lift."

Tira nodded sympathetically.

"It's frightening because you don't know where the threat is, or who might be next." A breeze stirred the leaves at our feet. I pulled my sweater tighter. "Do you think the same person is responsible for both deaths?"

"There are certainly a lot of similarities."

I felt a chill that had nothing to do with the weather. "It scares me to think there's some guy walking around our neighborhoods, snatching women off the street and killing them for the fun of it."

Tira nodded. "Unfortunately there's no shortage of sickos. Never has been and I doubt it's ever going to change."

The sentiment was one that had often played in my own mind. For all our scientific and technological advances, humankind had not progressed much in other regards.

"But I'm not sure," Tira continued, "that 'snatch' is quite the right word in this case."

"What do you mean?"

She shifted her weight to the other foot. "We have a witness who says he saw a girl fitting Julie Harmon's description on San Pablo Avenue about seven-thirty Friday night."

"Here in Berkeley?"

She nodded. "Near the intersection of University Avenue. He picked out Julie's photo from a collection of half a dozen."

"He's certain?"

"Says he is."

"What was Julie doing in Berkeley?"

"That's what we'd like to know. When our witness saw her, she was standing on a corner. That's why he was able to remember what she looked like. He thought she was looking for some action."

"Action? You mean . . . *hooking?*"

"That's what our witness thought."

I drew in a breath. "Was she?"

"You knew the girl," Tira said gently. "You can probably answer that better than me."

I felt a bubble of uneasiness in my chest. How well did I really know Julie? I had trouble imagining her as a woman of the streets. But if that wasn't the reason she'd been in that part of town, what was?

During the drive home, I continued to mull over the question of what Julie was doing in Berkeley. As soon as Libby came through the door that afternoon, I pulled her into the kitchen and asked her about it. She was as baffled as I was.

"What would Julie be doing in *that* area at *night?*" Libby asked, throwing back to me more or less the same question I'd put to her. "Why that part of Berkeley at all? There's nothing there."

Nothing but pawn shops and bars and the assortment of struggling businesses that are attracted to a low-rent district. But Libby was right—it wasn't an area of town that had much to offer a fifteen-year-old girl.

"Can I have one of these?" Libby asked, pointing to a plate of lemon bars Faye had baked that morning.

"Help yourself." I grabbed one also and bit into it, thereby dusting my chest with powdered sugar. "You said last week that Julie was expecting a change with the situation at the Shepherds. Could going to Berkeley have had something to do with that?"

"I don't know. Julie took BART in there a couple of times before, kind of on the sly. The Shepherds would never have approved. But it was always in the middle of the day and I assumed she was just, you know, cruising Telegraph." Libby grabbed another cookie. "All the kids do that."

Telegraph Avenue runs south from the main entrance of the University through Berkeley and into the heart of

Oakland. What most people mean when they talk about Telegraph Avenue, however, is the four-block stretch nearest the campus—a colorful, eclectic experience of coffeehouses, street artists, musicians, soothsayers, and eccentrics. It's also a mecca for local high school students who yearn for a taste of what they consider *Real Life*.

"Who did Julie usually go with?" I asked.

"She went alone."

I frowned. That was less common.

Libby's sense of guilt must have nipped at her again, because she added, "I asked if she wanted to come along the last time a group of us went in there to Amoeba Music."

"And she didn't?"

"No interest at all."

I leaned back in my chair. While the ambiance of Telegraph Avenue is certainly not what you'll find in Walnut Hills, the truth of the matter is that it's still far more refined than what passes for real life in many places, including the section of San Pablo where Julie was last seen. I couldn't imagine what she'd been doing there.

"Did she do drugs?" I asked.

Libby tucked a loose strand of hair behind her ear. "She might have tried pot or something, but she wasn't a dope-head if that's what you mean."

"What about other behaviors?"

Libby made a face. "Other *what?*"

"Did she have a wild side? You know, smoking, drinking . . ."

"Not that I ever saw."

I drummed my fingers on the table. "Maybe she liked to pick up boys and party."

"It doesn't sound much like Julie."

"Or maybe she liked to pick up girls," I added. This was, after all, a generation that seemed to have no use for the closet, literally or otherwise.

Libby frowned. "I don't think so."

I took another cookie and tried again to reconcile today's revelations with what I knew of Julie Harmon. It didn't work. And yet a pattern was emerging. Marlene, the hairdresser who lived across from the Shepherds, had told Faye that she'd seen Julie sneaking out of the house. According to Celeste Tira, Julie had been seen on a street corner in a sleazy section of Berkeley the night she disappeared. I remembered Julie's tentative interest in talking with me. Her troubling self-portrait. Had she merely been attempting to escape the tight thumb of the Shepherds? Or was there something more to it?

The next morning Mario surprised me, not only by showing up to class for the first time in over a week, but working diligently on the day's assignment. When the bell rang and the rest of the students darted for the door, Mario remained bent over his drawing, methodically shading a detailed array of foliage.

"It's nice to have you back again," I told him, peering over his shoulder. "I mean that sincerely."

His response was throaty and undecipherable.

"You don't have to finish this today, you know. There'll be time tomorrow."

"Yeah, I know."

It's always nice to see students engrossed in their work, so I was reluctant to interfere. But I knew we'd have to vacate the room soon for the studio art class that met after morning break. "I can give you a few minutes more, then you'll have to put it away and finish later."

He nodded silently and I went to the back of the room to tidy up. Each student had an individual plastic storage bin and segregated portion of shelf, but that didn't stop most of them from strewing supplies across the back counter. As I straightened loose paper into piles and sorted the soft-leaded drawing pencils, I was reminded that I hadn't yet cleaned out Julie's cubicle. It was something I was going to have to do eventually. The sooner I went at it, the less likely it was her drawings would become dog-eared.

A few minutes later, Mario stood beside me, clearing his throat. When I turned, he thrust a small leather-bound book into my hands.

"This was Julie's," he mumbled.

"Maybe you should give it to her family."

"I'm not so sure about that." He shuffled uneasily from one foot to the other.

I turned the book to examine the spine. *Selected Poems of D. H. Lawrence.*

"Look inside," Mario said. "At the handwritten message."

I flipped open the cover and leafed through a couple of pages. Scrawled in loopy penmanship on the title page was a message in black ink. It took a moment for me to decipher the writing.

What wild ecstasy it is, riding the waves of your desire. I too, yearn for another night like the last. Be patient and we will find a way. I am yours always in body and soul.

No signature, only a casually sketched heart, and below that, an initial so tangled I couldn't make it out.

I felt my pulse skip a beat. "Did you give this to her?"

Mario's cheeks took on the faintest hue of pink. "You think I'd be showing it to you if I did?"

"No, I guess not." Although to tell the truth, I wasn't sure why he was showing it to me at all. "How did you wind up with it, then?"

Mario looked at his hands. "Julie left her backpack in my truck last week. I didn't discover it until I got home. I called and said I'd drop it off, but she said not to bother. And then I thought, since I had her books and stuff, I might as well copy her notes from English. We did that a lot, so I knew she wouldn't mind." He gestured toward the book. "That was in her backpack."

"Do you know who did give it to her?"

"At first I thought it was Brian Walker. The two of them were seeing each other for a while and he's the kind of candy ass who'd write shit like that." Mario paused, looking uncomfortable. "She said it wasn't, though."

"What else did she say?"

There was a flicker of anger in his eyes, and then an icing over of emotion. "That it was none of my business."

Something in my mind clicked. "Is that what the two of you were arguing about Friday?"

"Pretty much." He turned away. "Julie was . . . well, I thought she was kind of special, you know. I mean, it's not like I expected that she'd see me in the same way at all, but . . ." He paused for a breath. "Well, I thought she could do a whole lot better than some jerk who'd write crap like that. Makes her sound like a slut."

There were a lot of years and a lot of living that separated my own experience from Mario's. To me, the scrawled message spoke of passion rather than bawdiness. But I was as uncomfortable as he was with the context.

"Anyone besides Brian come to mind?"

He shook his head.

"How about outside of school? Do you think she might have been seeing someone who wasn't a student here?"

Mario snorted in disgust. "It's pretty obvious she was *seeing* someone." His words were clipped, his voice angry. For an emotion that brings such joy, love certainly has its dark side as well.

"Libby says Julie used to go into Berkeley sometimes," I said. "Do you know anything about that?"

Mario shot me a sorrowful, beseeching look. "You think she was meeting some guy there?"

"I don't know. I'd like to take this book though, and show it to the police."

His face froze. "Ms. Austen, I don't want any trouble."

"You wouldn't be in trouble."

"My family would be real upset if I got involved with the police."

"Mario, you didn't do anything wrong." I stopped. "Did you?"

"Not like you're thinking, no." He stepped back, paused to shake his head. "Shit, no way."

Despite the words, I detected a layer of uncertainty. "But?" I said.

He hesitated. "Julie didn't get along with the Shepherds. She'd come to my house after school sometimes, tell them she was working on the newspaper or something. Mr. Shepherd found out. He didn't like it. He called my parents hollering and screaming, told them I should stay away from Julie. It was ugly, Ms. Austen."

"And what did your parents say?"

"To Mr. Shepherd, nothing. But they were upset with

me. They told me there's no sense in going looking for trouble, that I should do what the man says."

The injustice of it caused the heat to rise in my chest. "Did you?"

He shook his head. "My folks, they're both gone during the day. They'd be real angry if they knew she'd been coming over after they told me to keep my distance."

"I've got a friend who's a policeman," I said. "Can I give the book to him? He'll be careful what he says."

Mario hesitated. "He's a good guy?"

"A very good guy."

"I dunno, I don't want trouble."

"It might help find Julie's killer."

Mario scratched his cheek. "Okay, I guess."

As I ran my hand over the smooth leather of the cover, another thought came to mind. "Did Julie ever talk about the Shepherds' son, Dennis?"

"Yeah, a bit."

"What did she say about him?"

Mario shrugged. "That he was nothing like his dad."

"Anything else?"

Mario shook his head, "Nothing I can recall."

After he left, I tucked the book of poems into my canvas tote bag and then hefted Julie's portfolio under my arm.

On my way to the parking lot, I stopped by the office to pick up my mail and call Michael, who wasn't available. Then I headed over to Sharon's for the Fall Festival meeting, promising myself I'd be assertive about saying no to additional responsibility.

16

I spotted Susie's silver Mercedes and Laurelle's white one parked side by side in Sharon's driveway. In front of the house were several other cars I recognized as belonging to mothers of Anna's schoolmates—a BMW, a Lexus, and a brand-new Suburban. I pulled my dented and dusty old Volvo into the closest remaining spot, a rutted area under a large Monterey Pine where the car was sure to collect bird droppings as well as more grit.

Although they hadn't started the official meeting without me, they'd polished off half the pastries and were well into premeeting gossip by the time I got myself settled.

"Did you ask him?" Susie whispered, pulling her chair closer to mine.

"Ask who?"

"Michael. You know, the interview. I wanted to talk to him about the murders, remember?"

"I haven't had a chance," I told her, which was the

truth. Her request had also completely slipped my mind. "But I left a message for him. I'm sure we'll speak soon."

"Good," she said rather snippily. "You can call me this evening. I'll be home." With that, she scooted her chair back to join in the trashing of Cheri Dupres, who two months ago had replaced Beau who-required-no-last-name as the aerobics instructor at the club.

"That isn't her God-given nose," Laurelle said derisively.

"I bet those aren't her God-given boobs, either," added Marsha.

Sharon set her coffee cup down with a thunk of disgust. "For that matter," she said sarcastically, "I don't imagine she was born with holes pierced in her earlobes, either. And I know for a fact she had orthodontia as a child and now wears contact lenses. What difference does it make?"

Since I didn't belong to the club myself, I'd never so much as laid eyes on Cheri. But I knew that Beau had been the inspiration for many a woman's devotion to aerobics—or more precisely, devotion to aerobics classes at the Walnut Hills Country Club.

"She never even sweats," said Susie, sipping her coffee. "Maybe she's entirely synthetic."

Marsha laughed. "I doubt that. I saw her last week at Yoshi's. She was with a guy, draped around him like a hungry boa. They were both working up a sweat,"—she paused for effect—"if you know what I mean."

She turned to me. "You might know him, Kate. Cheri says he teaches English at the high school. Dick something, if I recall."

I mentally ran through the list of faculty and couldn't come up with anyone named Dick. I shook my head.

"Tall," Marsha said. "Blond hair, fair complexion, eyes that are almost turquoise. He teaches English."

"Marvin Melville?"

"Yeah, that's it." She laughed self-consciously. "The Melville connection. I guess I was thinking of *Moby Dick.*"

"Or maybe you were just thinking of dick," Susie said under her breath.

Sharon took a baby carrot from the largely untouched platter of vegetables on the coffee table. "I wonder if that's the guy she met over the Internet. Sounds like him anyway."

I rocked forward. "The Internet? When? How?"

"Some chat room or something. That's how they first met. Then they discovered they lived in the same area."

"You can *talk* over the Internet?" Marsha asked.

"You don't actually talk, you type your message."

"Seems silly to me," Sharon said. "But apparently there are all these different rooms or bulletin boards or whatever for different interests. I guess it's like those classified ads you see in the paper—*Sexy, gentle, fun-loving guy looking for beautiful babe*—only it comes over the modem."

"What I can't understand," Laurelle said, "is why anyone would agree to actually get together with someone like that. I mean, in person. You've got to figure any guy who's not a total weenie is going to have no trouble meeting women on his own. So odds are, you're getting the dregs to begin with."

"It's got to be dangerous," Sharon said. "Who knows what kind of psychopaths are out there disguising themselves as gentle, fun-loving guys."

I nodded. "That's what may have happened with the woman who was murdered out by the reservoir. She apparently gave out her name and address to guys she met on-line. Someone should tell Cheri to be careful.''

Marsha shuddered. "Especially now. I don't know about the rest of you, but having a killer on the prowl makes me nervous."

"So what's this Moby Dick guy like?" Susie asked, addressing her question my way.

"Not a psychopath."

"A weenie?"

"Hardly," I said with a laugh. "He's decent looking, although maybe a little anemic for my tastes. But he's got that quiet, sensitive, shy quality that some women seem to adore. I'm sure Marvin doesn't need to look far to find a date."

Sharon stood and stretched. "Who all wants a refill? And then we'd better get down to business."

The rest of the meeting was decidedly less interesting. We formed committees, divvied up chores, and finished off the wine. I embroidered the truth a bit, saying I had an appointment, and left early in the hope of catching Michael at the station.

He was just heading out when I arrived.

"Come take a ride with me," he said, throwing a jacket over his shoulder.

"A ride? Why?"

"She asks why?" he said dramatically. His expression was pure vaudeville. "The love of my life, a woman I've barely seen in days. I want to spend a little time with her, and she asks why?"

I laughed. "Okay, where to?"

"Berkeley. I need to take another look at Cindy Purcell's computer. It's a long shot, but after talking to this guy I told you about, the one who said he'd communicated with her on-line, I really think there might be a connection."

"The guy's name isn't Melville, is it?"

Michael shook his head. "It's not Hemingway, either."

"That wasn't a joke." While we walked to the car, I filled him in on the conversation at Sharon's, or the relevant parts of it anyway.

"It does boggle the mind a bit," he said, "the number of people who are reaching out and touching someone through cyberspace. And it runs the gamut from clever erotica to the genuinely sordid and disgusting. People get hooked on it. It can apparently be a real addiction."

It certainly boggled my mind. I slid over next to Michael and gave him a kiss before buckling myself in. "I think I'll stick to the tried and true. Speaking of which . . ." I reached into my canvas tote and pulled out the book of poems Mario had given me. "This belonged to Julie."

Michael's gaze bounced my direction for just a moment before returning to the road. "What is it?"

I explained and then read the inscription.

"The waves of your desire," he repeated, whistling softly under his breath. "And to think that when I was that age it took all my nerve to inscribe Marilyn Homer's yearbook with a 'roses are red' verse."

"Maybe you were just a late bloomer."

He looked at me and bit back a smirk.

"And who was Marilyn Homer?"

This time he laughed out loud. "Someone who would probably have preferred 'waves of desire' to 'roses are red.' "

"I always assumed Julie was more the red-roses type," I said. And yet it was becoming clear to me that she wasn't. "You've heard that she was last seen in Berkeley, on San Pablo Avenue?"

"Yeah, Gates told me." There was a brief pause. "Gates also told me that you dropped by to see him yesterday."

Michael's tone was neutral but I could well imagine that the tone of Jim Gates's message had been otherwise.

"I just wanted to be sure he knew about Dennis Shepherd," I explained.

"You didn't think I'd pass along your message?"

"It's not that—"

"And now. I suppose, you want to make sure he hears about the inscription in Julie's book as well?"

I nodded. "Will you see that he gets it?"

Michael sighed. "It would be better if you'd let this Mario kid call Gates directly."

"But he won't. He was even reluctant to let me hand it over to the police. I gave him my word that you'd tread carefully."

The sigh became a groan. "Tread carefully? The case isn't even mine. You must think I'm a stand-in for Houdini."

I leaned closer and traced a line along his inner thigh. "Aren't you?"

Michael had arranged to meet Cindy's roommate, Toby Perkins, at the apartment they'd shared.

"Like I told you on the phone, I only have an hour," Toby mumbled when she let us in. "I've got a class at two o'clock."

Michael introduced me. "We won't be long," he said.

Toby pulled her arms across her chest and uttered a blur of sounds that I pieced together as "s'okay."

"Are you familiar with Cindy's files?"

She nodded. "Some, anyway."

"How about her on-line account?"

Another nod. "She used Eudora for e-mail."

Toby was short and round, and so soft-spoken you had to strain to make out the words. It didn't help that she kept her gaze fixed on the floor and frequently used her hand as a veil. I was willing to bet that when she was growing up the "Toby" had mutated to "Tubby" in the mouths of her classmates.

She shuffled to a corner of the dining area where a computer sat on an old card table. "Here. Just be careful. All my reading notes are on there."

Michael pulled out the chair, sat, and was soon clicking on icons and pulling down menus so rapidly that the flickering screen made me dizzy. I joined Toby on the stained, Herculon plaid couch.

Toby slouched backward as though trying to burrow into the seat cushion. Her hand again drifted toward the lower half of her face, and then found her mouth.

"Would you like some soda or something?" she asked between nibbles on a well-chewed fingernail.

"No thanks, I'm fine." I gestured to the thick textbook in her lap. "What are you studying?"

"Paleontology."

I smiled. "My daughter is a great fan of the dinosaurs."

She forced a half-smile in return.

"It must be hard for you to concentrate on your studies with Cindy's murder on your mind."

The smile vanished as quickly as it had come. "It is. And I have to find a new roommate, too. I can't afford to keep this place alone."

"Didn't you find Cindy through an ad or something?"

She nodded. "I posted a notice in the housing office at school."

"You could try that again."

"I did. But now that the semester's started, most people are settled."

I could understand the problem. "Still, situations change. You're bound to find someone."

"Maybe." Toby glanced at Michael, then back to a spot somewhere near my knee. "Cindy was an easy roommate. She spent every weekend with her boyfriend. She worked twenty hours a week at the video store in addition to carrying a full load. She was hardly ever around."

I'd had a roommate like that once, and it did tend to spoil you. Somebody to pay half the rent who didn't really take up half the space. "Did the two of you get along okay when she was here?"

Toby nodded again. "Cindy was real friendly." She sucked on her bottom lip for a minute. "Do they really think it was someone Cindy met up with through the Internet?"

I waited for Michael to respond. He kept his back to us and didn't say a word. "It's a possibility," I said at last. "Did you know that she was active in these"—I looked for the right word—"these on-line sex groups."

Toby shook her head and pulled on the lip even harder. "I mean, I knew she did it once. We both did, together. It was all a joke. I had no idea she kept it up."

"What was it like?"

Toby's face grew flush. "Talk about what your fantasies are, your weirdest experience, things that turned you on. I think most people were just making stuff up. I know we were."

"What was Cindy's boyfriend like?" I asked, again eyeing Michael's back. I was dying to know what he'd found.

"Bright, kind of intense." She paused. "Cute. He's not as outgoing as Cindy, but I don't think that bothered her."

"Were they serious?"

"She wasn't dating anyone else, if that's what you mean. But I don't know if she planned to stay with him forever. She wanted to get into the movies. I don't think tying yourself down to an engineering graduate student is the best way to do that."

Michael muttered under his breath and pushed back the chair. "You sure we can't borrow the computer for a couple of days? It would make our job a lot easier."

She shook her head. "I need it for classes."

Michael sighed.

"It's mine, you know." Toby tugged at the sleeve of her sweater. "I let Cindy use it but it belongs to me."

When we were outside, I touched Michael's shoulder. "Well?"

"Well, what?"

"What did you find?"

"Nothing useful," he said with a groan. "I can check with the on-line service and see if they keep a record of messages. Probably have to get a court order to do it."

By the time we returned to Walnut Hills, I had barely ten minutes to hop into my own car and pick up Anna. It wasn't until I saw Susie's Mercedes parked by the flagpole near the front of the school that I remembered I'd promised to ask Michael if he'd grant her an interview. I told myself I would call him the minute I got home.

But when Anna and I walked in the door, Faye was

having it out with Max, in no uncertain terms. "You're a bad dog," she scolded. "Bad, bad dog."

"What happened?" I asked.

She turned angrily, hands on her broad hips. "Look what that dog did. Tromped across my fabric, tore the pattern to shreds. It's a wonder your house isn't a constant shambles, the way he behaves."

With one glance, I took in the mess on the floor. Scraps of flimsy pattern pieces were scattered indiscriminately over swatches of shiny golden taffeta, newly patterned with muddy paw prints. It was clear that Max had had a heyday with Faye's sewing project.

"Oh dear," I said, unable to think of anything more astute.

"He's a . . . a . . . ." Faye fumbled, near tears. "A menace, that's what he is."

A part of me couldn't help but think that maybe Faye was overreacting. But I could also understand her anger. Max was a sweet and loving member of our family, but there were times I, too, wanted to wring his neck.

"I'll replace the pattern," I offered, "and the fabric too, if necessary. I'm sorry he made such a mess."

Faye sighed with a great heave of her chest. "I suppose it's partially my fault. I put him out in the first place. I guess I must have forgotten to latch the door securely."

"He does like to be in the middle of things," I said, bending to gather the strewn pieces. "What are you making, anyway?"

"A princess gown for Anna. For Halloween."

Anna, who'd been heretofore watching silently, gave a sigh of her own, full of exasperation. "I'm going to be a vampire," she protested, "I told you that."

I sent Anna a warning glance. Her tone was far too shrill to use on her grandmother.

"But you'd look so much prettier as a princess," Faye cajoled.

"I don't care. I want fangs and black fingernails and some of that fake blood like Kyle has."

"Maybe you could be a vampire princess," I suggested.

Anna rolled her eyes and Faye huffed with distaste.

I back-pedaled. "Sorry, it was just a suggestion."

I kept my head down and my thoughts to myself as I finished picking up the remnants of Max's destruction. Then I scolded Max one more time for good measure, wiped the remaining mud from his feet and fur, and joined the others in the kitchen. On the way, I grabbed the day's mail, weighted heavily with election fliers, from the hallway table.

"Where'd this come from?" I asked Faye, holding up the small plastic skeleton I'd found with the stack of magazines.

"It was in the mailbox."

"In a package?"

"No, it was loose, just like that."

I clutched the skeleton in my hand. A Halloween toy. The kind you could buy at any dime store, along with plastic spiders and rubber bats. All the same, it gave me a queasy feeling. It looked an awfully lot like the plastic skeleton that had been found near Julie's body.

I slipped into the bedroom where we kept the extension phone and called Michael. Once again I neglected to pass on Susie's request for an interview.

17

"Tell me again where you found it." Michael angled his chair to better address Faye. He'd slipped the skeleton into a plastic bag and it now lay on the table between them.

Faye's expression was stiff, as it had been since Michael's arrival fifteen minutes earlier. "In the mailbox," she said, without looking at him.

"Under the mail or on top?"

"The mail wasn't here yet."

"What time was this?"

"Afternoon." Her voice remained cool and clipped.

"Mrs. Austen." Michael eased himself forward. "I realize that you might find the personal dynamics between us a tad awkward, but this is police business, not a social call. It could be serious. If you could be more specific about when and where you found the skeleton, I'd appreciate it."

Her eyes flickered in his direction briefly. "Early afternoon," she said, hardly moving her lips. "Before two o'clock."

"Had you checked for the mail earlier, by any chance?"

She shook her head.

"And I gather you didn't see anyone out front in the vicinity of the mailbox?"

"If I had," Faye snipped, "I'd have said so straight off."

Michael picked up the bag and examined the skeleton.

"You think it means anything?" I asked, trying not to let my anxiety show.

"Wish I knew." He frowned. "On first impression I'd say it's identical to the one found with Julie's body. Of course, with Halloween approaching, there must be thousands of these things floating around. I bet half the kids at Anna's school have talked their parents into buying them at least one Halloween favor."

I nodded. Anna had several, although she preferred black cats and pumpkins to skeletons. "How about the one found with Cindy Purcell?" I asked.

"That one was different. Smaller and lighter, made from a different sort of plastic."

Faye folded her arms across her chest. "I don't see how any of this is going to help you catch the killer. Isn't that what you should be spending your energy on?"

"We're doing that too," Michael said cordially.

Anna returned from her bedroom wearing the plastic vampire teeth she'd gone off earlier to retrieve. She sidled up to Michael's arm and pretended to nip him.

"Sorry, honey, vampires suck blood." He made a slurping sound. "They don't go around nibbling people's arms the way you would a bar of chocolate."

Anna tried again, drooling on his shirt sleeve in the process.

"Much better," Michael coached. He held a hand under Anna's chin and studied her. "Perfect vampire features, almost classic."

Faye frowned so intently I thought she might injure her face.

Just then, Libby arrived home with a slam, a thunk, and a muttered curse.

"What's the matter?" I asked.

"Life," she answered.

Faye took the opportunity to summon Anna, and they retreated together to another room.

I grinned at Michael. "At least she didn't bite."

"The teeth were only plastic."

"I meant Faye, not Anna."

As usual, Libby headed directly for the refrigerator. She opened the door and gave the contents a leisurely gaze.

Michael lifted the plastic skeleton. "Do you by any chance recognize this?"

She turned and glared, leaving the door ajar. "Duh, it's a skeleton. Now what's the punch line, I'm in no mood for games."

"No punch line, I'm afraid." Michael explained that Faye had found it in our mailbox.

"It's similar to the one found by Julie's body," I added, straining to keep my tone even.

Libby's expression froze for a moment, and then she turned abruptly back to the fridge. "So?"

"So we're worried that there may be a connection."

"What do you mean, a connection?"

I looked at Michael. "Well, like somebody wanted to

scare us." I swallowed and tried again. "Not somebody, really. The person who killed Julie. And maybe Cindy Purcell."

"That doesn't make sense. Why would the killer leave something in our mailbox?"

"I don't know," Michael said. "It might be a coincidence. But I'd like you both to be extra cautious."

"If he comes after me," Libby grumbled, "I'll direct him Skye's way."

"Libby! You don't mean that."

"Want to bet?"

"You and Skye having a problem?" Michael asked.

Libby settled on cheese and a soda. "Would you believe she asked Brian Walker to go horseback riding with her? A fox hunt, no less. It's some big to-do with important people and a gourmet brunch." She popped the tab on the soda. "I mean, that takes gall, pretending she's my friend and then trying to snag him behind my back."

"A fox hunt? Do people do that still?"

"It's so phoney." Libby's tone was full of disdain. "They don't even use a real fox, just some stupid scent."

The fox wasn't the problem. I sat back. "What did Brian say?"

"He just about had to say yes. Skye's daddy is Mr. Hot Shot Judge, after all."

"What does Steve Burton have to do with this?"

Libby arched her neck. "He controls Brian's money, that's what."

I shook my head. "You've lost me."

"He's like the executor of the trust or something. He's the one who decides how much money Brian can spend."

"Ah." Not that I understood, entirely. But I figured it was the best I was going to get at the moment.

"None of the boys like her," Libby huffed. "They whinny at her behind her back. Sometimes even to her face."

Skye tried so hard to belong that she ended up putting people off. I found her annoying at times myself, but I felt sorry for her, too. She had none of the natural beauty or charm that her mother and stepfather had.

"Ever since she found out that Judge Burton had been a friend of Brian's father," Libby continued, "she's been acting like . . . well, like they've been engaged since birth or something. And now she's moving in on him for real."

"It's only horseback riding," Michael offered mildly.

"You don't know Skye," Libby snapped in response.

Michael backed off and turned to me. "Didn't you tell me that Julie Harmon had gone out with this Brian fellow?"

I nodded and waited for Libby to add her two cents' worth. When she didn't, I continued. "It was only a couple of times, though. The Shepherds didn't approve of her dating."

Michael scratched his cheek, fiddled with the baggie-encased skeleton. "Is Walker a fan of poetry?" he inquired of Libby.

She shrugged. "Yeah, I guess. Some of it."

"D. H. Lawrence?"

"Never heard of him." Libby popped a wedge of cheese into her mouth.

Michael sighed. "How about Julie Harmon? Did she like poetry?"

"She liked to write it. I guess she read it too."

"What kind of poetry did she write?"

Libby shrugged. "Not like those English class poems

about bobbing daffodils and woods on snowy evenings. More modern stuff.''

Michael was silent a moment, lost in thought. He tapped his fingers lightly against the table top.

"She even belonged to a poetry group," Libby added as an afterthought. "Over the Internet. You can post your own poems and comment on other people's stuff. It's like being instantly published. Kind of cool, huh?"

Michael's fingers stopped their drumming. "How'd she manage that? Last time I checked, her computer didn't have a modem."

"The school is on-line."

"You guys can surf the net right from your classrooms?" His tone wavered somewhere between incredulity and envy. The Walnut Hills Police Department makes do with equipment so dated it's often more of a hindrance than a help.

"Some of the classrooms," Libby said. "And the library. We have two computers in the newspaper room, and Mr. Melville has one of them set up so that we can use his own browser. It's much better than the network server the school uses." She sliced off another chunk of cheese. "We're only supposed to use it for class research, but he's pretty lax about keeping track."

"You can exchange messages with people outside of school, one to one?"

"Sure."

Michael's expression was thoughtful. He hunched his shoulders and stroked his chin. Finally, he rocked back with a sigh. "I guess I'd better be going. Looks like I've got some digging to do." He grabbed the plastic skeleton. "I'll look into this, too. But remember, both of you, be careful."

I turned to Libby with a sudden, uncomfortable awareness. "You don't, uh, talk to people over the Internet,
do you? I mean those chat rooms or whatever they are."

"I have. Mostly, though, it's pretty boring stuff. Reminds me of when my dad got a CB radio back a few
years."

"But you wouldn't give out your name or address,
would you? Or agree to meet some guy you'd hooked up
with in that way?"

Libby gave me a withering look. "I'm not stupid, Kate."
She wrapped the cheese and turned her attention back
to the fridge before adding under her breath, "I might
send Skye a piece of anonymous hate mail, though."

Michael gave Libby's shoulder a gentle squeeze on his
way out. "If Skye's an experienced horsewoman, she'll
probably ride your friend Brian into the ground. He'll
end up with such a sore butt he won't want to go anywhere
near her again."

"Well, Skye certainly has more padding than he does,"
Libby said nastily.

Bits and pieces of the murders rattled in my thoughts
like loose change. I needed to get out, to stretch my legs
and my lungs, to settle the clamor in my brain. Max came
bounding when I grabbed his leash, and after checking
on Faye and Anna, we headed out in the direction of the
park.

The sky was a heavy, flat gray, much like my mood.
The plastic skeleton worried me more than I cared to
admit.

Perhaps it shouldn't have. How many times had I found
toys, hair ribbons, socks where they didn't belong?
Objects got dropped or misplaced. It happened daily.

The skeleton might have slipped from a child's pocket on his way to school and a neighbor, thinking it belonged to us, had returned it via the mailbox. Or maybe it was a present to Anna or Libby. After all, this wasn't like finding a bloody switchblade or a severed human hand on your doorstep. So it stood to reason that there might be nothing significant about finding a small plastic skeleton, especially with the approach of Halloween. But none of those arguments did anything to quell the tight knot of nervousness in my belly.

Max stopped to sniff the ivy at the corner. I ran my hands over my arms to warm them, realizing I should have slipped on a jacket before leaving. Although we would probably have another warm spell before chilly weather settled in for the season, the evening air had an icy quality to it I hadn't expected.

When we started on our way again, I put my mind to sorting and assembling what I knew. Julie had gone into Berkeley the night she was murdered. Since she'd been seen standing on the street corner alone, I had to assume she'd gone willingly.

Was she meeting someone there? Or maybe looking for somebody in particular?

And did the book of poems tie in to this? If Julie had been as involved in a relationship as the inscription suggested, surely there would have been someone who knew. Unless, of course, there'd been a reason for them to keep the relationship secret.

I backtracked. Whatever her reasons for going to Berkeley, it was clear that eventually Julie did meet someone there. Someone who drove her into the hills and killed her. And then removed her shoes, cut her hair, tucked a plastic skeleton under her body, and covered her with leaves. In that regard, she and Cindy Purcell had much in common.

The other thing the two women shared was on-line communication. But that was almost like pointing to the fact that they both had telephones or electric lights. These days everyone and his brother seemed to be on-line. Still, Michael thought it possible that Cindy Purcell's killer had found her through the Internet. Had he found Julie the same way?

My pace slowed as I mentally worked through the possibilities. All were tenuous, held together with gossamer strands of conjecture and coincidence. And more importantly, none seemed to jibe with the soft-spoken, reserved teenager who had been my star art student.

Max had grown impatient with my dawdling and was beginning to pull at his leash. I picked up my pace and turned toward home, my thoughts more scattered than when I'd started out. A block from the house, a red Mustang pulled slowly around the corner and then shot off at high speed, tires squealing. I didn't catch so much as a glimpse of the driver, but the name that came immediately to mind was Dennis Shepherd. He'd been driving the same color and make of car when I'd met him at his parents' house last week.

In my absence, Faye and Anna had worked out a compromise on the costume. Faye would make both a princess dress *and* a black satin cape suitable for vampire-wear. Anna could then decide. I had strong suspicions my daughter was using Faye's kindness as a ploy to get the black cape she'd been after me to make for the last month. Nonetheless, they both appeared happy with the arrangement so I kept quiet.

After dinner the three of us drove to Payless to garner the necessary supplies. I left Faye and Anna to handle the details of the cape while I went off to pick up a few household items we needed. As I passed the aisle of Halloween goods, I stopped to examine the selection of novelty items. They were numerous and varied. And, as I'd expected, there was a bin of skeletons just like the one that had been slipped into our mailbox.

A harmless holiday favor, I told myself, nothing sinister. As easily lost from a child's pocket or backpack as a gum wrapper. But the voice in the back of my head wouldn't let go. *What makes you think killers don't shop at the same places as everyone else?*

I closed my eyes against a terrible image. Had Julie's killer stood here in this very aisle and painstakingly selected the memento he would leave with her corpse? Had he also picked up one for us? And how many others had he procured? How many girls did he plan on killing?

"Oh, here you are," said Faye, edging in beside me. "We're all set with the fabric and such, but Anna wants to show me the talking parrot."

The shop next door sold tropical fish and birds, and was a favorite of Anna's. "I don't know that they're open this late," I told her. "But go ahead and see. I'll pay for these and meet you out front."

I grabbed the remaining items I needed and joined the throng of shoppers at the registers. None of the lines appeared to be moving with any speed, so I chose the best of the lot, pulling in behind a woman whose basket was practically empty. It was only after she turned that I recognized Patricia Shepherd.

She looked drained and tired, older somehow than she had only a week earlier. She smiled fleetingly, the polite, mouth-only smile one uses with strangers. Her eyes registered puzzlement, however. No doubt I looked familiar, but she couldn't pinpoint the context.

I helped by introducing myself and reminding her how we'd met. "I was terribly sorry to learn of Julie's death," I said, feeling, as I often did in such situations, the inadequacy of words. "I can only imagine how difficult this has been for you."

Mrs. Shepherd pressed her lips tight and nodded. "It's been very"—she paused for a breath—"very trying. On all of us."

"If there's anything I can do—"

"We did our best," she persisted, her tone strained.

"I'm sure you did. It can't be easy having a stranger move into your home." I'd learned that much with Libby. But I'd also found unexpected rewards in her company, which was something I doubted was true where the Shepherds were concerned.

"Not easy at all, but we tried to do what was right." Patricia Shepherd scowled. "Julie may have been family, but she'd been raised different. She didn't take to our ways, not willingly at any rate. It was especially hard on Walt. The two of them were like oil and water, about as different as can be."

"I bet you ran interference fairly often."

She smiled, but the gesture was stiff and fleeting. "I tried. Not that either one of them seemed to appreciate it." As we inched our carts forward, Mrs. Shepherd sighed. "Of course, Walt always thought I was too soft with Dennis as well."

I gave a knowing, mother-to-mother nod. "How is Dennis taking the news of Julie's death?"

"It's been hard on him. Despite what he said the other

day, Dennis was quite fond of his cousin. And he was hurt that she didn't return the affection.''

''I should think he might have resented Julie a bit.''

''Resented? Why?''

''She moved into his home, after all. Appropriated his parents' energy and attention.''

She shook her head. ''Dennis had already moved out on his own, and he always wanted a sister.'' She paused. ''Unfortunately, God chose not to favor us in that way.''

It was one of those comments I never know how to respond to. ''I'm sorry,'' I said after a minute.

She nodded.

The line moved forward again.

''It's nice that Dennis is close enough to come home fairly often.''

Mrs. Shepherd nodded again. ''Dennis is a sweet boy. It's too bad that he's never really fit in with his peers, never been very good at personal relationships. I sometimes think his being an only child contributed to the problem.''

I bit back a smile. She obviously didn't know about her son's numerous female companions. ''I ran into him at Macy's the other day. A friend and I were shopping for shoes and he waited on us. He's quite the salesman.''

This time the smile was softer and reached beyond the confines of her lips. ''Goodness, yes. He does enjoy that job. Of course, we hope that eventually he'll go on to something . . . well, something with more potential. But he's done very well there.''

Based on what I'd seen, Dennis was certainly handling his job admirably. Perhaps too admirably. ''Does Dennis have a computer with a modem, Mrs. Shepherd?''

She blinked in surprise. "He does have a computer, but I don't know what kind. Why do you ask?"

I gave a shrug and did my best to look nonchalant. "Just curious. Seems like more and more people do. I'm thinking of getting one myself."

"Well, you'd have to talk to Dennis. I'm afraid I know nothing about them." She pulled at the sleeve of her sweater. "He was asking about you just the other day, in fact."

"Asking? What about?"

"Just that he'd remembered you coming to the house when Julie first disappeared. I guess maybe seeing you again in Macy's reminded him."

The cashier pulled Mrs. Shepherd's cart into position and began ringing up her items, putting an end to our conversation. Not that she'd have been able to shed any new light on her son's idiosyncrasies, or tell me about Julie's interest in the poetry of D. H. Lawrence, even if I'd had the courage to ask. But it struck me that both were avenues which could use further probing.

And as I joined Anna and Faye outside, I had a sudden inspiration about who might be able to help round out the picture.

18

As soon as class was over the next morning, I called Marlene and set up an appointment to have my hair done. Lacquered curls weren't really my style, but I considered them a small price to pay for information— as long as they were only a temporary phenomenon.

"You off to a big party tonight, honey?" Marlene asked, wrapping a towel around my dripping, freshly shampooed hair.

"Don't I wish."

The salon was small, only two chairs without much space in between. The walls were gray, the floor a marbled turquoise linoleum. It smelled like the beauty parlor my mother had gone to every Thursday afternoon when I was growing up.

"Most gals your age don't get themselves done regular. Takes something kind of fancy to bring them in."

I gave her a smile by way of the mirror. "I'm just feeling down, I guess. Thought I'd do something to cheer myself up."

"That's smart thinking. Pamper yourself a little. Does a world of good." She wiped a rivulet of water from the side of my face. "You want to go for something completely different? I could cut off a couple inches easy, and put a little more wave near the front."

With a shudder, I flashed on Julie's dead body and the chunk of lopped-off hair. "Nothing quite so . . . drastic."

"How about something upswept then? Pulled back on the sides, curls up top?"

"Okay, just so long as it's not irreversible."

Marlene gave a knowing smile. "A pickup, not a makeover. I understand." She poured a dollop of purple gel on her palm and worked it through my hair. I wound up smelling like grape bubble gum. "What's got you down, if my asking isn't too personal."

It was a perfect lead-in to the reason for my visit. "The high school girl who was murdered in Berkeley last week—she was a student of mine. And a friend of my . . . niece's." Explaining Libby's relationship wasn't worth the trouble. "It's shaken me, I guess."

Marlene nodded in sympathy. "You're talking about Julie Harmon, right?"

I nodded in return and gave her a quizzical look.

"The couple she was staying with," Marlene announced. "Her aunt and uncle, they're neighbors of mine."

I'd been wondering about the best strategy for garnering information. But Marlene seemed ready enough to talk, so I decided to stick to the truth. "I know. My mother-in-law was in earlier this week," I explained. "She mentioned that Julie sometimes took care of your granddaughter."

Marlene grinned. "You must be the gal married to Andy, am I right?"

I opened my mouth to clarify her use of the term "married" but she cut me off.

"No wonder you're feeling down, honey. When things aren't right in a marriage, seems like the whole world's against you. I know, I've been there. So has my daughter. The key is to work on fixing the problem instead of letting it take over."

"Well, actually Andy and I are—"

"Relationships are like everything else, they sometimes need a little tuning up."

"Yes, but—"

"If you have a leaky sink, you don't walk away and sell the house. You call a plumber, right? Same with a marriage. You got maintenance and upkeep, and sometimes some major repairs. But that doesn't mean the whole thing is about to crumble." She squeezed my shoulder gently. "With a little effort you and Andy might be able to make a go of it yet."

I nodded numbly and weighed the advantages of setting her straight. None that I was able to discern. Certainly not in terms of getting the information I wanted.

"About Julie," I said, easing back on the subject. "I got the impression from Faye that she spent a fair amount of time at your place."

"Over the summer, yes. Once school started, she wasn't there as often. Karen's none too happy about that."

"Karen?"

"My granddaughter. She's with me a couple of afternoons a week, plus Sundays. My daughter works part-time at the pasta shop."

"Sounds like you have your hands full."

Marlene's laugh was gentle and colored with affection. "She keeps me on my toes, all right. Karen idolized Julie. And to tell the truth, I think the feeling was mutual in many ways. Julie would drop over to see her even when she wasn't babysitting. An excuse to get out of the house, probably, as much as anything."

"Did Julie talk much about herself?"

"Not in an obnoxious way. But I could tell she was unhappy with the Shepherds, poor thing. They didn't show an ounce of sympathy for what the girl had been through. Silenced her every time she started to talk about her mother. I tried to let her know she was welcome to talk to her heart's content at my place."

"Did she?"

Marlene sectioned my hair and began winding it on rollers. "You want full curls on the sides or just on top?" she asked.

I didn't want full curls anywhere, which is why I usually left my hair to dry with only a little finger fluffing. "Whatever you think best," I told her, wondering if I would be able to make it home without running into anyone I knew.

Marlene dabbed on more purple goo. "I wish now I'd been a little less inclined to offer her refuge. Walt and Patricia are as narrow-minded and insensitive as they come, but maybe if Julie had been stuck by their rules, she'd still be alive."

"Faye said you saw her sneaking out to meet boys."

Marlene nodded. "Well, there was only one time I actually saw her. But I knew she was going places and doing things the Shepherds wouldn't approve of. Nothing out-and-out bad, mind you, just the kind of stuff most kids do."

"Was there one special boy she was involved with?"

"She never mentioned anyone special."

"How about the boy you saw her sneak off with?"

"The one with the blue truck. He'd give her a ride home from school sometimes, too. Used to hang around, gaze at her with those dark puppy-dog eyes of his."

I didn't know whether Mario's truck was blue or not, but the rest of the description fit. "Did you ever see her with anyone else?"

Marlene took her time winding a strand of hair around the curler, tucking the ends in with the tail of her comb. "How come you're so interested in all this?"

I told her about the book of poems and the fact that Julie had been seen in Berkeley the night she was killed. "There was a side to Julie that no one seems to know much about. So if you saw her with someone in particular . . ."

"I never did, no." Marlene paused to secure the curler with a clip. She seemed to weigh something in her mind, then reach a decision. "But my daughter thought she did. An older man."

"Older?"

"Not old, but clearly of a different generation. When I asked Julie about it later, she said he was a family friend. But she was mighty quick to change the subject. It was clear she didn't want to elaborate."

"When was this?"

"About a week before she died. Nan, that's my daughter, saw them sitting at a picnic table out by the reservoir, talking. She probably wouldn't have thought anything about it except that it was during the school day." Marlene paused. "That's what I meant about Julie bending the rules. Nothing so terrible in itself. Not that I approve of cutting class, but it didn't seem right to go tattling on her to the Shepherds either.''

''I can understand your reluctance.''

Marlene sighed heavily. ''I've been kicking myself ever since.'' She picked up another roller and partitioned a second strand of hair. ''You think maybe this man had something to do with her death?''

''I honestly don't know, but he might have.''

''I thought she was killed by this so-called Parkside Killer.''

''That's one theory. And maybe he's the same man your daughter saw her with at the reservoir. Do you know what he looked like?''

''You'd have to ask Nan. She never mentioned anything about him looking sinister though.''

''Unfortunately most killers don't look any different from the rest of us.''

I had her write down Nan's address and phone number, explaining that I was going to pass it on to a friend who was a policeman. I was hoping Michael would talk to Nan himself rather than leave it to Gates.

Marlene finished the last rollers and stuck me under the dryer with a tattered and dated issue of *Good Housekeeping*. While the hot blast from the dryer fried my head and the back of my neck, I scanned an article about the perils of yo-yo dieting and drooled over recipes for chocolate cake. But I did so with half a mind. The other half was engaged in speculation about Julie's *family friend* and her motive for being in Berkeley on an evening when she was supposed to be at the high school football game in Walnut Hills. Was there a connection? And if so, how had it led to her murder?

Lots of questions, but no answers. Finally, I gave up

and went back to my reading. I was well into a survey about men's sexual fantasies (which, I'm not proud to say, did manage to hold both halves of my mind) when Marlene came over to test a coil of hair. I could tell by the way it bounced back against my scalp that these were not going to be wimpy curls.

"Okay, let's comb you out," she said, shutting off the dryer. Since my former chair was now occupied by another customer, Marlene led me to the second station by the window.

"You doing okay, Mrs. Burl?" she asked the older woman whose thinning gray hair had been slicked in white foam during the time I was frying under the dryer. "You want a magazine or anything?"

Mrs. Burl appeared to be asleep, but she obviously wasn't because she opened her eyes at the question. "What kind of playthings?"

"Not playthings, Mrs. Burl. I said 'anything,' like maybe a magazine or some coffee." Marlene's voice was several decibels higher this time, and the words formed with exaggerated precision.

"A magazine might be nice."

When Marlene had set Mrs. Burl up with several publications aimed at an audience half a century younger, she began removing the rollers from my hair. As I feared, the curls were as tight without the benefit of plastic as with.

"You know," she continued, as though there'd been only a momentary lapse in our discussion, "if it had been anyone else besides Walt and Patricia, I might have spoken up. I do believe parents should know what's going on with their children. God knows that's what I wanted with my own two. But the Shepherds are so . . ." She paused, searching for the right word. "So touchy, so firm in their vision of how things should be, that it's hard to know how they would have reacted."

"It's not easy to know what's right."

"To my mind, they were a good part of the problem. I don't know about this *other side* of Julie, as you call it. Maybe she did bend the rules a bit, but she was a sweet girl, level-headed too. If Walt and Patricia had been more accepting, she'd never have had to go sneaking off the way she did."

"Sneakers are the best," piped in Mrs. Burl. "That's all I wear anymore. I'll go for comfort any day. Who gives a hoot about style when you've got sore feet."

"You're right about that," Marlene responded.

I wasn't overly fond of the Shepherds myself, but given what I'd learned recently, it seemed Julie might have been pushing the limits of what any family would find acceptable. On the other hand, I had to agree with Marlene that I'd seen nothing in Julie that fit with the picture that seemed to be emerging after the fact.

"Of course, they were strict with their son, too," Marlene continued. "Though I never got the feeling it much bothered him."

"You're talking about Dennis?"

"You know him?"

"I've met him. And I ran into him again the other day at Macy's. He sells women's shoes there." I waited, for what I'm not sure. A reaction or comment, maybe, that would confirm my sense of something odd about his interest in feet. None was forthcoming. Instead, Marlene squinted at my reflection in the mirror as she ran a brush through my hair. The curls sprang to twice their former size.

After a moment, I tried again. "I understand he had some emotional problems when he was younger."

She nodded. "I guess it might have bothered him, after all. Only he handled it in a different way."

"Any idea what kind of emotional problems?"

"My kids were gone by then, so I didn't pay much attention." Another swipe of the brush and I looked like Hillary Clinton at the first inauguration. Not that I have anything against Hillary, but her hairdresser would not be among the names in my Rolodex.

"What about problems with the law?" I asked.

"None that I ever heard about."

Mrs. Burl leaned forward, the magazines still unopened on her lap. "You got problems with the law, Marlene? It's that danged government, minding everybody's business but their own."

"Not me, Mrs. B. We're talking about a mutual acquaintance. Why don't you just look at those magazines there, and I'll be with you in a minute."

Marlene pulled the sides of my hair back with an upward twist and pinned them securely against my scalp. "You want my opinion," she said, "he might well still have some problems."

"Dennis?"

She nodded. "Julie caught him going through her things. She was madder than a hornet's nest. Not only at Dennis, but at Walt and Patricia, too. They acted like it wasn't any big deal. I'd forgotten about that. It was over the summer when she was down at my place a lot. Maybe they smoothed things out, but she was absolutely livid at the time. Can't say as I blame her, either."

"Going through her things? You mean personal things?"

178 *Jonnie Jacobs*

Another nod. "Snooping through her bureau drawers, if you can believe it. She caught him at it red-handed."

"What was Dennis's explanation?"

Marlene humphed in disgust. "That he was looking for his high school ring, thought maybe it got stuck in one of the grooves or something. About as lame an excuse as I can imagine. And even if it was true, he should have asked first."

"Was anything missing?"

"Nothing she could prove. What with the move and all, and she had stuff in storage . . . Well, you know what it's like when you can't find something, but you can't say for sure the last time you saw it either." Marlene fluffed the top section of curls and pulled a few wisps loose at the temples. Then she took a large can of hairspray and emptied half of it on my head. "There you go, and mighty nice if I do say so myself. You ought to go dangle yourself in front of that husband of yours." She passed me a hand mirror, then turned the chair slowly for a 360-degree perspective.

I no longer resembled Hillary Clinton. Maybe a Miss America wannabe from 1963 or Tammy Faye Bakker in a poodle look-alike contest.

"What do you think?" Marlene asked, clearly more pleased with the result than I was.

"I . . ."

"You look like a Hollywood starlet."

"It's certainly a new look," I conceded.

"Looks like rain to me," Mrs. Burl volunteered.

One thing was certain, I looked like a woman who'd been to the beauty parlor.

*   *   *

When I returned home, Faye was working away industriously on Anna's costume. Max was on the back porch, separated from any prospect of trouble by several securely closed doors.

I was trying to slink down the hallway to the bathroom where I could stick my head under the faucet when Faye looked up.

"I like it," she said, referring to my new do. "It's more polished. You look like you could be selling cosmetics or something."

I scanned her words for a glint of sarcasm, and didn't find any. "Why would I want to sell cosmetics?"

"Well, furs then. Whatever. I just meant that it gives you an image. Classy." She bent back over the fabric. "You had a call while you were out. Your . . . um, your suitor."

Suiter? I didn't even own a suit. "Who?" I asked, puzzled.

"The policeman."

Ah, that I understood. I retired to the bedroom to return the call.

Michael must have been sitting at his desk because he picked up halfway through the first ring. "We compared the plastic skeletons," he said without preliminaries.

"And?"

"The one from your mailbox matches the one found near Julie's body."

I felt the intake of breath against my ribs.

"Although the things are fairly common, they aren't as widely carried by stores as you'd think. Lots of places are cutting back on seasonal novelties. There's apparently not enough profit to justify the space and effort.''

''But you're sure they're the same?''

''For all practical purposes. That doesn't mean it's related to the murder, of course. There are plenty of other explanations.''

I nodded mutely.

''Still, until we get a better handle on these murders, I think you should be extra cautious. Libby and Anna, too. Stay in well-populated areas and keep clear of strangers, no matter how innocuous they seem.''

''Why us? Why our mailbox?''

''I don't know that. As I said, it could be unrelated. Then, too, we don't know that yours was the only mailbox where one of these things showed up. This skeleton business wasn't mentioned in the newspapers so most people wouldn't make the connection. They'd simply toss off finding one as a mistake, or at worst, a prank.'' Michael was trying hard to be reassuring, but I could sense the uneasiness behind the words.

''I thought I saw Dennis Shepherd's car drive by our house the other day.'' I waited, and when Michael didn't respond, I asked if Gates had questioned Dennis yet.

''He doesn't answer to me, Kate.''

''I know that, but . . .''

But what? Looking at it objectively, there was little about Dennis to raise one's suspicions. It was more the feeling I got being around him.

''Julie found him going through her drawers,'' I said.

''Not polite, but not a crime either.''

''There's someone else you might want to question as well.'' I told him about my conversation with Marlene.

As I expected, the older man Julie had met near the reservoir caught his interest.

"You have a description?" Michael asked.

"No, but I have Nan's number." I read it into the phone.

"Nice work, Kate." The soft rolling pitch of his voice made it clear the compliment was genuine. "And I'll talk to her myself," he said. "Before I pass the information onto Gates, okay?"

I smiled. My *suitor* knew how to please. Then I remembered Susie's appeal for help setting up an interview. "There's one other tiny thing," I said slowly.

"What's that?"

I explained. "I'm not asking you to do it, understand. Simply passing along the request. It won't bother me if you say no."

To my surprise, Michael agreed. "If I don't talk to her, God knows what she'll write."

"Either a sensationalist, panic-inducing piece fit for the *National Enquirer* or a scathing indictment of the Walnut Hills police force."

He laughed. "Actually, I was thinking she'd do both. Have her give me a call and I'll see what I can do. But I can't promise I'll be able to tell her anything she doesn't already know."

As soon as we hung up, I picked up the phone again and called Susie to give her the good news.

"Thanks, Kate. This will be a big help. I've already done a small article that should be appearing this week, but now I can do a much more comprehensive piece. Maybe I can even parlay it into a major magazine article once the case is solved. This is truly a golden opportunity."

I felt my skin prickle. How could a dead girl ever be a golden opportunity?

"There's the doorbell," she said breathlessly. "I've got to run. But I wanted to invite you to brunch on Saturday. Nothing fancy. Just a few friends. Michael, too, of course."

I dropped the phone into the cradle and went to check on Max, then wandered back into the living room.

"The dress is just about done," Faye said. "I'll fit it to Anna this afternoon and then do the final stitching." She held up a gown of gold taffeta and chiffon, trimmed in lace. I thought it might be the fanciest dress Anna would ever own, certainly more elaborate than anything of mine. I only hoped Faye wouldn't be too disappointed when Anna chose beast over beauty for Halloween.

"Did you check the mail?" I asked.

"No. I thought it didn't come until later."

It didn't, but our mailbox had recently assumed a prominent place in my mind, and checking it had become something of a nervous habit.

I wandered out front, took a breath, and yanked the box open quickly, the way you pull a Band-Aid off tender skin. It was empty save for a stray ant near the front. I brushed him aside, hoping he hadn't already sent for reinforcements, and felt my breathing return to normal.

Judy Belson walked by with her twin preschoolers rattling along behind on their Big Wheels.

I greeted her with a wave. "Your kids didn't happen to lose a miniature plastic skeleton, did they?"

She shook her head. "They're more into bats and spiders anyway." There was a moment's pause. "New hairdo?"

"An experiment. I'm going to wash it out as soon as I get a chance."

One of the boys screeched to a halt at my feet. "You like my Ferrari?" he asked, peddling up the driveway with a throaty "Vroom, Vroom."

"Mine's a Mustang," said his brother.

Judy laughed. "Until recently it was a Porsche. But he was intrigued by the Mustang parked on our street the other day."

"There was a Mustang parked on our street?" It came out more as a croak than a question. "What color?"

"Same as mine," the boy said. "Fire engine red."

I turned to Judy. "Did you see who it belonged to?"

"Sorry. I'm not much into cars myself."

"It belonged to a man," her son said. "And it had a Garfield in the back window. They do it with suction cups."

I told myself I was being ridiculous. Mine was not the only house on the street. Dennis was not the only person who drove a red Mustang. And perhaps more important, I couldn't think of any reason he'd choose to park in our neighborhood. But once the idea was there, it wouldn't go away. Like the song of the Siren, it masked reason and drew me in. The difference was in the melody. There was nothing pleasurable about it.

19

I told Faye I had to run an errand and might be gone for the remainder of the afternoon. Then I called Sharon to enlist her help in case I wasn't back by the time Anna's school got out.

"Are you sure," Sharon asked, "that it was Dennis's car the boys saw?"

"No, I'm not sure at all. That's why I want to see if his Mustang has a Garfield in the back window."

"And if it does?"

"I don't know. I haven't thought that far."

"It's spooky. I mean, if it really was him. Maybe after we saw him at Macy's, he remembered who you were."

"That," I told her, "is one of the things that concerns me."

"Do you think it was Dennis who put the skeleton in your mailbox?"

I gave an exasperated sigh. "Do I sound to you like a woman with answers?"

Sharon laughed. "Kate, you always have answers. It's

just that half the time they don't make sense to anyone but you." She paused. "He might not be home, you know. What are you going to do then, go around asking his neighbors if they've seen a red Mustang with Garfield stuck to the rear window?"

In fact, that was exactly what I planned to do. Only it was neighbor, singular—Luke Martin.

Despite the low clouds and heavy mist, the traffic into Berkeley flowed smoothly. It was a good thing, because my mind was on Dennis and what it might mean if I discovered that a Garfield adorned the rear window of his Mustang. I was still lost in thought when I turned onto Sacramento Street, which is why I didn't see the policeman with the radar gun until after he'd seen me.

"Any idea how fast you were going, lady?" The cop was young, probably only a couple of years on the job, but his words held the intonation that comes with authority.

I shook my head. If I'd been observant enough to know how fast I was going, I'd have seen the stupid radar gun.

"You clocked in at thirty-two miles per hour."

A regular speed-demon.

"That's seven over the limit." He checked my license, then uncapped the pen with his teeth, wrote out a citation. He handed me the narrow slip of pink paper with a gruff, "Have a good day, ma'am."

I waited until he was out of earshot to grumble my reply, then drove off well under the posted limit.

When I got to Dennis Shepherd's street, I slowed to a crawl, checking the cars parked along the curb. There wasn't a red Mustang anywhere to be seen. I circled the block to the right, and then to the left. The closest I came was a rusted burgundy Toyota.

Time for the backup plan, then. A plan that had
sounded reasonable enough when I'd first thought of it,
but now gave me pause. After all, I knew next to nothing
about Luke Martin aside from the fact that he'd caught
me tailing one of Dennis's women friends. Luke Martin
might be crazy, or dangerous. He might slam the door
in my face.

But it was the opposite response that worried me most.
Would he misinterpret the reason for my visit and think
I'd come there primarily to see him? Might there, in fact,
be a small element of truth in that?

Pushing the thought aside, I parked at the end of the
block and walked resolutely toward Luke Martin's house.
I'd come all this way and I did want to know about the
car. As I neared Dennis's pink bungalow, I noticed the
gravel area at the far end of his driveway, behind the
house. Barely visible from the road, but easy to spot from
the walkway between the houses, was a red Mustang. And
grinning out at me from the back window was a wide-
eyed and springy Garfield.

My skin grew prickly in spite of the cold. So it *had* been
Dennis parked across from my house. But why?

With a shiver, I started back to my car. After a moment
the shock passed and the backfill of mental gymnastics
set in. Dennis might have been visiting a friend in our
neighborhood, I told myself. Or maybe he'd begun taking
piano lessons from Mrs. Doyle down the street. Or perhaps he was simply passing through the area when his
car suddenly succumbed to engine trouble.

There were plenty of innocent explanations. In any
event, I'd found what I'd come for. As soon as I got
home, I'd call Michael and . . .

And what? When I stopped to think about it, there

wasn't a whole lot Michael could do. Even if he agreed to question Dennis about parking on our street, which was unlikely in the first place, what would that get me? Parking wasn't illegal, and I couldn't say for sure that it had been Dennis.

With a resigned sigh, I turned and headed back again in the direction I'd come. If I wanted to know more about Dennis Shepherd, I'd have to make inquiries myself. And at the moment, Luke Martin was my best shot.

Martin's house, a deeply weathered brown shingle, faced sideways on the lot. The entrance was down a path that ran parallel to the driveway. I made my way boldly along the walk, then hesitated at the door when I saw the placard over the bell.

We do not sign petitions, answer surveys, give to charity or buy anything at the door. If you don't have an appointment, please don't bother ringing.

I shifted my weight. He'd invited me, hadn't he? Anytime but Thursday evening. Without giving myself time to reconsider, I punched the bell.

A moment later, Luke Martin's gruff voice boomed from over my shoulder. "What is it?"

I jumped, turned to my left, in the direction of the sound, and noticed a small grill mounted on the wall.

"Hi," I called out. "It's Kate." I wasn't sure whether I was supposed to address the grill or the door, so I tried doing both. "Remember me from a couple of days ago?"

There was a stretch of silence during which I imagined him racking his brain for a woman named Kate.

Feeling my face redden, I added, "I was the one tailing

your neighbor's girlfriend." I was still talking to the speaker grill when Luke Martin himself opened the door.

"Hey," he said with a grin. "I never expected to see you again. Come on in."

He wheeled his chair back, pulling the door open further. I stepped inside, pleasantly surprised at the sleek and simple beauty of the decor. Bare hardwood floors, sparse furnishings, lots of natural light, and a stunning array of paintings and photographs.

"Did you decide to take me up on that offer of a latte?" he asked.

I cleared my throat. "Actually, it was more the other part."

"The other part." He put a finger to his forehead. "You mean, information?"

I nodded.

He waved his hand in a theatrical gesture of disappointment. "I should have guessed."

"Sorry."

"I'm not about to let you off the hook, though." He raised his gaze to mine and I caught a glint of amusement in his eyes. I began to relax. "Since you're not dead set on coffee, how about mulled cider instead? I've got some already made. That way we won't have to go out into the cold and damp."

"Cider sounds good," I told him, eyeing the painting in the hallway. A mountain meadow filled with wildflowers, and beyond them the snow-capped peaks of early summer. I could almost feel the gentle rustle of wind against my skin.

I stepped closer. "This is beautiful."

"It's one of my favorites."

"You painted it yourself?"

He laughed. "Hardly."

"Someone you know?"

"I've met him, but I hadn't when I bought it." Luke Martin rolled his chair to a position where he had a better view of the painting. "The Wind River Mountains in Wyoming. You ever been there?"

I shook my head.

He stared at the picture for a moment longer. "My magic carpet," he said softly. "It takes my mind where my body can't go."

My eyes slid from the painting to his strong, almost Slavic profile. I would like to have known how he came to be in a wheelchair.

"I've always loved the mountains," he said. "The exhilaration of being alone in the wilderness is one of the things I miss most."

Before I could fashion a suitable reply, he turned his chair abruptly. "Make yourself comfortable. I'll get our cider and be right back."

Luke Martin disappeared into the kitchen and returned a few minutes later with two heavy ceramic mugs. "You changed your hair," he said, handing me one.

Self-consciously, I touched the topknot of rigid curls. In my concern about the red Mustang, I'd forgotten Marlene's makeover.

"It looks nice," he added, without conviction.

I laughed. "No, it doesn't. And it certainly doesn't look like me. I just haven't had a chance to wash it out yet."

He laughed too, a full, rich sound that dispelled any lingering tension about my visit. "I did like it better loose."

I took a sip of cider. It was warm and spicy and not too sweet. "You said you were a writer. What do you write?"

"Most of what I'm doing these days involves computers. Articles for computer magazines, some technical stuff—and, of course, the great American novel."

"About computers?"

"About everything but."

"Are you close to finishing?"

"The novel? I don't know. Some months I think I'm almost there, and then the next thing I see is how it needs to be changed. Like Mrs. Winchester and her mystery house. Maybe I'm simply afraid to declare it done."

Luke Martin set his mug on the wooden chest that served as a side table, then crossed his arms. "So what's your interest in Denny? I take it you're not with a collection agency or some such thing."

"Is he a deadbeat?"

"Not that I know of. But like I told you the other day, I don't know him well."

I wondered how best to explain my interest in Dennis Shepherd. The story was so convoluted that no matter what I told him it was bound to come out jumbled. Finally I said the first thing that came to mind. "His parents were the legal guardians of a fifteen-year-old girl, a student of mine, who was murdered last week."

Luke's eyes clouded. "Jesus, how terrible."

"You might have heard about it. They found her body in Tilden Park."

"Are you talking about the Parkside Killer? It's been in the news all week. He killed another girl a couple of weeks ago, too."

I nodded. "Only it might not be a serial killer. That's only one theory."

"And you're looking into it?"

"Certain aspects anyway."

He ran a hand along his jaw. "How come?"

"I knew Julie Harmon. She asked for my help just before she was killed, so I guess I feel guilty as well. In retrospect, I realize that she was troubled by something but I have no idea what. And there are a string of things that don't make sense, too many to go into at the moment."

"And Denny?"

"Julie wasn't happy living with his parents. In fact, she thought she'd found an alternative arrangement."

I filled him in a bit on Julie's background and her excitement at the prospect of leaving the Shepherds. Luke listened attentively without interrupting.

"I don't know exactly where Dennis fits in," I said. "For one thing, Julie caught him searching her bureau drawers. And he didn't seem particularly fond of her, for another." I took a breath. "And he was parked on my street the other day, near my house. None of this makes sense objectively, I know, but it has gotten under my skin. I want to learn more about him."

Luke frowned, sipped his drink. "I'm afraid I'm not going to be able to help you much."

"Anything you can tell me, I'd appreciate it."

"Well, he goes by Denny rather than Dennis. Moved in less than a year ago. He's fairly quiet, except for when he plays the saxophone. Keeps to himself mostly. He's got a job and goes to school, so I guess that doesn't give him a lot of time."

"Friends?"

"I've seen people around, but I never paid much attention."

"Except for the women."

The corners of his mouth twitched with humor. "Right, except for the women. They're the only ones who visit with any regularity." Luke paused. "At first there was just the one."

"Did she spend a lot of time there?"

"No. I don't think so anyway. She might have spent the night once or twice, but then sometimes she wouldn't show up for a week or so."

"Is she the one I saw the other day?"

"No, that's one of the others. She started showing up about four or five months ago. That's when I started taking note, really. A kid his age, not exactly an Adonis, and he's stringing along two, maybe three gals. I guess I found it curious."

"You said you saw a young girl there as well?"

He nodded. "She stood out as being different from the others. Different look, different attitude. And she didn't have a key the way the others do."

I wished I'd thought to bring a picture of Julie. "Can you describe her?"

"Blond, slender, kind of a regal bearing."

The description fit. "Did she stay long?"

"Couldn't say for sure, but I don't think so. One time I can tell you about for certain, she was only there ten minutes or so."

I slid back in my chair, running my fingers over the worn leather upholstery. "What's your impression of the guy?"

"Before you showed up, I'm not sure I'd taken the time to form one. We nod to each other when we pass on the street, which isn't that often, mumble about the weather if we happen to retrieve the morning paper at the same time. I invited him over to share a pizza one rainy night when I couldn't get my demons into their cages alone.'' He paused. ''Figuratively speaking.''

Our eyes met and Luke gave me an apologetic smile.

''Do you have a lot of demons?'' I asked.

''Probably no more than the next guy. Or gal.'' Another smile, self-conscious but not without humor. ''It's just that they are terribly ill-behaved at times.''

I'd had similar moments, although I had a feeling that Luke Martin's demons were far more obstreperous than mine. ''From what little I've seen, you appear to handle them pretty well.''

''I guess so. Most of the time. But it's been a lot of years getting there.''

There was a moment's silence, and then before I realized what I was doing, the words were out of my mouth. ''What happened? With your legs, I mean.''

He gave me a quizzical look. ''I thought you wanted to know about Denny.''

''I do.'' I nodded vigorously, feeling my cheeks grow red.

Luke's gaze drifted to the maple outside his window. ''My story isn't all that interesting.''

''I'm sorry, I didn't really mean to ask.''

''Hey, it's not a problem. Most people pretend the wheelchair's invisible. Like it's an embarrassment. That drives me nuts.''

I sipped my cider and kept silent.

''Anyway,'' Luke said, pushing the hair off his forehead. ''Denny came over one night. We had pizza, talked a little, watched some stupid made-for-TV movie as I recall.

We don't have a lot in common, so the conversation was kind of stiff at first. The *where'd you move from, what do you do for a living* kind of stuff.''

"What did he say about himself?"

"Let's see." Luke scratched his chin. "Denny said he was a goof-off in high school, wished now he'd applied himself. He's at a junior college, but hoping to transfer next year."

"Do you know what he's studying?"

"General stuff, I guess. His dad is apparently a real bear. Wanted Denny to go to some small Bible college in the Midwest. Said the old guy just about disowned him when he refused."

It sounded like Walt, but not Dennis. "Funny, I wouldn't have guessed Dennis had the mettle to go against his parents' wishes."

"It was his dad's wish primarily. I got the feeling theirs has never been the easiest of relationships."

"Did he seem bitter about it?"

"More resigned than anything."

"How about Julie?" I asked. "Did he ever mention her? Anything about a cousin or someone who'd moved into his family home?"

Luke shook his head. "If he did, I don't remember it."

"What about his job? Did he talk about it?"

"Sales of some kind. Macy's, Mervyn's, some place like that. It's just part-time while he's going to school. You want some more cider?"

"I'm fine, thanks." I leaned forward with my arms on my knees. "Tell me, based on what you saw of Dennis, did he strike you as . . . as stable?"

Luke threw back his head and laughed. "What's stable?

Especially at twenty. He didn't act like he was on drugs, or about to take a dive off the Golden Gate, if that's what you mean. On the other hand, he's not going to win any awards for charisma or social grace.''

I sighed. I'd been hoping for something more.

Luke set his cup down and wheeled the chair forward a couple of feet. "Look, if you're so interested, let's go talk to him.''

"Talk to him?'' My voice spiraled to an ungodly pitch.

"Yeah. We'll go borrow a cup of sugar or something.''

"He might recognize me.''

"All the better. You can ask him what he was doing parked in front of your house yesterday.''

"It wasn't in front, really. I mean, not right in front—''

"Heck, I'll ask him if you want. You can pretend to be surprised, like you didn't know he lived next door.''

"I don't know if—''

"But that's why you're here, isn't it? You're bothered by the fact that he was parked across from your house. And beyond that, you're wondering if he might not be implicated in the girl's death. Right?''

The man was perceptive, if not particularly cautious. "That's why I really don't think . . .''

But Luke was already at the door. "You coming, or am I doing this alone?''

I sighed and, against my better judgment, followed.

When we arrived at Dennis's front landing, I held back, afraid that Luke might find the step something of an obstacle. But without so much as a pause, he pulled the chair onto its rear wheels and propelled himself up and over.

"That's impressive," I said.

"That's nothing," he replied, with the merest hint of a smile.

"But I still think this visit is a stupid idea."

He grinned and didn't answer.

The doorbell hung loosely by a single wire. Luke tried it, and then after a few moments knocked on the door. I stood off to the side, torn between a mesmerizing curiosity and a strong desire to flee.

The landing was cramped, in part because the mailbox was just that, a wooden box sitting on the ground by the side of the door. Ever the snoop, I peered in. *Time* magazine, a mailing from a national music club, a supermarket throwaway, and an envelope of gray linen. With calculated nonchalance, I reached down and turned it over. And then let out a squeak.

"What is it?" Luke asked.

"A letter. Addressed to Julie Harmon at this number." As I was holding it out for him to examine, the door suddenly opened and a familiar-looking woman with flaming red hair glared at us. She had a heavy jaw and strong features that, although not unattractive, seemed somehow mismatched.

It took only a moment for me to recognize her as the woman I'd followed the other day after she'd emerged from Dennis's house. Surprisingly, she seemed to have no difficulty recognizing me either. Her face registered shock, then indignation and something else that was hard to read. Her eyes flickered from my face to Luke's and then to the letter in my hand.

And then, in a voice that was recognizably Dennis Shepherd's, she said, "Well, what *is* it you want?"

20

"Denny?" Luke's voice cracked with disbelief.

"Denise," the figure at the door replied. "At the moment, anyway." Denny-Denise turned and pointed a finger accusingly in my direction. "And you! What is it with you, anyway?"

I stepped back, too astonished to do more than sputter. "I, um . . ."

With a forward lunge, he grabbed the letter from my hand. "And now you're going through my mail?" He gave me a scorching look. "This is too much. It's just really too much."

Luke cleared his throat. "Uh, maybe it would be best if we talked inside."

"I don't see why." Denny, who was sounding more and more like Denise, crossed his arms over an amazingly well-endowed chest. He continued to glower in my direction.

"Fine," Luke said. "If that's the way you want it, we'll

talk out here. I've got my chair, I'm comfortable. And I'm sure our neighbors would like to hear more.''

Dennis glanced at Luke, cursed under his breath, then stood back, holding the door open. Luke popped another wheelie up and over the doorsill, and propelled himself inside. I followed, my heart racing.

We stepped into a room furnished, if that is the proper term, almost exclusively with fish tanks and a colorful variety of shimmering fish. There were three large rectangular aquariums, two cylindrical vats, and one bowl, whose sole occupant, a bug-eyed goldfish, observed us with curiosity. Dennis sat in the only armchair and folded his skirt around his knees. I took a straight-back chair near the door.

For a moment nobody said a word, and then Luke burst out laughing.

"I don't see anything particularly funny about this . . ." Dennis paused. He scowled and gestured toward me. "This She-Devil with a bee in her britches. She harassed me at work, followed me the other day—"

"I'm sorry," Luke said. "It's just that . . ." He struggled to contain another bout of laughter, only partially succeeding. "Aw, Denny, you sure had me fooled. These gals I've seen coming and going, this mini-harem of yours . . . it was you. In drag."

Denny's eyelids dropped to half-mast, revealing lids of periwinkle. "I don't see *that* as particularly funny either. Nor what concern it is of yours."

Luke grinned and held up his hands in a gesture of accord. "It's not. And I'm not laughing at you, buddy. I'm laughing at myself. I can't tell you the nights when envy was breathing so hard down my neck I didn't sleep a wink.''

I shifted in my chair, glad that Luke found the situation amusing, and perhaps reassuring. But it seemed to me he'd lost sight of the reason we were there.

Dennis, however, had not. He again turned his attention my way. "You," he snarled over the hum and gurgling of the aquariums. "What are you after, anyway?"

"*Me?*"

"When I saw you shopping for shoes the other day, I knew you looked familiar. And then next thing I know, you're staking out my house, slinking along behind me like some two-bit Sherlock. What's your game, lady? You got on some kind of twisted moral crusade?"

"Not at all, I'm simply . . ." My mind was still reeling, trying to make sense of the latest turn of events. Finally, I seized on the only piece of the whole mess that was within my grasp at the moment. "Why was there a letter addressed to Julie Harmon in *your* mail?"

Dennis was not about to be sidetracked. "Fooling with the mail is a federal offense, you know. I could have you arrested for that. I could have you arrested for harassing me, in fact. I could probably even have you arrested as a public nuisance." His voice grew harsher with each threat.

Indignation rose in my throat. "Yeah?" I shot back. "Don't forget you were snooping around my neighborhood the other day." I bit back any mention of the plastic skeleton in my mailbox. If Dennis had put it there, airing my suspicions might not be smart.

"Snooping? What makes you—"

"Hold on," Luke said. "Both of you. Yelling at each other isn't going to accomplish anything."

Dennis sighed, fingered the chunky gold bracelet on his wrist. "So, let's cut to the chase," he said. "What's the bottom line, blackmail? Or are you one of those *guiding lights* from my folks' church?''

"That's what you think?" Luke asked, his voice rippling with amusement. "That Kate cares whether you wear flannel boxers or pink silk panties?"

It was actually an intriguing question, and one I hadn't had time to consider in the rush of the day's revelations. But Luke was right that I didn't much care either way.

"You're not a cop," Dennis said. "I know because I checked it out."

"I'm here because of Julie Harmon," I explained.

He drummed his fingers on his knee. "She told you, didn't she?"

"Told me what?"

His widely arched brows furrowed, his mouth pulled into a rose-bud pout. Dennis looked a lot like the drawings I'd seen of Cinderella's stepsisters.

"Why was she getting mail at your address?" I asked again.

"Because she didn't have any privacy at home." Dennis stood and moved to one of the larger fish tanks, where he tinkered with the dials. "My father pries into everything. Thinks it's his God-given right to read your mail, search your room, listen to your conversations."

"Rifle through your bureau drawers?"

"Yeah, you got it."

I waited a beat. "The same way you went through Julie's?"

He rocked forward. "She *did* tell you. I knew it!"

"Seems to me you're in no position to complain about your father's behavior."

Dennis glared at me, his eyes blazing through lashes heavy with mascara. "It wasn't the same."

"No?"

"I only wanted to have a look at her stuff. I was admiring, not prying."

"I don't see—"

He returned to his chair. "Julie's things were silky and delicate. Some of them so tiny they'd fit into the palm of your hand. Different from the stuff my mother wears."

"That's no excuse."

"It was only a couple of times." His voice was soft, almost wispy. "And I never did it again after she caught me at it."

Luke pressed his fingers to his temples, shaking his head. "Christ, Denny. It doesn't matter the reason, you still went through her private possessions without asking. I don't imagine she was happy about it."

"She was pretty mad," Dennis conceded, without looking at either of us. "Livid, in fact. Came storming in here to my place to have it out with me." He paused to examine his nails, which were short and square, but polished in a crimson red. "That's when she met Denise. I thought sure there was going to be trouble."

"Trouble?"

"You know, that she'd freak out, tell my parents. Tell her friends and the kids at school, not that I really care about them. My dad, though, he'd rather see me dead. And I'm not shitting you, either."

Having met Walton Shepherd, I thought that might be true. But it also gave Dennis a pretty good motive for wanting to make sure Julie wasn't able to talk.

"Did she threaten trouble?" I asked.

Dennis brushed at a strand of hair. "We made a deal."

"What kind of deal?"

"She promised to keep her mouth shut if I'd let her use my address for mail. That was fine by me. There weren't all that many letters anyway. Although she sure was anxious about them. You'd have thought she was waiting to see if she won the national sweepstakes or something. Whenever I told her a letter had arrived, she'd come charging in here just as soon as she could manage it."

A young woman's understandable desire for privacy, or something more? "Who were the letters from?" I asked.

Dennis shook his head. "She never volunteered and I didn't ask."

"How about a return address?"

"A couple of different places, I think. To tell the truth, I didn't pay much attention."

"The letter that came today, can I see it?"

Dennis shrugged and gave a nod toward the table where he'd tossed it. "Help yourself."

Luke, who was sitting nearest the table, picked up the envelope, and brought it to me. "You going to open it?"

"You think I shouldn't?" It was, I suppose, technically a sticky issue.

He grinned. "No, I think you most definitely should."

The envelope was addressed with a typewriter rather than a computer. No return address. Although the postmark was blurred, I could read enough to know that it had been mailed from somewhere in Minnesota. I opened the envelope and pulled out a sheet of paper that matched the gray linen of the envelope. The message was short and to the point.

> *Dear Julie,*
> *Sorry, wrong guy. Best of luck.*
> *T. L. Wiley*

Luke had pulled his wheelchair alongside and was reading over my shoulder. "Not exactly helpful, is it?" he
asked.

"No, it's not." I read the letter aloud to Dennis. "Does
it mean anything to you?"

He shook his head, giving an artful toss to the shoulder-
length tresses. Dennis was watching the fish in the closest
aquarium, and appeared to share none of my curiosity
about Julie. After a moment he turned back my direction.
"So if it's Julie you're interested in, how come you were
following me the other day? And why did you come by
the store when I was at work?"

So we were back to that. I took a breath. There was
no easy explanation to the first of his questions, so I tried
a pared-down version of the truth. "I came to ask you
about Julie," I explained. "When I saw you, uh Denise,
leaving the house, I assumed she was a friend of yours.
I was hoping she could help me. But then she, that is
you, got on the bus before I had a chance to ask."

It was a lame answer if you stopped to think about it,
something I hoped Dennis wouldn't do. I felt the need,
in spite of everything, to proceed with caution. After all,
Dennis had piqued my interest initially because I was
worried that he might have had something to do with
Julie's death. And I still wasn't certain that I'd been
wrong.

Dennis compressed his lips in thought, cocked his
head. "And Macy's?"

That was easier. "Pure coincidence," I said. "My friend
and I were shopping. She wanted a pair of shoes."

He appeared to mull this over.

"My friend was impressed with your talent for fitting

shoes," I added. "She thinks you have an unusual knack for it, and an impressive understanding of feet."

"Thanks," he said with the hint of a smile. He sounded more like Dennis than he had all afternoon. "Shoes are a passion of mine."

And of the killer's, I thought uncomfortably.

"Julie didn't tell you about Denise, then?" he asked.

I shook my head. "Not even a hint."

He moved his head slightly, as if easing a stiff neck.

"My turn," I said. "What were you doing in my neighborhood the other day?"

"I wanted to catch a glimpse of you. After you and your friend left, I remembered where I'd seen you before. Or I thought I did. It was at my parents' house. Then when I saw you following me, I wanted to see if you really were the same person."

I wondered if his answer was as skewed a version of the truth as mine had been. "May I keep the letter?" I asked.

"Fine with me. I've got no use for it."

I tucked the envelope into my purse and stood. "I'm sorry about disturbing you. And I'm not going to say a word to your parents. I'm only interested in Julie."

Dennis nodded.

Luke wheeled himself over and held out a hand to his neighbor. "You want to come over and share a pizza again some time, you let me know."

"Who are you inviting, Dennis or Denise?"

Luke laughed. "If it's all the same to you, I think I'd feel more comfortable with Dennis."

"That's a hang-up you should get over," Dennis said, not unkindly.

Luke laughed. "Maybe, but don't count on it."

21

Rain had begun falling by the time I started back to Walnut Hills. Limited visibility and slick pavement slowed the commute to a crawl. As I inched along the incline toward the tunnel, I tried to make sense of the jumble in my brain.

The mail delivered to Dennis's address, Julie's Friday night foray into Berkeley, the book of poems, the older man at the reservoir. A veritable tapestry of secrets. I wondered if any of it pertained to her death.

Questions were plentiful, but what did I actually know? Despite the Shepherds' tight reins, or maybe because of them, Julie had become involved in a romantic relationship. Sexual relationship, I amended, remembering the inscription in the leather-bound collection of poems. A relationship she hadn't talked about and had, in fact, done her best to conceal from her friends.

I put Mario's name on my mental list, although I found him an unlikely candidate. Brian Walker? Perhaps. But why would Brian and Julie feel the need to keep the relationship secret? A more probable prospect was the older man Julie had been with at the reservoir. Maybe he was someone she'd met on-line through her poetry connections, or through one of those discussion groups like Cindy Purcell belonged to.

Or maybe it wasn't one single relationship at all, but several. A whole string of them. Men she met in Berkeley rather than on-line. Was it possible that she really had been turning tricks? Or maybe she simply enjoyed the excitement of picking up guys. That might explain the clandestine correspondence.

There was a roiling nervousness in my stomach, and my mouth tasted sour. Julie had been barely fifteen. Little more than a child. True, she had an aloofness that might, under certain circumstances, be mistaken for sophistication. But you didn't have to look hard to see that it was a pretense. At heart, Julie was like a young colt, eager and a little unsteady. A girl on the brink of adulthood yet still possessed of the ingenuousness of youth.

Or so I'd thought. But perhaps there'd been another, radically divergent persona, as well. Was it possible?

The letter from T. L. Wiley was a new piece of the puzzle. Not that it meant much yet. If Michael could track down a phone number, talk with him, then we'd know why Julie had written, what the connection was. Sometimes that was all you needed, Michael had told me. It was like playing a game of dominoes. Turn over the right one and the rest of the hand fell neatly into place.

My thoughts were still on Julie when a trailer-truck merged from my left without signaling. I slammed on the brakes, holding the steering wheel firm against the oil-slick pavement, and then slowed further to give him ample room. My reflexes were quick enough to avoid a collision, but not to protect my windshield from the wet road muck of his tires. I hit the wiper spray and cursed under my breath. Neither effort had much effect.

By the time I reached home, my mind and my nerves were equally frayed. Luckily Anna was curled up on the couch with Faye, wedded to one of Faye's afternoon programs. I waved at them both as I passed through on my way to the phone.

I called Michael and left a cryptic message about Dennis and the letters Julie had received there. I told him about Susie's party as well, then took a long, hot shower and washed the stickiness and what was left of the stylized curls from my hair.

When I emerged, the television program had ended. Anna was standing with her back to me, rigid as the Tin Man, while Faye adjusted the seams of her princess dress. I thought from the tension in Anna's shoulders that she was probably gritting her teeth in exasperation, but when Faye had her turn around, I caught instead a wide, unabashed smile—which she quickly reined in when she saw me watching.

"You look lovely," I said.

Anna was noncommittal. "It's prettier than I thought it would be."

I nodded and left it at that. With Anna, I've learned it's better not to push.

Before starting dinner, I pulled out the atlas and tried matching the postmark on Wiley's letter with a name in the index. I came up with only two possibilities, and they were both a stretch. Nonetheless, I called Information. Neither locale had a listing for Wiley.

I'd gone back to the atlas for a second go-around, when

Libby emerged from her room in search of a soda. She found me bent over the map with a magnifying glass.

"Planning a trip?" she asked.

I shook my head, and told her about my visit with Dennis, omitting reference to Denise. "Julie was getting mail there," I said. "It must have been correspondence she didn't want the Shepherds to know about."

Libby took a swig of soda. "Guess that explains why she went into Berkeley so often, and always by herself."

I nodded and leaned back in my chair. "I don't suppose you have any idea who she was writing to?"

Libby shook her head. "Could have been kids from her old school."

"That's a possibility, I suppose."

"She was expecting something to change, remember? Something that meant she wouldn't have to live with the Shepherds anymore. She'd want to keep that from them until it was settled."

"They didn't seem any too pleased to have her living there in the first place," I remarked. "You'd think they'd be happy if she'd found another arrangement."

"Except for the money." Libby opened a cupboard and scanned the contents.

"What do you mean, money?"

"They got money for keeping Julie. From her inheritance." Libby grabbed a handful of pretzels and plopped into the chair to my right. "Supposedly it was to cover the extra expense of having her live with them, but she thought they were probably using more than they were supposed to. Mr. Shepherd bought a new truck, and they were going to have the kitchen remodeled."

And Walton had quit his job to open a new store. Had he used Julie's money for that?

"Wasn't there some way she could check on it?" I asked, more thinking out loud than posing the question to Libby.

Libby shrugged. "Maybe that was the change she was talking about, but I don't think so. It wasn't like a big deal to her or anything. In the beginning she was mostly just sad about her mother's death and unhappy about living with the Shepherds. Then lately, it was like, well, things are going to change soon anyway." Libby peered over my shoulder at the atlas. "You think she was planning on moving to Minnesota?"

"Not based on the letter I saw today." I handed it to her. "Have a look."

"This Wiley guy doesn't believe in wasting words, does he?"

"Any idea what he's talking about?"

Libby took another swig of soda. "Haven't a clue. I can't even tell if he's mad or just indifferent."

I gave up on the atlas and started dinner. "One of Julie's neighbors saw her at the reservoir with an older man. Did she ever mention anyone like that?"

"How old?"

"I don't know. Probably early thirties at least, maybe older."

Libby shook her head. "Unless it was someone she was interviewing for her class project."

"The newspaper project? I thought you didn't know what her topic was."

"I don't, but I know she was talking to people, or trying to talk to them anyway. It was all very secretive, like she was worried we were going to steal her idea or something." Libby twisted a strand of hair around her index finger, then let it spring back. "Like we'd even care. No one else took the assignment as seriously as she did."

It didn't make a lot of sense to me that she'd interview someone at the reservoir, but Libby was trying to be helpful so I nodded without comment.

Libby bit her bottom lip and studied the soda can. "What did Michael decide about that plastic skeleton? Does he think it's connected to Julie's murder?"

"I don't know that he's *decided* anything. Most likely it was just a coincidence." I gave her a hug. "You should stay alert, but try not to worry about it too much."

"I'm not really worried, just curious." She stood and looked out the rain-spattered window into the evening gray. "It's really raining out there, isn't it?"

I nodded.

"You think it will continue all weekend?"

"Probably not. It's too early in the year for a major storm. Why, do you have plans?"

"I was just thinking about Skye's fox hunt."

And Brian Walker, I added silently.

"It can't be at all pleasant to go riding in the rain," she said after a moment.

"No, I imagine not."

Libby started to smile and then cut it short, but not before I caught the glint of smugness in her expression, like the cat with the taste of canary still fresh in his mouth.

22

Susie Sullivan's simple little brunch on Saturday was, as I'd expected, neither simple nor little. Because of the wet weather we were confined to the house, but there was still ample room for mingling. And with the cheer of three blazing fireplaces, the gloomy dampness of the day was recast into a backdrop for cozy comfort.

When I arrived, Susie was standing at the far end of the living room talking with, or more aptly fawning over, a man I didn't recognize. Silver-haired and slight of build, he was not unattractive. But he had none of the smooth self-confidence or monied polish that typified Susie's usual taste in men.

Since they were deep in conversation with another couple, I decided to save my greeting for later. I looked around for Michael, who'd said he'd try to make it but would offer no promises. When I didn't find him, I snagged a glass of champagne and a small pastry, and joined Sharon by the hearth in the den. Between bites, I told her about my visit with Dennis and Denise.

She laughed. "Must have been quite a sight."

"It was. Interestingly, though, I found Denise more appealing than Dennis."

"George has a cousin who wears skirts around the house on the advice of his shrink. Something about getting in touch with his 'feminine inner self.' " She paused and cocked her head. "Do you imagine it's the same sort of thing?"

"You think I asked?"

"It does help explain Dennis's knowledge of women's shoes, though."

It did. To a degree. But I wasn't convinced it was the full explanation.

I'd started to explore the matter further with Sharon when I spied Marvin Melville across the room talking to a pert young brunette dressed for a warm summer's afternoon. While the rest of us were bundled up against the cold, she wore a short, sleeveless sheath made of something soft and clinging. And it looked terrific. She had the body of one who either worked hard at it or was born blessed.

"I wonder what Marvin's doing here," I murmured.

"Who?"

"That guy in the blue shirt." I gestured as unobtrusively as possible with my champagne glass. "He's a teacher at the high school. Marvin Melville."

"So *that's* who he is. He came with Cheri."

"The aerobics instructor?"

Sharon nodded. "And the only reason *she's* here is because she promised to bring her father. That's him talking with Susie. He's the owner and publisher of *Focus West.*"

Well, that explained the dazzle in Susie's smile. A piece

in *Focus West* would be a coup for any aspiring journalist. Doubly so for one whose clips were limited to the society page of *The Walnut Hills Sun*.

Sharon paused for a sip of champagne, then continued. "I was there when Susie found out he was in town. You could practically see the lights come on and the wheels begin to churn. Next thing you know she'd thrown together this little brunch. You have to hand it to her, she doesn't let opportunity slip by."

I nodded agreement, then excused myself to seize an opportunity of my own. I made my way across the room and eased into the corner next to Marvin, whose fingers were caressing Cheri's bare shoulder.

"Can I talk to you a minute, Marvin?" I asked. "It's about Julie."

Cheri looked at him with a coquettish pout. "Not a wife or girlfriend, I hope."

Marvin blushed. "A student."

"The one who was murdered last week," I added.

Cheri's expression changed from playfulness to genuine chagrin. "Me and my big mouth. I'm sorry. I didn't know." She turned to Marvin. "You never said anything. I didn't realize she was one of your students."

He nodded, swallowed. "It's not exactly a fun topic."

"No, of course not." She unwrapped herself from Marvin's grasp. "I'll go freshen my drink and let you two talk."

Marvin watched her wander off, mesmerized no doubt by the rhythmic pull of fabric across her tight little backside. I was fascinated myself, for a moment or two, then I turned to address Marvin.

"I'm interested in the article Julie was researching for the newspaper," I told him.

"Huh?" His attention was still clearly fixed on Cheri.

"Didn't you give an assignment for a story involving research?"

Reluctantly, he shifted mental gears. "It wasn't for the paper necessarily. It's a more general assignment, like a term project. A piece that might, conceivably, be published in something other than a school paper."

"Okay, project then. What can you tell me about it?"

"Like I told you before, I don't know what Julie was doing."

"Not even what the general subject was?"

He shook his head. "I got the feeling it was something Julie felt emotional about, maybe related in some way to her mother's death. She seemed reluctant to discuss it, though, and we're only a couple of months into the term so I didn't push."

"Are most of the kids as secretive as Julie about their research?"

He looked at me, amused. "Most of the kids haven't even begun to think about a topic yet."

I saw Michael at the door, looking around uncertainly. I tried to catch his eye, but Susie beat me to it, cornering him even before he had a chance to grab a glass of champagne. I could tell from his expression that he wasn't pleased. Guilt tugged at my consciousness, but I pushed it aside. He'd have to fend for himself for a bit longer.

I turned back to Marvin. "Julie may have written some letters in connection with her research. Would there be copies at school?"

"I doubt it."

"What about notes or a rough draft? Do you think there might be something in the computer?"

"Possibly." He cleared his throat. "Someone from the police department came by yesterday to have a look. I don't think he found much."

"What about the Internet?" I asked. "Libby mentioned something about a poetry group Julie participated in."

Marvin shifted his position, rocked back a bit on his heels, looked a little sheepish. "I don't know much about poetry."

"But you do know about the Internet."

He shifted again and rolled his shoulders. "What do you mean?"

"That's how you met Cheri, isn't it?"

"Ah, that." Marvin's face grew flush. "I wish she wouldn't go around telling people that story. It seems so, I don't know, shallow."

His embarrassment amused me. "Hey, what works, works. She's certainly attractive."

"Yes," he said, flushing a deeper shade of red, "she is."

"I was thinking maybe Julie met someone that way too, through the poetry group."

"I'm afraid I wouldn't know about that."

I glanced again in Michael's direction. His gaze found mine, and he shot me a pleading look. "I've got to go rescue a friend," I told Marvin. "If you find anything, let me know."

He nodded. "See you Monday."

Susie was winding down by the time I joined them. She'd apparently pinned Michael down on a date for a formal interview and pried loose enough answers to sustain her until then. I was able to wrest him away without much of a struggle.

We were standing at the buffet with plates half-loaded,

when Michael nudged me with his shoulder. "What are we doing here, anyway?"

"Getting something to eat."

"No, I meant here at this party."

"I know Susie's not—"

Michael leaned closer and whispered in my ear. "You've obviously got Anna covered for a few hours. I'm off today, and Don is out of town for the weekend so his apartment is all mine—" He looked at me expectantly, then set his plate down and took my arm. "Come on, let's go."

"You mean, just leave?"

He grinned. "That's exactly what I mean."

It was obvious from the look of Don's apartment that he was single. The furnishings were bare-bones stark, the rest of the place cluttered and dusty. Not that I spent much time taking in the decor. What I focused on first were the tiny buttons on Michael's shirt, then the buckle of his belt and the familiar contours of his body. After that, I stopped looking altogether and concentrated instead on the weightless, shimmering swells of pleasure.

"You didn't really want to stay at Susie's, did you?" Michael asked afterwards, his arm draped comfortably across my breast.

"You needed to ask?"

He smiled. "Just wanted to make sure."

"It wasn't very polite, though, sneaking off the way we did."

"I'm willing to bet Susie never noticed." He adjusted the pillow under his head. "Is she really trying to make a name for herself as a serious journalist?"

"For now. Although I suspect that if Cheri's father

were better looking, she might settle for being married to a serious journalist. None of Susie's passions are very enduring."

Michael traced a pattern of interlocking circles on my skin. "I hope yours are."

"You're not worried about your own?"

He smiled. "I have only one passion and it is much too hot to ever burn out."

"Speaking of burning passions," I said, twisting sideways, "what did you find on the school computers?"

Michael stopped his tracing and poked me gently. "Love of my job was not the passion I was referring to."

"No?"

"Most decidedly not." He kissed me lightly. His fingers moved again across my skin.

"Were there any messages to Julie?" I asked after a moment.

"Do we have to talk about this stuff now?"

"I don't see you as often as I used to, remember? It may be now or never."

Michael sighed.

I pulled myself upright and tried again. "Any lewd messages?"

"No. And nothing that struck me as significant. I took a look at the poetry groups. All pretty tame." He rolled over on an elbow. "Cindy Purcell's stuff, on the other hand, was anything but tame."

"Pornography?"

"No, mostly just kind of . . . kinky. Definitely erotic. Funny that her friends had such a different impression of her. But I guess that's one of the attractions of these groups. When you're anonymous, you can let your hair down, become an entirely different person."

"Anonymity didn't protect Cindy," I pointed out. "Assuming your theory about how she met her killer is correct."

"I suspect that Cindy gave out too much information about herself."

Through the break in the curtains I could see the rain falling in a slow, steady drizzle. "Does Jim Gates still think the same person is responsible for both murders?"

"More or less. He's looking for other unsolved cases that might be similar. I think the guy's already got his eye on the talk show circuit."

"I thought you said he was good."

"He is. It's just that he also likes the limelight."

"You'll remember to pass along what I told you about the Shepherds using Julie's money? And about the letters she had sent to Dennis's place?"

Michael nodded. "Meanwhile, they've found a witness who might have seen Julie getting into a car on San Pablo the night she was killed."

"Getting in or being dragged in?"

"Sounded voluntary from what I heard." Michael kissed my ear. "Can we stop with all the questions now? Seems to me we can find better things to do."

"Like what?"

He kissed me again. And then again. "This is nice," he murmured, his breath soft and warm against my cheek. "Even better than being at home. No worry about interruptions."

"You're right." I curled to face him and was just about to return the kisses when a high-pitched squeak sounded from next to the bed.

Michael groaned and rolled away to pick up his beeper. "I'd better call in," he said grudgingly.

I sighed. Not so different from home, after all.

Michael punched in the number, carried on a monosyllabic conversation, and then scratched a quick note on a sheet of paper by the phone before hanging up. "The techs have identified a guy Cindy Purcell communicated with over the Internet," he said, turning to me. "A guy by the name of Frank Davis, with a record. Seems he was visiting his mother in Berkeley when Cindy was killed. They'd apparently set up a date to meet a week earlier." He grabbed his shirt. "I need to talk to Mrs. Davis."

"Now?"

Michael tossed me my own clothes. "I'd like to get to her before her son has a chance to coach her."

I rolled over and reached for my underwear. Worse than home, I thought. There, at least, I could take my time getting dressed.

23

"Frankie's a good boy," Mrs. Davis said for the second time since ushering us into her house in north Berkeley. "He wouldn't be involved in any murders. Wouldn't hurt anybody."

She sat upright on the edge of an armchair and brushed at a wisp of gray-blond hair that had sprung loose from its mooring at the nape of her neck. She was dressed in gray slacks and a sweater, and still clutched the book of crossword puzzles she'd been working when we arrived. Mrs. Davis wasn't the frail, impoverished woman I'd somehow envisioned, but it was clear Michael's questions were causing her considerable agitation.

"When did he last visit you?" Michael asked.

"He comes to see me every year. At least once every year. He's a good boy."

Michael leaned forward. Although he spoke gently, his words were blunt. "He's a convicted sex offender, Mrs. Davis."

"It was all that girl's fault. She lied in court. Frankie

would have never done those things she said. I know my son."

I huddled at one end of the sofa, arms wrapped across my chest, and wondered why I'd agreed to come along. Michael's company, I suppose. But at that moment, I would rather have been almost anywhere else. I didn't want to witness the woman's distress, didn't want to hear in her voice the dying embers of a mother's dreams.

Michael's fingers formed a steeple. "Can you tell me how long ago he left?"

She shook her head. "Couple of weeks ago."

"Did he visit with friends while he was here? Maybe go out some evenings, rent a video?"

"He's a good son. He fixed my drain, cleaned the garage. He took me to Spenger's for dinner."

Michael nodded and tried again. The woman was adamant; Frankie was a good boy.

"Tell me about him," Michael said. "What does he do for a living?"

"He's a computer programmer, in Dallas." There was no mistaking the pride in Mrs. Davis's voice. "He stays clear of trouble."

"He's single?"

She nodded, ran a hand across her knee. "He hasn't met the right girl yet."

"Did your son go out in the evenings while he was here visiting you?"

Mrs. Davis straightened. "He might have gotten together with friends. I don't remember for sure." The cadence of her words made clear her unwillingness to talk further.

Eventually Michael coaxed from her a vague approximation of the dates of her son's visit, which coincided with Cindy Purcell's death. But he got little more in the way of relevant information. After we left, he dropped me at my car, still parked in front of Don's apartment.

"I'm going in to work," he said. "Looks like I may be flying to Dallas. I'll let you know if I do."

"Do you think Frank Davis is the killer?"

"I don't know. Might not know after I talk to him, either, but I've got to give it a shot."

I kissed him lightly. "Remember, Faye leaves Monday. Don't stay away longer than you have to."

He smiled. "As if there were any chance of that."

Saturday evening I made a few more phone calls in search of T. L. Wiley, residing somewhere in Minnesota. I fared no better than I had earlier. Presumably the police would have better luck when they got around to checking. *If* they got around to checking, I corrected.

Although Michael had begun an initial search, he'd done so with little enthusiasm. And he'd turned the information about Julie's correspondence over to Gates, with a reminder to me that it was, after all, Berkeley's case. I was afraid that might be the end of it.

After dinner, I carried Julie's art bin and portfolio to the table and began sorting through them. Her supplies were neat and organized, and it was clear they'd been used with care. This was in marked contrast to many, if not most, of the classroom bins—which were catchalls for everything from chewing gum wrappers to dirty gym socks.

Julie's portfolio was orderly as well. I went through it slowly, appreciating once again those pieces I'd seen before, and finding myself equally admiring of those that were new to me. All of her work was skillfully rendered, and much of it exhibited a passion, a uniqueness of vision, that was the mark of true talent. It brought home to me again the sorrow I felt at her death. A sorrow made all the more acute by the lingering feeling that I might have been able to prevent it.

I pulled out the featureless self-portrait she'd done that Friday morning in class. A drawing so obviously the work of a troubled mind, I kicked myself now for not reacting more strongly. But I'd been caught up in the routine of the class and my own nervousness about being summoned to Combs's office, and I'd let it slide.

With a wrenching awareness of my own complicity, I set the portrait aside and pulled out a Picasso-like drawing of Mario Sanchez. Three eyes and an angular mouth that emerged in segments, but he was nonetheless clearly identifiable. I remembered Julie working on the piece, and Mario's brusqueness at seeing himself so portrayed. But I thought that he might now appreciate having it to keep.

I leafed through the portfolio a second time, pausing at a watercolor, a garden scene that had struck a familiar chord the first time through. Now, coming back to it, I recognized the view from the Burtons' dining room. The brick patio and large oak in the foreground, fading into the sun-burnished gold of California hillsides. I chuckled to myself when I saw a horse, which looked very much like Skye's, standing on a knoll just beyond the fence and gazing longingly back toward the house. I set that aside too, thinking Skye might enjoy it.

On Monday I'd take the rest of the portfolio, as well as the bin of supplies, to Combs so that he could return them to the Shepherds. I approached the task with a certain reluctance, however, because I suspected that they would dispose of the entirety by way of the trash.

By Sunday morning the rain had stopped. Anna and Faye were going to spend the day with Andy. Miniature golf, lunch in the Napa Valley, and no doubt, a hefty dose of Andy on Andy. Faye was disappointed that I wasn't joining them.

"I have work to do," I told her.

"You can do it another time."

I shook my head. "I have an appointment with clients."

"You know, Kate, maybe if you tried harder you'd find that you and Andy could make your marriage work."

"We did try, for almost seven years."

She looked at me over the rim of her cup. "The easy times are easy; it's when problems arise that trying becomes important."

In truth, the easy times had not been all that easy. There'd been wonderful moments, of course. Many of them. But the tension had been there as well. We'd both stepped around it, I far more often than Andy. And then he'd decided that the good times weren't good enough, that trying was too much effort. That, ultimately, marriage was too confining.

I'd endeavored to explain this to Faye, more than once. But she heard only what she wanted to hear.

"You need to make an effort," she said.

"We're beyond that, Faye. We're no longer interested in trying, either one of us. Sooner or later you're going to have to accept that."

Faye set her cup on the table and leaned forward. "He loves you, Kate. I know he does."

Just like Frank Davis was a good boy, I thought. But I

felt a certain sympathy, too, for both women. You didn't stop being a mother just because your child was grown.

Yvonne and I had agreed to meet at her house at eleven o'clock. I'd collected twenty slides, taken at various galleries in the Bay Area. They were works I thought she and Steve might like. We'd use the slides to narrow the field before looking at the actual pieces, thus saving time and effort on everyone's part. I'd also brought with me a lithograph that I thought would be perfect for the den.

Steve poured coffee for the three of us, and brought out a tray of bagels and fruit. I set up the projector and we went through the carousel twice. Of the twenty slides, two were a near miss and three were promising enough that both Steve and Yvonne expressed excitement. And they loved the lithograph.

I leaned back in my chair, accepted a second cup of coffee, and relaxed into the quiet glow of success. I didn't yet have a check in hand, but I felt reasonably certain we'd get to that point. It wasn't only the money that buoyed my spirits, however, although I certainly could use it. I was also in need of referrals, and I was hoping the Burtons would prove to be a valuable resource in that respect.

Skye strolled in and grabbed a bagel. She smeared it thickly with cream cheese and jam.

"Stupid weather," she mumbled, dropping onto the chair next to Steve.

I looked outside. The day had dawned bright and clear, and as far as I could tell, it hadn't changed.

Yvonne sighed. "It's yesterday's weather she's upset about. There was a fox hunt scheduled, but it was canceled because of the rain."

"They have one practically every month," Steve pointed out. "Besides, it isn't as though you need an excuse to go riding."

Yvonne caught his eye. "There was a little more to it than that, darling. Remember?"

"Ah, yes," he said dryly. "Young Brian."

Skye scowled and stomped out of the room.

"He's quite the heartthrob," I said. "I think half the girls at school have a crush on him."

"Well I, for one, am just as happy that yesterday's hunt was called off," Yvonne announced. "Brian is much too slick for a girl like Skye."

"In what way?"

"It's his attitude more than anything. Most of the girls he's been involved with are a lot more, uh, worldly than Skye."

"I understand that he put a big rush on Julie Harmon at the beginning of the year."

Steve's attention had wandered, but now it pulled into focus again. His expression was dark. "I hope they catch the bastard who killed her," Steve said with unexpected vehemence. "Catch him and fry him."

Yvonne turned, and a look passed between them. She gripped her coffee cup with both hands and sipped. "This murder has been very upsetting to those of us with teen-aged daughters," she explained.

I nodded agreement. "To those of us without teenaged daughters, as well."

Yvonne gave me a wan smile. "I guess it helps to remember there are worse hazards than slick, smooth-talking boys."

The discussion reminded me of something Libby had

said the other day. I turned to Steve. "I understand you're involved somehow in Brian's trust."

He raised a brow. "Only in an administrative capacity."

"Did you know his family?"

"His father was a client of mine. He died of melanoma when Brian was sixteen."

"What about Brian's mother?"

"The short of it is, she went nuts." Steve looked grim. "Guess she always was nuts. It's just that after Alan died, she couldn't pretend anymore."

"So she's in a . . ." I searched for the right word. ". . . a mental facility?"

"That would be an improvement," Steve said bitterly. "Last I heard she was still living on the streets in Los Angeles, killing whatever brain cells she has left with heroin."

"How awful."

"You're right."

"And there was no one else in the family to look after Brian?"

"There were some distant relatives, none of them particularly eager to take Brian in. It's a sad situation no matter how you slice it. But the boy's done okay."

Skye wandered back for another bagel.

"I almost forgot," I told her. "I have something for you. Why don't you come out to the car with me."

I boxed up my slides and projector, and Skye helped me carry them out front. I opened the rear hatch and brought out Julie's picture. Skye looked at it, blankly at first, then with recognition.

"Where'd you get this?"

"Julie painted it. See, there's your horse in the background."

She didn't move.

"I thought you'd be pleased."

"I'm just . . . I mean . . ." Skye held her breath for a moment. She looked pale and overwrought. "Julie painted this and now she's dead. It's just spooky, is all."

Yvonne called to me from the house. "Kate, it's Libby, for you."

I handed Skye the painting and darted for the door. In the fifteen or so seconds it took me to reach the phone, I'd envisioned a long sequence of disasters, each worse than the preceding. By the time I grabbed the receiver, my throat was so dry I could hardly speak.

"Sorry to bother you," Libby said breezily.

I felt the constriction in my chest ease up. Not, apparently, a disaster after all.

"A man called," she continued. "Luke Martin. He wants you to call him, says it's important. I wouldn't have bothered you except that he said he'd only be at that number for another hour and I didn't know how long you'd be out."

Luke Martin. The name brought with it an unexpected quiver of anticipation. "It's not a bother," I told her. "I was just about finished here anyway."

Yvonne had gone back into the other room. I could hear her talking with Steve in low, soft tones. I punched in Luke's number.

"I guess you got my message," he said.

"Just now. I'm calling from a friend's house, so I can't talk for long."

"I've got something you might be interested in."

"What's that?"

"Another letter addressed to Julie Harmon in care of Denny."

"Another one came today?" And then I realized that it was Sunday; there wouldn't have been delivery.

"Came last week. Denny apparently tossed it into the recycle bin. Found it there today when he was setting the bins out for Monday's pickup. He brought it over a bit ago."

"Is it postmarked from Minnesota?"

For a moment there was only Luke's breathing and the rattle of paper. "No," he said. "It was mailed from Santa Barbara. There's a return address, too. Someone by the name of Claudia Walker."

There was a flutter in my chest. Claudia Walker, a name from the list on Julie's computer. "I'd like to come by and pick it up. Will you be there?"

"Horses couldn't drag me away."

24

Luke Martin was waiting by the door when I arrived. "I hope I haven't delayed you," I said. "I got here as soon as I could."

"I don't have to leave for another thirty minutes or so, and it's not critical anyway. You want a cup of coffee?"

"Thanks, but I'm about coffeed out."

"Soda?"

I shook my head.

He gave me a wry smile. "In the old days I could have offered you a beer."

"I'd have passed on that, too," I said with a laugh.

He looked at me for a moment without speaking. His eyes were a soft, liquid gray. "Guess you want that letter," he said finally. He wheeled himself to a wide oak desk in what had originally been the dining room and was now a home office. I was struck again by the ease with which he maneuvered, almost as though he and the chair were one.

"Have you figured out yet what this is all about?" Luke asked.

"The letters?"

He nodded. "Do you think they're somehow connected to the girl's death?"

"I don't know what to think. Julie was apparently involved in a romantic relationship that she didn't want people to know about, so it would make sense that she'd want to keep the correspondence secret, too. That might be all there is to it. I was hoping Mr. T. L. Wiley could clarify a few things, but I wasn't able to find a number for him."

"Me neither, although I did manage to locate a Thomas R. Wiley outside of St. Paul."

I did a double take. "You tried to find a number for Wiley?"

Luke shrugged, a gesture that was somewhere between sheepish and smug. "Figured if I did, it would give me an excuse to call you." He paused. "Besides, that kind of search isn't difficult. I used an on-line service that claims to have every listing in the country."

His eyes locked on mine for a moment, then he turned abruptly. "The letter's in here."

Luke opened the desk drawer, grabbed the envelope, and handed it to me. Marbled blue stationery, addressed by hand. The return address was engraved on the back. I slipped a finger under the flap and pulled out a single sheet of matching paper. My eyes scanned the short message quickly, then I read it aloud.

> *Dear Julie,*
> *I have recently learned that*
> *Ted Wiley passed away last year.*

Sorry if I've complicated matters further. If there's anything more, please don't hesitate to call on me.

*Sincerely Yours,
Claudia Walker*

Luke frowned. "Doesn't say much, does it?"

"No. But now I've got a name, address, and with luck, a telephone number. At the very least Claudia Walker ought to be able to tell me what Julie wrote to her about in the first place."

"Telephone's in the kitchen," Luke said, nodding toward the hallway.

"I can call when I get home."

"Her number's on the scratch pad next to the phone."

I stared at him. "You've already looked up her phone number?"

He grinned. "I got you the letter, Kate. At least allow me a peek at what comes next."

Unfortunately, all that came next was the brief recording of an answering machine. I left a message and turned to Luke with an apologetic shrug.

"Not home, huh?"

"Not answering anyway."

Luke scratched his cheek, propelled his chair to the center of the kitchen. "You sure you don't want some coffee?"

"No thanks."

He opened the fridge. "Orange juice?"

I laughed. "I'm fine."

There was a beat of silence, then he asked, "Was that your daughter who answered when I called a bit ago?"

The abrupt change of topic caught me off guard. "No. Why do you ask?"

"Just curious."

"That was Libby," I told him, then went on to explain her presence in our household. "My daughter, Anna, is only six."

"Six is a good age."

"Sometimes."

Luke's hands stroked the outer chrome wheel of his chair. "I notice you aren't wearing a wedding ring."

Reflexively, I bent my thumb toward my ring finger. It was a habit I'd yet to break. "Divorced," I said. "Well, almost."

"You seeing anyone? I mean, anyone in particular?"

His words hung between us for a moment. I felt a flutter in my chest. Finally, I nodded. "Yeah, I am."

Luke grunted, then laughed apologetically. "Figured as much. But it's always best to make sure. Hope you aren't offended."

"Offended? I'm flattered." Curiously, more so than I'd have imagined. There was an impish but genuinely sexy quality about Luke Martin that I found very appealing.

"Do you mind if we stay in touch? Casually. I'd like to know the outcome of this whole mystery with the letters."

"I'd like that. Very much." I felt a flicker of regret, not for the path I'd taken but for the others I had to pass over. "And I really appreciate your help. I'd never have had the nerve to go next door and talk to Dennis if you hadn't dragged me along."

"Remember," Luke said as I headed down the front path, "the invitation for coffee is still open. Anytime." He paused. "Anytime at all."

*   *   *

When I got home, I was surprised to find Anna and Faye already back from their outing with Andy. I hadn't expected them until late in the afternoon.

"You're here early," I said, wrestling with the bag of groceries I'd picked up on the way home from Luke's. Since this would be Faye's last night with us, I thought I'd fix something special.

"Andy had to get back," Faye said.

"He needed to watch the football game," Anna added.

"Needed to?"

"A friend of his just bought one of those big screen televisions," Faye explained.

It shouldn't have surprised me. Andy often had trouble separating necessity from indulgence in matters that concerned him personally. "And what about the afternoon he promised the two of you?"

"Anna got her game of miniature golf," Faye said. "And we had a nice lunch."

"Except we didn't have time for dessert 'cause people were expecting him."

"He made you rush through lunch?" My voice rose with exasperation.

Faye brushed the air dismissively. "I had a headache anyway. In fact, I was just going to lie down when you pulled up."

I wondered to what degree Faye's headache was kindled by Andy's professed need to watch the game. "Did you take something for it?" I asked.

"Yes, only I'm feeling a little queasy too, so I don't want to overdo it."

"Go ahead and lie down. Let me know if there's anything I can bring you."

"I'll be fine. I just need a nap."

Before unloading the groceries, I checked the answering machine and found a message from Michael. He was calling from the airport, on his way to Dallas. I was unaccountably irked. I'd have to wait until he called to tell him about Claudia Walker, although by then maybe I'd have some answers.

Both Anna and Max were hovering around the grocery bag when I returned to the kitchen.

"Did you get anything good?" Anna asked.

"You think I'd buy something bad?"

She sighed heavily and without a trace of humor. "You know what I mean."

I started putting things away. "Apples," I told her, pulling out a plastic bag.

She made a face of disgust.

"For apple pie."

The dour expression gave way to a smile. "Did you hear that, Max? We get apple pie tonight." Her mood much improved, she sank down in her favorite kitchen chair to watch me work.

"I don't want anyone picking at this pie before dinner, understood?"

"Tell Libby and Grandma too."

"I will." But I knew where the real risk lay.

A short while later, as I was tossing the apple peelings into the garbage, I saw bits of black ribbon and a ball of rumpled wrapping paper on top of the morning's toast crusts. It was Halloween paper, with grotesque, warty witches riding on broomsticks.

"Where'd this come from?" I asked. "Did Daddy give you a present?"

She shook her head. "It was for Libby."

"From whom?"

A shrug. "It was by the front door when we got home. But I think there was a mistake."

"Oh?"

"The tag had Libby's name, but they must have meant the present for me. She gave it to me anyway."

"That's nice." I pushed the can back under the sink. "What was it?"

"Doll clothes."

"Doll clothes?"

Anna slid from her seat and returned a minute later with a small cardboard box from which she withdrew a pair of miniature shoes. Ladies shoes, red. With pointy toes and spike heels.

"That's all?" I asked, poking through the papers in the trash. Nothing but wrapping paper and ribbon and a small tag with Libby's name on it. "That's the whole present?"

Anna nodded, and then added graciously, "The important thing is the thought, not the present."

That was my feeling too, and the very reason that my heart was suddenly pounding in my chest.

"Where's Libby now?"

"With Brian," Anna replied. "She said she'd be back in time for dinner."

I could feel panic rise up and grab me by the throat. "Where did they go?"

Anna shrugged.

"Did he call her?"

Another shrug.

Was the timing a coincidence? "Why Brian?" I asked aloud, talking as much to myself as to Anna. But this time she had an answer.

"I think Libby likes him."

I tried to quell the sense of dread. Brian was, after all, a boy she'd been out with before. A boy, as Anna pointed out, she was eager to spend time with. What possible reason would he have to hurt her? Looking at it rationally, there was nothing about Brian Walker to make me nervous except for an overly cocky attitude.

The shoes were what put me on edge. They weren't a present, I felt certain. They were meant as a threat. Like the plastic skeleton in our mailbox days earlier.

I picked up the phone and dialed Brian's number. Nothing, not even the message machine.

I forced myself to finish making the pie, chatting with Anna while I rolled out the dough and sliced the apples. But as soon as I'd put it in the oven, I tried Brian again, and then Michael's number at work, on the off chance one of the other detectives might answer. I left a message asking Michael to call me, but I knew he'd do that anyway. I checked on Faye, straightened the kitchen, washed lettuce for the salad.

There was nothing to do but wait.

By four o'clock I was pacing in front of the living room window, holding my breath with every passing car, willing Libby's return. My mind was so ensnared with worry about Libby that I'd forgotten my earlier message to Claudia Walker. When she returned my call, it took me a moment to sort out the two Walkers, Brian and Claudia.

"I was calling about Julie Harmon," I told her finally.

"I hope she's finding what she needs."

I hesitated. "Unfortunately there's some bad news." With Libby's safety in doubt, the words were raw in my throat. "Julie was killed about a week and a half ago."

"Killed? How?"

"She was murdered."

"My God, how terrible."

I explained how I'd come upon her letter to Julie, how I'd been trying to make sense of the puzzling fragments of Julie's last few weeks. "I was hoping you'd be able to enlighten me," I told her.

"I wish I could. I'm afraid I can't be of much help, though. I barely knew Julie."

"Maybe you could start by telling me why she wrote to you."

"She wanted to know about her mother."

"Know about her? In what way?"

"As a person," Claudia said. "At least that's the impression I got. She wanted to know what Leslie's life had been like, what Leslie herself was like when she was younger. I was grown when my own mother died, but I felt the same need to talk to her friends, to hear the stories that would fill in the gaps of my memory."

"You were a friend of Leslie Harmon?"

"I worked with her."

"Recently?" I remembered Libby saying she thought Julie's journalism project might have been related in some way to her mother. Could Julie have picked up on an issue her mother had been exploring before her death?

"We worked together on a freelance assignment last year," Claudia replied. "But I've known Leslie since she first started out in broadcasting. We were at KSFK together in San Francisco. That's why Julie wrote to me, because I'd known Leslie for so long."

"Were you personal friends as well?"

"We were friends, yes. But not close friends. That's

what I told Julie. She really needed someone who knew her mother better than I did."

I sat back a bit. "Can you remember what, in particular, Julie was interested in knowing? Assignments her mother was involved with? Or maybe . . ." I paused, wondered why I hadn't thought of this before. ". . . or maybe something having to do with the boating accident that caused Leslie's death?"

Claudia was quiet with thought. "I didn't keep Julie's letter, but as I recall, it wasn't so much projects or events as people who'd known Leslie when she was younger. I gave Julie a few names. I thought that if nothing else, they could at least give her other names."

"Was T. L. Wiley one of those names?"

"Yes. Ted was the station manager when we first worked together. I knew he'd retired to the north somewhere, but I didn't have his address. He and Leslie stayed in touch, though, even after she left San Francisco. She told me about his retirement when we worked together last year."

"What were the other names you gave her?"

"Well, there was Marianne Bailey. She's another reporter who'd known Leslie for years. And Jill Morely, the film editor on our most recent project. She worked with Leslie in New York as well. And then there was Dulcey Haggerty. She and Leslie shared a house for a number of years before Julie was born."

"Could you give me the addresses you gave Julie?"

There was a pause. "I suppose so. Just a minute."

She set the phone down and returned with a rustle of pages. "I'm not sure any of them are current, but Jill's was correct as of last year."

Marianne Bailey lived in Paris, Jill Morely outside Chicago, and Dulcey Haggerty in Berkeley. The leads might turn out to be as ephemeral as morning mist, but they were at least somewhere to start.

"I appreciate your calling me back so promptly," I told her. "You've been a big help."

"Let me know if there's anything else."

My eyes fell again on the pair of miniature shoes that had been delivered to Libby. And again I felt the swell of uneasiness in my chest. Brian had said he didn't know anyone named Claudia Walker, but that didn't necessarily mean it was true.

I approached the question in reverse. "Do you by any chance know a Brian Walker?" I asked Claudia.

She hesitated for a moment before answering. "No, I don't believe I do."

Two for two. Not that it changed a damn thing. Julie's clandestine correspondence hadn't proved to be the key piece to the puzzle I'd hoped it would.

25

After checking on Faye, who was sleeping fitfully, I tried Chicago information for Jill Morely. No listing under that name, or for any Morely at the address Claudia Walker had given me. I had similar luck with Dulcey Haggerty. At least she lived close enough that I could visit in person.

I penned a quick note to Jill Morely explaining the situation and asking her to call me, then I walked to the mailbox at the corner and deposited it. Dulcey would have to wait until tomorrow.

While I continued my vigil by the front window waiting for Libby's return, I tried again to find a pattern in Julie's behavior. It was almost as though I'd collected a handful of snapshots, each capturing Julie from a different perspective. But the girl herself, someone I thought I'd known, was becoming more of an enigma each day.

And so was the reason for her murder.

* * *

It was almost five-thirty by the time Libby came through the door, looking flushed and animated. She dropped her sweater and backpack in the corner of the hallway, then ran a hand through her tousled curls.

"Where have you been?" I screeched from my spot by the window.

Her face registered surprise. "With Brian. I told Anna and Faye. Didn't they give you the message?"

"Yes, but 'with Brian' didn't tell me much. Like where you were going and why."

Libby looked at me, surprise giving way to a tight scowl. "What's that supposed to mean?"

I crossed my arms. "Where did you go?" Despite my best intentions, the words came out as though barked by a drill sergeant.

"The reservoir."

"The reservoir?" This time I didn't even try to fight the shrill edge in my tone. "Don't you think that was pretty stupid?"

Libby shook her head, more in confusion than denial. "It was a nice day. Brian wanted me to help him with Spanish. What's the big deal?"

"Haven't we talked about being careful?"

"It's the middle of the day, Kate. And I wasn't alone."

I folded my arms. "How come Brian's answering machine wasn't picking up?"

"I don't know, maybe he didn't turn it on." Libby's expression grew wary. "What were you doing, checking up on me?"

"As a matter of fact, yes. That's exactly what I was doing."

Libby scowled. Her face flushed with indignation. "You

sound just like my dad, you know that? Like you're dictator of the world.''

"I'm dictator of this house, and don't you forget it.''

She stepped back. "You've no right to treat me this way. I left word that I'd gone with Brian and would be home by dinner. I didn't do anything wrong.'' She spit out the words with contempt, but I could see her eyes were glistening with tears.

I dropped down into a chair, feeling suddenly deflated. Libby was right. I'd worked myself into such a state of alarm that her safe return had only opened the floodgates of worry.

"I'm sorry,'' I told her. "I was concerned. I guess I got a little worked up about it.''

"A *little*?''

"Okay, a lot." I gave an apologetic smile, which she ignored.

"Geez," Libby huffed, "you act like I threw a wild party and trashed your house or something.''

I held up my hands in surrender. "I was way out of line. But it's only because I was worried about you.''

I tried another smile and got a halfhearted one in return. If not absolved, I was at least working my way back in her good graces.

"I still don't see the problem," Libby said after a moment.

"That Halloween present you found by the door—''

She brushed the air with her hand in a gesture of dismissal. "It was nothing, I gave it to Anna. Either it was a mistake or somebody's got a weird sense of humor. What would I want with doll clothes?''

"Not clothes, honey, shoes.''

She shrugged. "Okay, shoes.''

I hesitated. "Both Julie and the other girl, Cindy Purcell, their shoes were missing. The killer seems to have a thing about feet."

"So?" Libby turned away and then swung back slowly. I watched the color drain from her face as the connection dawned. "Oh, my God, I never even thought of that. Oh, Kate . . ." She was breathing hard. "And the skeleton in our mailbox. They were meant as warnings, weren't they?" Her voice cracked. "Oh, my God. I'm next."

Good going, I told myself. You couldn't have handled this any worse if you'd tried. First you jump on her without cause, then you scare her half to death.

I went to Libby and hugged her. "It may be nothing. I'm probably letting my imagination get the better of me."

"But what if you aren't?"

"I'll call Detective Luce. He's a friend of Michael's. He'll know what to do."

"Why me? What did I ever do?" She was breathing hard.

"I could easily be overreacting, honey. Let's wait and see what Luce says."

"I'd rather ask Michael," Libby said shakily.

"He's in Texas looking into Cindy Purcell's death. I'm hoping he'll call soon."

Libby brushed her cheek with the back of her hand. Although the look of terror had left her face, I could tell she was upset. "You thought it was Brian, didn't you? That's why you jumped on me so hard."

"I was worried, Libby. I don't know what I thought."

"It couldn't be. I mean, why? It makes no sense."

"None of it makes any sense. But someone has killed two girls in the last three weeks."

"And now he has his eye on me." She wrapped her arms across her chest and drew in a deep breath. "I can't believe Brian had anything to do with it."

"Still, I think you shouldn't go off alone with him, or with anyone, until the police have a better handle on these murders."

"I know the way he acts, all cool and stuff. But that's not really the way he is." Her face had regained some of the love-struck radiance I'd seen when she first came through the door.

"Did you have a nice time with him this afternoon?"

She nodded. "Brian was glad it rained yesterday. He hates horses."

"Then why did he agree to go riding in the first place?"

She gave me a look, exasperation tinged with a modicum of uncertainty, and then a shrug. "You know Skye. Sometimes it's just easier to go along with what she wants."

As soon as Libby left to put her things away, I went into the kitchen and called Don Luce at home with apologies for bothering him on a Sunday afternoon. I explained the situation, hoping he'd laugh at my worries and dismiss then as meaningless. But I also braced myself for the alternative—an intense and solemn official visit and the dinner-hour disruption that would ensue.

Luce's response, however, fell squarely in the middle.

"Could be coincidence," he said. "Or a prank of some sort. Maybe even an honest, if misguided, gift. I don't recall a similar pattern with either of the other victims."

"But it could be for real," I argued.

"Could be. I'd be nuts to tell you otherwise. And as a

friend, I gotta say I can understand why you're nervous. But to be honest, there's not a whole lot we can do."

"Can't you run a forensics test or something? Look for fingerprints or fibers or . . . or whatever it is you look for."

There was a pause. "We could, but I doubt we'd find anything. The best advice I can give you is to stay alert and be careful. And keep me posted. You get an actual threat, or someone trying to intimidate you, you call me right away."

I sighed. Why were things rarely as clear cut as I expected? "I don't suppose you know where Michael's staying in Dallas."

"No. I could find out tomorrow if you'd like."

"That's okay, I'm sure he'll call by then anyway."

"Michael's involvement in this case is more personal than mine," Don said gently. "And I'm sure he'll share your concern for Libby. But he's going to tell you the same thing I did. There's not much you can do but be careful."

I could see the logic of his position, but I didn't like it. I stuck the pair of doll shoes in the drawer where I wouldn't have to look at them and took out my frustration by chopping the broccoli into pieces the size of peas.

When I went to wake Faye for dinner, she begged off, saying she didn't feel like eating. She wasn't interested in the late-night snack I offered, either. And by the next morning it was clear she would not be catching her plane that afternoon. She'd developed a fever and chills in addition to the relentless headache.

The doctor, who took his sweet time returning my call, told me to make sure she got plenty of fluids and suggested Motrin to bring down the fever. For that, it took a medical degree?

I thought about skipping class, but there was little I could do to help Faye, who seemed to want nothing but quiet. Still, with everything else that was going on, my mind was not on teaching. I gave the students a simple assignment and set them to work. When the bell rang, I hurried them out the door and then followed quickly in their footsteps. I headed into Berkeley in the hopes of finding Dulcey Haggerty.

Half an hour later, I pulled up in front of a spacious home in one of Berkeley's more desirable neighborhoods near the Claremont Hotel. From the street, I took a stone walkway, planted with rhododendrons and ferns. A thick-stemmed and undoubtedly very old wisteria climbed the posts of the porch overhang, and a huge redwood towered over the roof from the rear. I rang the bell, hoping Dulcey still lived there.

The door was opened by a tall, bearded gentleman of mature, but indeterminate, age. He held a half-wound spindle of red yarn. The remaining yarn was looped over his forearm.

"I'm looking for Dulcey Haggerty," I told him.

He smiled. "It's Dulcey St. John now. I'll get her for you." Before he had a chance, however, a woman appeared from the room to his left. "Dulcey," he said, turning toward her, "there's a woman here for you."

Dulcey Haggerty St. John was almost as tall as her companion, with a wide, flat face and silver hair that she wore pinned loosely in a knot atop her head. She was dressed in an oversized peasant blouse, a batik print skirt, and Birkenstocks.

I introduced myself and explained how I'd gotten her

name. "I'm sorry to show up at your door without phoning first, but I couldn't find a listing in the book."

"Not if you were looking under Haggerty," she said amiably. "Bill and I have been married for almost three years now." She opened the door wider and stood back. "Why don't you come in and I'll tell you what I can, but I'm afraid it won't be much."

"I'm grateful for any information you can give me."

"Would you like some tea? I have only herbal brews."

"Tea would be lovely."

While Dulcey headed for the kitchen, Bill ushered me into the living room, where a grand piano, a harp, and a large loom vied for space.

He saw me look around the room and smiled. "It's a little tight, I know. But when you combine two households, space is always a problem."

Like his wife, Bill St. John was casually dressed. A black turtleneck, baggy corduroy pants, argyle socks with his Birkenstocks. He sat on the edge of a wooden chair and worked the yarn from skein to spindle.

"I read about the murder," Dulcey said when she returned with our tea. "It was a shock, I'll tell you that. And a real tragedy. It wasn't but a month or so ago that she sat right where you're sitting now talking to me about her mother."

"So Julie managed to reach you?"

"Oh yes. She looked just like Leslie."

"You and Leslie Harmon roomed together from what I understand."

Dulcey's green eyes held a spark of amusement. "I suppose so, in a manner of speaking."

"What do you mean?"

"I used to let out the second floor of the house. It's

a separate apartment really, although it doesn't have its own kitchen or entrance. Leslie rented it from me for several years."

I held the mug between my palms, warming them. "When was that?"

"I don't recall the dates exactly, but must have been about sixteen, seventeen years ago. It was right before she took the job in New York."

"Before Julie was born."

"Goodness, yes. I wouldn't rent to someone with children. Too much noise, too much of a chance that things would get broken or damaged. Not that I have anything against children in and of themselves."

I took a sip of tea and nodded. I understood all too well about the noise and the damage.

"Leslie didn't have time for a child anyway," Dulcey added. "Not at that stage of her life. She was devoted to her job. Made her an easy tenant, though. Wasn't always tromping around the way some of them do."

"Had you met Julie before last month?"

Dulcey shook her head. "Never laid eyes on her. Leslie and I kept in touch, but very irregularly. I probably knew more what she was up to by watching TV than from her letters."

The tea had a heavy, eucalyptus flavor. I didn't like it, but I didn't want to offend my hostess by leaving it untouched so I took another small sip. "You must have been surprised when Julie contacted you."

"Could have knocked me over with a feather. Isn't that so, Bill?"

He nodded, while continuing to transfer the yarn from his arm to the spindle. "Julie was quite the charmer, though. Very polite and well spoken. A lot of kids today aren't.''

"What was it Julie wanted to know?" I asked.

"Oh, all kinds of things," Dulcey said. "About her mother's friends from the early days, the stories she worked on, what she did in her spare time—that sort of thing. She wanted to know if her mother and I were close. I think she was disappointed to learn that it was more business than friendship. I had my life, Leslie had hers.''

"But you must have been able to tell Julie something.''

"Unfortunately, nothing important.''

"I think simply meeting you was important to her," Bill said encouragingly. "She seemed to hang on everything you said.''

"Do you have any idea *why* she was interested?"

Dulcey frowned into her cup. "I suspect she was trying to deal with her loss. It's understandable. Julie was visibly moved when I showed her the apartment her mother had rented. It's been repainted over the years, of course, but otherwise it's the same as it was then. Only now we keep it available for out-of-town guests." She looked at her husband and chuckled. "Bill's family, mostly.''

Trying to deal with her loss. It was pretty much the same thing Claudia Walker had said. And it made sense. It even made sense that Julie would want the letters sent to her in care of Dennis. She must have known the Shepherds wouldn't have approved of her inquiry into her mother's life, just as they hadn't approved of her mother. Julie might have been using her mother as the subject of her newspaper project as well. That would explain why she approached the assignment so eagerly.

Not such a big mystery after all.

While it was gratifying to have the matter settled, I couldn't help but feel a tinge of disappointment. I'd been hoping the letters might shed light on Julie's death, but that apparently was not to be.

Unless she'd somehow, inadvertently, stirred up trouble that had been buried all these years.

I made one last attempt at a connection. "Julie was in Berkeley the night she was killed. A witness saw her getting into a car. Did you by any chance give her the name of another of her mother's friends, someone local she might have been meeting that night?"

Dulcey shook her head. "No. As I said, I didn't know much about Leslie's personal life. The only thing I could give Julie was a box of her mother's mementos. If she'd come six months earlier, I wouldn't even have been able to do that."

"Mementos? What sort?"

"Books, some costume jewelry, maybe some letters and papers. I didn't go through it myself. Leslie left a number of boxes here when she moved to New York, asked me to send them to her once she was settled. This one must have been somehow overlooked. We found it when we were clearing out the basement to make a darkroom for Bill."

Funny that nothing like that had shown up when the police went through Julie's belongings. "Do you remember anything in particular from the box?"

Dulcey thought a moment. "The only book I remember was a cookbook. One of those books churches and schools sometimes put together as a fundraiser. I can't remember the name of it though. And a silver picture frame. I could tell it was real silver because of the tarnish."

"What was the picture of?"

"There wasn't one, just the frame. Oh, and there was an envelope. It fell out of the box when Julie was leaving. I picked it up and handed it to her."

"What kind of envelope?"

"Business size. It wasn't thick so there couldn't have been much in it."

"Addressed to Leslie Harmon?"

"It wasn't addressed at all. Just a blank envelope. From some law firm in San Francisco."

A further lead Julie might have pursued. "Do you remember the name?"

Dulcey Haggerty spent another moment in thought, then shook her head. "There were three names. Emerson something, I believe. On Pine."

"Do you think you'd recognize the name if you saw it again?"

"I might."

If the firm was even still in existence. "Did Julie give any indication of other people she'd contacted, or was planning to?"

"Not besides Claudia Walker."

I'd sipped about all of the foul-tasting tea I could stomach, and I'd about run out of questions, as well. I thanked Dulcey for her help and left my phone number. "If you think of anything else, I'd appreciate it if you'd call me."

"I'll do that." She rubbed the bridge of her nose. "It seems so sad, first the mother and then the daughter. Both of them such lovely people too. Some families seem to attract tragedy."

26

The Walnut Hills library is a bustle of activity on week-ends and after school, but at midday on Monday it was practically deserted. A small cluster of retired men sat at the table by the window poring over the stock market and business newsletters, and a mother with her two preschoolers had spread out in the children's room. I had the rest of the place to myself.

I pulled out the San Francisco yellow pages and scanned the listing of law firms. There were an astonishing number of them, but none that began with the name "Emerson." Of course the envelope Dulcey had seen would have been close to twenty years old. The firm could easily have broken up. It could have moved too, but I glanced through the addresses anyway, looking for firms on Pine Street. I was almost ready to give up when I found a listing for Richards and Emerson, still on Pine. I let out a squeal of delight, which elicited a quick and stern frown from the reference librarian. As soon as I'd copied the phone number, I left for home.

* * *

The first thing that caught my eye when I entered the kitchen were the slivers of broken glass scattered across the floor near the sink. A larger piece remained on the counter's edge, and a pool of clear liquid dripped down the face of the cabinet.

"Faye?" I called. Guilt washed over me. I should never have left her alone when she wasn't well, not for the whole morning.

I scurried down the hall to the bedroom, where I found her curled on her side in bed, seemingly unhurt. With a sigh of relief, I started to back out of the room. As I was leaving, she stirred and opened her eyes.

"I broke a glass, Kate. Left such a mess." Her voice was dry and tired. "I just didn't have the strength to clean it up."

I felt a flicker of irritation, soon doused by another wave of guilt. "Don't worry about the mess," I told her. "Did you hurt yourself?"

"No, I'm fine." Faye managed a weak smile. "I'm afraid your poor kitchen isn't, though. I knocked over the bottle of ginger ale as well as the glass. It's going to be sticky by now."

"I have plenty of experience with sticky. How are you feeling?"

"Better, I think." She tried to sit up, then flopped back down on the bed. "Those pills helped my head and I think my fever's gone down. But I'm so drained I can barely move."

When I'd poured her a fresh glass of soda and helped her sit up to drink it, I tackled the kitchen. Faye was right about it being a mess. It was almost half an hour later when I sat down to make my call.

The firm's receptionist answered after the fifth ring, rolling out the name "Richards and Emerson" in a flat, bored monotone. I opened my mouth to speak and then closed it again with the realization that I had nothing to say.

Hi, I found an unaddressed envelope, almost two decades old, with a return address similar to that of your firm's. Can you tell me what the contents of the envelope might have been?

It was hardly the sort of query that would net me anything but being stamped a kook. Conceivably, I could ask whether Leslie Harmon had been a client and whether Julie Harmon had been in touch recently. I doubted I'd get answers though, and certainly not from the receptionist.

"Can I help you?" she said again. A note of annoyance had crept into her otherwise indifferent tone.

I cleared my throat. "Could I speak to Mr. Emerson?"

"He's in court."

"How about Mr. Richards then?"

"It's Ms. Richards, and she's out of town on a deposition. I can take a message if you'd like."

I slouched back in the chair. "I think it would be better if I tried again later."

Without another word, the woman hung up—just as I thought of something else I wanted to ask. I redialed, trying on this go-round to pull off a Southern drawl and thereby disguise my voice. Not that she probably cared one way or another if it was the same caller she'd spoken with moments ago.

"Ah was wonderin'," I said, slow and sweet, "if you could tell me how long Richards and Emerson has been located on Pahne Street?"

"It's Pine Street, ma'am. They've been here a long time, but I couldn't begin to say how long."

"Ten, fifteen years?"

"At least."

Chances were, it was the same firm listed on the envelope. How had some of its papers come to be in a box of Leslie Harmon's belongings?

"Cahn you tell me," I asked, "does the firm have some sort of specialty?"

"They'll take on a civil case if they're interested, but the primary emphasis is on criminal defense. Are you in need of representation?"

"No, uh, just inquiring for future reference." I could feel my Southern ties evaporate with each word. "Thanks for your help."

Criminal defense? Why would Leslie Harmon have needed the services of a criminal defense attorney? My mind was sifting through this latest bit of information when it struck me that her involvement might not have been as a client, but as a journalist. An important, newsworthy case, perhaps. Or maybe she'd been working on a documentary pertaining to some sociological aspect of the justice system.

And then I was struck by another thought. Could this investigation of Leslie's have been something Julie was pursuing anew for her own class assignment? Had it also gotten her killed?

While the scenario was at least plausible, it left enough holes and unanswered questions that it was of little practical use.

Which is exactly what Michael said when he called that evening. "We don't exactly have the manpower of the U.S. Army," he added.

"Can't you find out if Leslie Harmon was one of the firm's clients?"

"Maybe. Maybe not. Depends on how cooperative they want to be."

"But you'd know if she'd been charged with a crime?"

"I could find out."

"You could also find out who her attorney had been."

"Probably." His voice was about as animated as a sleep-walker's.

I tried the other tack. "How about any big trials Leslie followed? Or investigative assignments concerning the legal system?"

"Again, it depends. We're talking about a long time ago, don't forget. More to the point, I don't see how it's going to help find Julie's killer."

"What if it was a Mafia case?" I suggested, my own enthusiasm for the notion growing in direct proportion to Michael's lack thereof. "Or a high-profile murder trial where the defendant got off when he shouldn't have. What if Leslie's papers contained important information, information Julie pursued—"

"I have to tell you, Kate, I think you're way off base here."

"But it's possible, isn't it?"

"More possible in Hollywood than elsewhere."

I let out my breath in an irritated huff. The frustrating part was that he was probably right. "What about the doll shoes?" I asked. "Am I off base there, as well?"

There was a moment's hesitation. "I wish to hell I knew."

I think a part of me had expected him to dismiss the episode outright. When he hadn't, I'd felt my anxiety mount. The uncertainty of this latest response didn't help.

"I don't like what's happening, Michael. I'm scared."

"I know, and I don't blame you. I'm worried as well."

"But why Libby?" I asked, feeling my stomach tighten anew.

"She was a friend of Julie's, so that might be the tie-in. Then, too, it might be for my benefit." There was a strained quality to his voice.

"What do you mean?"

"The skeleton in the mailbox, and now the shoes. They might both be a bid for my attention. Julie Harmon lived in Walnut Hills. I'm the local detective on the case. Probably in most people's minds, I'm in charge."

I wasn't sure I followed. "A bid? You mean the killer is, like . . . taunting you?"

"It's not unheard of. I doubt the fact that I've temporarily moved out is common knowledge."

"Isn't there something you can do?"

"Like what?"

"I don't know." Uneasiness gave way to frustration. "Something."

"Unfortunately, there's not." The same thing Don Luce had said when I'd called Sunday evening.

I wound the phone cord around my thumb. "When are you coming home?"

"As soon as I can, probably in a day or two. I don't like leaving you alone there."

Michael sounded tired. I knew he was worried about us as well as worn down by his own investigation.

"I miss you," I told him.

"I miss you, too. How's Libby doing?" he asked after a moment.

"About what you'd expect. I've started driving her to school and picking her up afterwards. She doesn't like the idea, but she's not arguing about it either."

"Tell her she'll be okay as long as she stays alert and uses her head. It wouldn't hurt to get her a can of pepper spray, and make sure she knows how to use it. You too, Kate."

"Can't you just make an announcement that you're *not* heading up the investigation of Julie Harmon's murder?"

"I am in charge of the Purcell case, though," Michael said.

"You think *that's* what this is about?"

"Sweetheart, if I knew what it was about, I wouldn't be spinning my wheels."

I leaned against the wall. "But if Frank Davis is in Texas, then he couldn't have been the one who left the skeleton or shoes at our place. Did you find him yet?"

Michael groaned. "For all the good it's done."

"He's not a suspect anymore?"

"Davis says Cindy stood him up. They'd been communicating back and forth on the Internet for a month or so, and when he came out to visit his mother, they set up a time and place to meet. Cindy never showed. Never answered another e-mail of his, either."

"Do you believe him?"

Michael sighed. "This meeting where she never showed, it was a couple of weeks before she was killed. I guess that might have made him angry enough to go after her, but he claims he was back home here in Dallas when she was killed. That's one of the things I want to check on. Gates is following through with the Internet stuff as far as Julie is concerned. Maybe we'll get lucky and come across a name that shows up on both lists."

"You really think that's the connection? That it was the same killer?"

"I don't know what to think at this point."

"Are you going to tell Gates about Julie's letters, and about Leslie's tie-in with a criminal defense firm?"

I could hear Michael pause midway through an intake of breath. I expected grumbling, but what I got instead was a weary laugh.

"Christ, Kate, you demand a lot of a guy."

Tuesday morning I got to school early and stopped by the newspaper lab in hopes of catching Marvin. He was working on the computer at the back of the room.

"Have you got a minute?" I asked.

He jumped, flipped off the screen, and stood.

"Sorry," I said. "I didn't mean to startle you. I thought you heard me come in."

Marvin ran a hand through his fine blond hair. "I was just finishing up a few things before class. What can I do for you?"

I told him what I'd discovered of Julie's efforts to learn more about her mother. "It ties in with what you were saying about her class project. I'm wondering if you found any notes. Or maybe some papers that belonged to her mother. Julie had a box of her mother's things from years ago."

"Sorry. Nothing's turned up."

"You've checked the cupboards and drawers at the back of the room?"

"Several times." Marvin rocked back on his heels.

"Could I take a look through her computer files?"

"The police went through everything already." He sounded a little peeved about the whole thing.

"But they were looking for something different," I said. "It won't take long. I'll be very quiet and I promise not to bother you."

"Use the computer over by the window." Marvin's tone was brusque. "It's the fastest. Most of the kids keep their stuff on floppies. They're filed alphabetically by last name in the bottom drawer of my desk."

I retrieved Julie's disk and scanned the files, following the instructions Libby had written out for me the night before. It was far easier than I'd anticipated, but I found nothing that made reference to Leslie Harmon or any stories she might have researched.

"This is Julie's only disk?" I asked Marvin when I'd finished.

He was busy with some activity that required a lot of mouse-clicking. "The only one I'm aware of."

He didn't look up when I left.

In the afternoon I called the Berkeley police department and talked with Celeste Tira. She was polite, and listened to my ramblings with sympathy, but offered little in the way of encouragement.

"This case is one of our highest priorities," she told me. "We've got a number of leads already, potentially a new witness or two, and forensics has found some fiber samples on Julie's clothing. It's slow work, as frustrating to us as it is to you, but there is progress being made."

"You haven't come across the box that Dulcey Haggerty gave Julie, though."

"Right," she said. "We haven't."

"You didn't even know about it until I told you."

"Right again." Tira, to her credit, didn't appear to take offense.

"And you didn't know about the letters Julie wrote. You didn't even follow up on that list of names Patricia Shepherd found after Julie disappeared. Claudia Walker and Dulcey Haggerty were both there."

"A list of names, by itself, isn't much to go on. They could have been childhood friends, or the girls' tennis team from a rival school. And we did look into it." She paused. "It's a big jump from Julie's wanting to talk to her mother's friends to thinking she'd uncovered a secret that cost her her life."

"Besides," I said pointedly, "the department is more likely to stay in the limelight if it's a serial killer and not simply someone Julie managed to anger."

"That's only one avenue we're looking at." Officer Tira's voice made it clear that her patience was wearing thin.

"There was something on Julie's mind, something that was troubling her. I'm certain of that. Whatever it was might explain why she went to Berkeley that night and who she met there. But you folks don't seem particularly interested in knowing what it was."

There was a long pause. "With all due respect, Mrs. Austen, we are every bit as interested in seeing this killer caught as you are."

I backed off. It wasn't fair to take out my frustrations on Celeste Tira, who had been more than accommodating. "I'm sorry. I'm upset and I'm worried."

"That's understandable," Tira said with surprising kindness. "And we have talked with her family and friends. So far, that line of inquiry hasn't helped us."

It hadn't helped me either, not in the sense of bringing answers. But I couldn't let go of the feeling that it might.

* * *

Wednesday dawned bright and warm, the return of Indian summer. Faye moved her chair outside and sat with the sun on her back while I planted primroses and pansies for spring. I was on my hands and knees digging in the soft soil when the phone rang. I'd have let the machine pick it up, but Faye had shuffled inside before I could stop her.

"For you, dear," she called. "It's Marlene, the woman who did our hair."

Brushing the dirt from my hands and clothing, and grumbling under my breath, I slipped off my shoes and went inside.

"I'm sorry to bother you," Marlene said. "But you told me to call."

"Did you remember something more?"

"It was something I found. Something of Julie's. In the closet where my granddaughter keeps her toys."

"What did you find?"

"A bag. One of those gallon-size Zip-loc things. There's a computer disk and some newspaper clippings inside. My daughter says the man in the news photo is the one she saw Julie with at the reservoir."

27

With Marlene's call, my interest in gardening took a nosedive. Unfortunately, Marlene was at the salon and wouldn't be free to show me what she'd found until after work. We agreed to meet at her house at five. I spent the remainder of the afternoon devising errands to keep my mind off the painfully slow progress of the clock.

I was waiting at the curb when she pulled into the driveway almost exactly on the hour. Two large cats, one gray and one black, greeted us inside the door. Marlene scooped them up, one in each arm.

"Come into the kitchen with me," she called over her shoulder. "I'll get you that bag of Julie's stuff just as soon as I break out a can of food for these fellows. Patience is not their strong suit."

I followed her into the breakfast nook, where she plopped the cats down on the linoleum, then opened a family-sized tin of real tuna and scooped it into matching ceramic bowls. She disappeared into another room and returned a moment later with a plastic freezer bag.

"This is it," Marlene said, handing me the bag. "My daughter found it yesterday when she was looking for a sweater Karen had misplaced. She might have thought nothing of it, even though she knows *I* have no use for computer disks, except that she recognized the man in the news photo. He's the one she saw with Julie at the reservoir."

"Did she tell the police?"

"She tried to reach the detective who questioned her last week. He's out of town."

So Michael had contacted her himself. "She didn't ask to speak to someone else?"

Marlene shook her head. She rinsed out the cats' water bowls and refilled them. "Nan didn't want to make a big deal out of it. Especially when she saw who it was."

"It's someone your daughter knows?" I opened the bag and pulled out a handful of newspaper clippings.

"That's the article there." Marlene pointed to the one on top. "And there's the photo, partway down."

The article she pointed to was clipped from the *San Francisco Chronicle* and appeared to be about the upcoming judicial election. The face in the photo was Steve Burton.

"Your daughter's sure this is the man she saw with Julie?"

"Not positive, no. That's partially why she was reluctant to go to the police. Besides, it doesn't seem likely their meeting had anything to do with Julie's death."

"I wonder why Julie didn't tell you when you asked her who it was?"

Marlene shrugged. "You know kids."

I nodded. "Julie and Steve Burton's stepdaughter, Skye, were classmates. It was probably easier to say 'family friend' than get into a full explanation."

Quickly, I looked through the other clippings. All of them, it appeared, pertained in some way to Steve Burton, but not all were current. One was dated six years earlier and another, although the date was missing, was so yellowed it had to have been even older.

Marlene sat in a nearby chair, her two cats tucked into the folds of her lap. "Nan feels silly now for ever mentioning that she'd seen Julie with an older man." She drew her hand along the cats' fur. "You don't think it means anything, do you?"

Although the reservoir was an unlikely place for either Steve or Julie to be on a weekday, their meeting could most certainly have been coincidence. But why the clipped news articles? And why hide them at a neighbor's?

Then, too, I couldn't completely discount my original impression that Julie's clandestine meetings were somehow related to the provocatively inscribed book of poetry.

There were no ready answers, only tremors of apprehension in my belly.

"Can I borrow these?" I asked. "Maybe I can figure out what was going on."

"Sure." Marlene paused. "Judge Burton has an outstanding reputation. I've never heard even a hint of indiscretion or scandal."

I hadn't either, but that did little to quiet my uneasiness.

When I got home, I put a pot of water on the stove—pasta was my standby quickie dinner—then slipped the disk into the computer. Unfortunately, I had not the slightest idea what to do next.

I called for Libby, and after a few minutes of mouse-clicking and icon-hopping, the screen opened to a document that appeared to be the outline for a biographical sketch of Steve Burton. There were key dates, educational and professional histories, a section of personal data, and an annotated bibliography of pertinent news articles. All in all, it was pretty bland reading. While I hadn't known that Steve had narrowly missed an appointment to the appellate court bench or that his first wife was a prominent socialite, there was nothing in the write-up to hint at any sort of impropriety.

And then, when I scrolled to the third page of the document, I saw that Steve Burton had at one time been employed at the firm of Richards, Walker and Emerson in San Francisco.

Located, no doubt, on Pine Street.

I felt the tingle of excitement at the base of my spine. Could there really be significance to the fact that Leslie Harmon had had some long-ago connection to a firm where Steve Burton had once worked?

But it wasn't just that, I reminded myself. Steve had said that Brian's father was a client. Had he neglected to mention that Walker was also his former employer? Or was I grasping at straws?

"What is it?" Libby asked, looking at me. "You seem bothered by something."

"Not bothered so much as perplexed. Has Brian ever talked to you about his father?"

"He was a music teacher, I know that."

"A music teacher?"

She nodded. "I guess he was a musician, really. It's just that teaching was kind of like, you know, his job."

Maybe it wasn't the same man, after all. "A musician, not an attorney?"

"Brian's grandfather was a lawyer. Why?"

His grandfather, maybe that explained it. "Judge Burton told me that Brian's father was a client of his. But according to this, Walker was one of the law partners. It must have been Brian's grandfather."

Libby frowned. "I didn't know judges had clients."

"I guess he meant former client." But that didn't explain how Leslie Harmon had come to have one of the firm's letterhead envelopes in her possession. Nor, more to the point, did it shed any light on Julie's interest in the matter. And it was clear that she *had* been interested.

I closed the file and pushed my chair back from the desk, discouraged. "Did Julie ever talk about Judge Burton?" I asked Libby.

Libby's face scrunched in thought. "She may have mentioned him in passing. I don't recall anything in particular, though. Why?"

"I'm wondering why Julie would be doing research on him. Is that the sort of thing Mr. Melville had in mind for the term project?"

"What he'd really like," Libby said with a sardonic laugh, "is for us to do an innovative, cutting-edge piece. You know, like blowing open the next Watergate, or finding a hidden toxic waste dump in downtown Walnut Hills. But I think he'll settle for a whole lot less. I hope so anyway."

"So it's possible that Julie could have been planning to do an article on Judge Burton?"

"Sure. Although I don't see why. Even with the election coming up. I mean, he's probably a nice man and all, but if you're going to spend time and energy on an assignment why not choose something you can get a bit more psyched about?''

That was my thought as well. Unless Julie had discovered something about Steve that made the piece more than a simple profile. I pressed my fingers to my temples in an effort to clear my mind. "What about Julie and Brian?"

"What about them?" Libby's tone became defensive.

"You said they went out."

She shrugged. "Just a couple of times. It wasn't any big deal."

Had Julie known about the connection between Brian's family and Judge Burton? Was that somehow the key to this mystery?

I tried to put the uncertainties out of my mind until I could turn the whole thing over to Michael, but that was like trying not to think of a tune that kept running through your head. After dinner, I called Sharon, who knew Steve and Yvonne much better than I did.

"Any skeletons in his closet?" I asked, after filling her in on the latest.

"Steve's about as upstanding as they come."

"He was apparently passed over for an appointment to the court of appeals."

"There was talk of his name being on the list of possible candidates, but it wasn't like he was the governor's first choice or anything."

"How about any big cases he tried as a prosecutor?"

"I didn't know him then. He only moved to Walnut Hills after he married Yvonne. But if there were some secret in his past, don't you think it would have come out before now? As I recall, the last election was pretty hotly contested. And finding dirt on your opponent seems almost *de rigueur* these days.''

"A couple of the newspaper clippings were old. They may have been in that box of things Dulcey Haggerty gave Julie. What if they were part of some investigative piece Leslie Harmon worked on? She might have had information that's never been made public.''

"And she just sat on it? Not likely. Besides, why would her fifteen-year-old daughter suddenly be interested in exposing it?''

"Well, Julie knew Skye, so there was the personal connection. And according to Libby, Julie was taking this term project far more seriously than the rest of the class. Who knows, maybe she was trying to emulate her mother.'' And then I thought of something else. "What if Julie tried to blackmail Steve? Maybe that's what Leslie had done, too.''

"Kate, I think you're going overboard here. There's an election coming up. It doesn't seem odd to me that Julie would decide to write a profile piece about one of the candidates running for re-election. Especially if it was someone she knew. Maybe she figured she'd even get an interview or something. It could have been Steve, himself, who gave her the old articles. What did they say, anyway?''

"The usual stuff. There were a couple that pertained to cases he'd heard, one that was sort of a feature piece that apparently ran when he joined to the DA's office. A number of the older clippings were actually from the society page. Steve's claim to fame there was his wife.''

Sharon laughed. "Yvonne has said that Lucinda was a hard act to follow. And even now Steve does what he can to oblige his late wife's father. Politics is a tricky business.''

Yes, it was. Which brought me back again to the question of what Leslie Harmon might have known and what Julie might have discovered. What ultimately, someone might have been willing to kill to keep hidden.

I gnawed at it the rest of the evening and finally concluded that Sharon was probably right, I was going overboard.

Still, when I happened to catch sight of Brian Walker's broad shoulders rounding a bay of lockers at school the next morning, I scurried after him. He darted off in the other direction at a quickened pace once he saw me.

"Brian," I called after him, breaking into a trot. For a moment I thought he was going to ignore me. Finally, he hesitated and turned, but didn't return the greeting. His arms were crossed and his face unsmiling.

"I wanted to talk to you for a minute," I told him.

"I gathered."

"Do you have time?"

"Would it matter if I didn't?" He shifted his weight to one leg.

"What's with the angry tone?"

Brian laughed without humor. "You're like all the other snooty, two-faced women in this town. Quick to judge, quick to blame."

"What are you talking about?"

"You really think I'd send Libby some stupid Barbie doll shoes if I was the Parkside Killer? Especially if I were going to whisk her off and do her in a few hours later?"

Libby had obviously told him about my afternoon of panic. "I was worried, I—"

"Worried, yeah. Because she was with me."

"I didn't accuse you, Brian, I just—"

A spasm of irritation crossed his face. "Look, I'm kind

of pushed for time. If you got something to ask me, do it."

I'd work on mending fences another time. "How well do you know Judge Burton?" I asked.

"Hardly at all."

"He handles your trust, doesn't he?"

Brian shrugged. "A name on a piece of paper."

"But you've met him?"

"Of course I've met him."

"Did you know that he used to work for your grandfather's law firm?"

A shadow of uneasiness crossed his face. "So?"

"Was that the connection between your father and Judge Burton?"

"I wouldn't know."

It felt like we were playing a game of *Twenty Questions*, but with Brian being less than forthcoming, I couldn't think of any other way to handle it. "Did you know that Julie was writing a paper on Judge Burton?"

"She might have mentioned it."

"You have any idea *why* she was interested in him?"

He shook his head. "She kind of hinted at something big, but I'm not sure it was actually about him." Brian glanced in the direction he'd been headed. "Hey, I gotta go. Catch you later."

Once again I tried to put the matter out of my mind, and once again I failed miserably. After class I used the phone in the teachers' room to call Celeste Tira at the Berkeley PD, having decided the wisest course was to turn the matter over to her. She was more directly involved in the investigation of Julie's murder than Michael anyway.

Officer Tira was not available, the brusque voice at the

other end informed me. Did I wish to speak with another officer working on the Harmon case?

"Fine," I said. I was tired of worrying over the possibilities alone. I waited through a series of clicks while the call was transferred.

"Gates here," barked a new voice.

Just what I didn't need. I groaned silently, then forged ahead, explaining about the computer disk and the newspaper clippings and as much of the background as I could squeeze in before I was interrupted.

"Tidbits from the society page, you say? And routine news articles?"

"But they were all about Judge Burton."

"Nothing that hinted at scandal or controversy though?"

"Not that I could find, but that doesn't mean—"

"Mrs. Austen, we can't go charging off to question a public figure just because a high school girl may have been writing a paper about him."

"A high school girl who turned up dead," I reminded him. "Besides, it's not just that. There's the connection with her mother, don't forget, and—"

Gates interrupted again. "I'll make a note of your call," he said in a voice devoid of any warmth. "We'll get back to you if we need further assistance. We appreciate your interest." The phone clicked in my ear.

Frustration boiled in my veins. While part of me still agreed with Sharon that I'd gone off the deep end, somewhere in the recesses of my mind was also the specter of doubt. What if I hadn't?

There seemed only one way to find out. I called Steve Burton and asked if we could talk.

"Sure," he said, sounding rather uncertain. "Is there a problem? Something about Skye?"

"No. It's about Julie Harmon."

If my response took him by surprise, he didn't let on. "Why don't you come by the courthouse, say around four-thirty. My calendar is fairly full this afternoon but things should be winding down by then."

It wasn't until after I had hung up that I thought to wonder if I'd given in to a lapse of good sense.

28

Judges don't have offices in the usual sense. A judge's chambers are accessible to members of the public only through the courtroom and only after they've been cleared by the court deputy. When waiting to see a judge who is otherwise occupied, as I was, you either wait in the courtroom or in the hallway outside where the benches are few and far between, and not very comfortable.

I'd started out in the hallway, but when court adjourned, I moved into the newly emptied courtroom, introduced myself to the deputy, and told him I had a four-thirty appointment. He made note of my arrival and explained that Judge Burton was in conference. I took a seat near the front of the visitors' section and waited. The buzz of voices from the hallway outside grew fainter as the crowds thinned and the judicial process wound down for the day.

I checked my watch—four-fifty. The deputy shrugged. "Lawyers like to talk," he said. "Sometimes these sessions go on for a while."

Finally, at five-fifteen Steve Burton appeared. "I'm sorry, Kate. I thought for sure I'd be finished before this. Some days take on a momentum of their own. There's no predicting when that will happen."

He led me through a short hallway, where he stopped to confer with the court clerk and pick up a handful of message slips. Then he turned back to me. "Would you like some coffee or a soda?"

"I'm fine, thanks."

"Come in and have a seat. I just have to make a couple of quick calls, people I want to catch before they leave for the day."

While Steve made his calls, I tried my best to appear engaged in something other than eavesdropping. Given the tedious nature of the conversations, it wasn't difficult to tune out. The most interesting call was to the veterinarian who needed to clarify some point relating to gum disease, a malady from which Skye's horse apparently suffered.

Steve's office was good-sized, and lined on three sides with heavy, leather-bound volumes. The wall without bookshelves held a credenza on which a silver-framed picture of Yvonne and Skye was prominently displayed. On the wall above were various degrees and certificates along with a smattering of photographs depicting Steve with prominent politicians. I recognized the portly gentleman with his arm around a much younger Steve as Steve's former father-in-law, who was a former California senator and current Washington official. It had to have been taken about fifteen years earlier, before Steve's hair had begun to go gray and the lines of his face deepen. He'd been handsome as a younger man, but I thought he'd grown even more attractive with age. Softer in the best sense of the word.

Finally, his calls completed, he turned to catch my eye. "So, what can I do for you? You said it was something about Julie Harmon."

I nodded, finding my mouth suddenly dry. I'd had all afternoon to prepare for this meeting, plus the hour I'd been waiting here at the courthouse, and I still wasn't sure how to best approach the matter.

"It's awful what happened to her," he said. "Just terrible."

I nodded again, licked my lips. "I don't know if you were aware of it," I said at last. "Julie was writing an article about you." I couched the words in a smile, keeping my tone conversational.

Steve shook his head. "An article? No, I didn't know."

So much for my theory that she'd arranged an interview at the reservoir. "I thought she might have talked to you about it, tried for the personal angle."

He shook his head again, smiled stiffly. "She never mentioned it."

There was an awkward silence while we each waited expectantly for the other to continue. His secretary knocked on the door and stuck her head inside. "Is there anything else you need before I leave?"

"No. Have a good evening, Betty."

"Oh, I will." She chuckled. "My husband and the boys have a Scout meeting tonight. I get the house to myself. Shall I lock the outer office on my way out?"

"Good idea, given the hour." Steve looked at me and explained. "This place empties out fairly quickly once court is no longer in session."

The door of Steve's office clicked shut, and then the

outer door. The room seemed suddenly smaller, the sur-
roundings quieter.

Steve folded his hands. "You were saying."

I swallowed. "A friend of mine saw the two of you by
the reservoir a couple of weeks ago, talking. I guess I
assumed Julie was interviewing you for her article."

His eyes locked on mine. They were the color of
autumn haze. "I'm having trouble following what it is
you want to know."

"Well, I thought, uh, about the article, that she might
have mentioned it." I knew I wasn't making a lot of
sense, but I didn't want to hit him over the head with
my suspicions either.

"Did Julie show you the article?" Steve asked, leaning
back.

"No. I'm not sure she'd even written it yet. But she'd
put together a fairly thorough biography, as well as a
bibliography of news stories about your career."

Steve pressed his fingers together steeple fashion. His
face was expressionless. "I see."

"She had some news clippings too, some of them from
a number of years back."

"Anything else?"

My mouth felt like sawdust. "What else would there
be?"

Another moment of strained silence. Steve's chin
rested against his fingers. "Perhaps a letter," he said at
last. "Or a book of poetry."

"Poetry?" The word was so soft I barely heard it myself.
"D. H. Lawrence?"

He nodded.

My stomach took a dive, like a kite on a string. A
romantic liaison, something I hadn't wanted to consider.

Political scandal would have been preferable. "It was yours? The inscription—"

"So you *have* seen it." He rocked back in his chair and looked away. "Utter foolishness from one who should have known better. Melodramatic and overdone, as well." He seemed embarrassed but not ashamed, as though the melodrama was worse than the rest of it.

"You and Julie ..." My voice had an unpleasant squeaky quality.

Steve's expression was hard to read. There was the faintest trace of a smile. "All these years, and I never dreamed ..."

I dug my nails into my palms, forced myself to breathe normally. I was appalled. How could he treat what he'd done so casually?

"When Leslie said she needed to see me again—"

"Leslie?"

"Julie's mother." His gaze settled somewhere over my shoulder. "It's funny, I can remember the day I gave her that book as plainly as though it were yesterday. We'd taken a drive down the coast, toward Monterey. It was one of those clear, picture-perfect days where everything is so beautiful you want to etch it forever in your memory."

"You gave the book to Leslie, not Julie? That's who it was inscribed to?"

Steve recoiled. Embarrassment flooded his face. "You thought that I'd inscribed the book to Julie?"

I nodded, feeling my own face grow flushed.

"Oh, Lord." He laughed nervously and then fell silent. "So that's what this was all about," he said after a moment. "You thought Julie and I ... that we had a ... romantic relationship?"

"That was one possibility. I mean, I knew about the book of poetry but I didn't know it was from you until just now when you told me. But I suspected that Julie was involved with someone. And she was so secretive about it . . . Or rather, I thought she'd been secretive. It never crossed my mind that the book had been her mother's."

Steve pushed back his chair. "I think I need a drink. How about you?"

I accepted, more as a gesture of congeniality than out of need. Anything to soften the brunt of my foolishness.

"Scotch or sherry?"

"Scotch, lots of water."

He opened the credenza and poured two glasses, adding water to mine from a pitcher on his desk. Instead of returning to his chair, he leaned against the edge of his desk, smiling self-consciously.

"So you didn't know about me and Leslie Harmon?" he said. "I assumed that's what you were leading up to."

I shook my head, took a small sip of my drink. "Leslie had an envelope from the law firm in San Francisco where you used to work. I thought maybe she'd been following a trial you worked on, or even that she'd been a client. It never occurred to me that you and she might have been lovers."

Steve swirled his scotch before taking a sip. "My affair with Leslie Harmon is not a facet of my life I'm particularly proud of. She deserved better than I was willing to offer, and my wife deserved better than I was giving at the time. It happened before I really stopped to think about it. I had great difficulty explaining that to someone as young as Julie."

"She knew then?"

Steve nodded.

"How did she find out? The inscription wasn't signed."

"There were some letters tucked inside. A couple from me, one that Leslie had written and never mailed."

"So Julie found them and figured out that you'd known Leslie? And then came to you to learn about her mother." Just as she'd gone to see Claudia Walker and Dulcey Haggerty.

Steve sucked on his cheek and nodded. "More or less." He took several long swigs of scotch. "Guess I'm still confused, though. If you didn't connect me with the book until a few minutes ago, what was it that brought you here?"

"I was curious why Julie would be writing an article on you. At least, that's what I assumed her interest was. The journalism teacher has assigned a term project, something to do with investigative reporting, and Julie seemed to be working on it so intently. She was so secretive about it . . ."

I trailed off, wondering if I hadn't just stumbled across a skeleton in Steve's past after all. Not political scandal but an illicit affair.

His first wife was no longer alive, but her father, an eminent political figure, was. Could Steve Burton have killed Julie to keep the fact of his affair quiet? But then why had he just now freely admitted it to me?

I sat forward. "Where are the letters now?"

"I have most of them. Or had them. They've since been destroyed."

A sour taste rose to my mouth. "Something that happened so long ago, it's not really the kind of scandal that could hurt you now, is it?"

He looked at me oddly. "It depends on what you mean by 'hurt.' "

"You think it might cost you the election?"

Steve took another swallow of scotch. And then I caught a flicker of something in his eyes, surprise maybe, mixed with a degree of sadness. He set the glass down on the desk.

"Ah, Kate. I think now I finally understand the purpose of this visit of yours. You think that I might somehow be implicated in Julie's death. Is that it?"

I sat back. "Well . . . not that you . . . but when you think about it . . ." That was it exactly, but I couldn't find the words to agree. My stammering seemed to go on forever.

He shook his head sadly. "Don't apologize. I can see how you might jump to that conclusion. Personally I'm very sorry that you would, however. This project of Julie's, her secretiveness, our meeting by the reservoir, the old clippings—you thought she'd discovered some fiasco or shady dealing from my past. Perhaps simply my involvement with Leslie. You suspected that I might have killed her to silence her."

I tried the kind of dismissive shrug Diane Keaton does so well, but in truth I was appalled to hear my own musings stated so succinctly. "You didn't?" I asked.

"I did not." He looked me in the eye. "I hope you believe me."

I nodded. I wasn't sure whether I believed him or not, but since we were alone, maybe the only two people left in the entire building, I decided it was best if he thought I did.

Steve gave me an odd look. He stood and refilled his glass. "You're a lousy liar, Kate."

I back-pedaled. "It wasn't that I necessarily *suspected* you."

"But you had your doubts." His smile was thin. "Have them still, I imagine."

"It was so clear to me that Julie had been up to something. I simply assumed this journalism project might have been the key."

Silence stretched between us, taut as an arched bow. Steve looked at me, then away. He sighed.

"It was a personal project," he said, draining his glass. "Julie used the journalism assignment as a cover."

I nodded vigorously, not at all sure what I was agreeing to. "She was interested in talking to people who had known her mother in the past, right?"

Steve picked up a pen from his desk and rolled it between his palms. "What she really wanted was to find her father."

"Her father? Did she?"

He walked to the other side of the room. "Yes," he said. "She found him."

"Where? How?" And then it hit me, broadside. "You?"

He nodded.

I was stunned into silence.

"Julie was a lovely girl." There was a ragged edge to Steve's voice. "I wish now that Leslie had told me earlier."

"You didn't know?"

"Not until a couple of years ago when Leslie needed some medical history. She asked me not to contact Julie. And to be honest, I wasn't sure I wanted any contact. Yvonne and I had been married less than a year at that time, and Julie was already twelve years old. It seemed best just to let things be."

I'd barely touched my drink. I took a sip now and

sorted through what Steve had told me. "You really had no idea?"

He seemed to retreat into himself for a moment. "My affair with Leslie was brief, lasting only a couple of months. I was married at the time, happily—believe it or not. But I loved Leslie too, in a very selfish way. She left abruptly to move to New York, ostensibly because of a promotion. I never knew she was pregnant. I doubt I'd have done anything differently if I had. I would never have left my wife. Leslie knew that."

"What did Julie know about you?"

He sat at his desk. "She was told her father had died before she was born. A few years ago she discovered her birth certificate. It listed the father's name as unknown. Julie confronted her mother, who apparently told her that she didn't have a father, that she should forget about it. But of course she couldn't. Who could? That's when Julie began her search. But she didn't get serious about it until after Leslie died and she went to live with the Shepherds."

It was an amazing undertaking for one so young. "How did she ever figure out that it was you?"

He smiled with a hint of pride. "Brains, hard work, and luck. Julie tried to learn about her mother's life during the time preceding her birth. She tracked down old friends and associates of Leslie's, but she'd probably have gotten nowhere without the box Dulcey Haggerty gave her."

"You must have been astonished when Julie actually contacted you."

His smile held the shadow of sadness. "That's putting it mildly."

"Does Yvonne know?"

"She does now. As I'm sure you're aware, Julie was unhappy living with her aunt and uncle. She was unhappy, period. Lonely and scared and hurt. I realized that this would be my last chance to get to know my daughter." He paused. "Julie was going to move in with us, become part of our family."

I swallowed. "Yvonne was okay with this?"

"Not thrilled, but she has a daughter herself. She understood that I couldn't simply turn my back. We both knew it wasn't going to be easy, but we also felt it was the right thing to do."

So that was Julie's surprise, the big change that was going to make her life so much better. She wasn't going to be stuck with the Shepherds after all.

"But why the delay? Why keep it secret?"

"That was Julie's idea. She thought we should wait until after the election. It's only a couple of weeks away. I didn't think the news would have much impact on voters, but you can't predict these things. And you never know what media will do with a story. Then, when she was killed, well, there didn't seem to be any reason to bring it all out in the open."

I sat back and took a moment to let the information settle. Julie's project, Julie's secret—a father, not a lover. A story of reconciliation rather than political scandal. I had been chasing my tail after all, just as Michael had predicted. None of what I'd been worrying over had anything to do with why she'd been killed.

"Do you have any idea why Julie went to Berkeley on Friday night?" I asked.

"None. I wish to God I did."

"The police have a witness who thinks he saw her getting into a car on San Pablo about seven-thirty that evening. One of those sport utility things. I'm guessing that it was a planned meeting, not a pickup."

"Do they have a description of the car?"

"Dark. That's all. They're looking into the possibility that it might be someone she met on-line. Same with Cindy Purcell."

He shook his head. "It doesn't seem like the kind of thing Julie would do. One thing that was clear to me was that she was a level-headed girl. Of course, where boys are concerned, it seems none of them at that age act like they've a head on their shoulders."

"I'm not so sure adults are much better."

He looked at me and laughed. "Touché. I'm hardly one to talk, am I?" He rocked back in the chair. The furrows in his face grew pronounced. "It's funny the way life turns out. My affair with Leslie was a mistake, something I knew was wrong even at the time. And yet as a result of it, I had a daughter. I was still reveling in the wonder of it when she was killed. And now there's a heaviness in my heart that will be there forever."

I nodded in sympathy. It had to have been hard on him. There were few people with whom Steve could even share his grief.

"I'll tell you this, losing Julie has made me appreciate more than ever before the fact that I have Yvonne and Skye."

As I headed for home in the gray dusk of early autumn, I, too, offered silent words of gratitude for those who were near and dear to me.

29

When I rounded the corner of Wisteria Road and saw Michael's car parked in my driveway, I felt a rush of delight, followed quickly by the sinking realization that he would have expected Faye to be gone by now. I had no trouble imagining his surprise at finding her still here, or hers at having him march in and make himself right at home. God only knew how long he'd been there and what they'd found to say to one another.

I gave half a thought to driving on and letting them handle it alone. But my cowardly bent was overshadowed by my eagerness to see Michael. Resigning myself to an evening shaped by tension, I pulled into the driveway.

The aroma of roasted garlic was what I noticed first; the ring of conversation and laughter struck me next. Both were coming from the direction of the kitchen.

"Mommy's home," Anna announced, looking up from her glass of chocolate milk. And then to me, "We couldn't imagine what was taking you so long." Faye's intonation and, no doubt, her words as well.

"Sorry, I expected to be home before this."

"Not to worry," Faye said brightly. "We've got things under control." Her smile was immediate, her cheeks rosy. The half-drained glass of red wine in front of her probably accounted for both.

"Hi, sweetheart," Michael said, kissing my cheek while he layered ricotta cheese on the lasagna he was making.

After glancing at Faye, who seemed unperturbed by this display of affection, I gave Michael a hug around the middle.

He whispered into my ear, "I thought she was leaving."

"She was. Is," I whispered back. "On Saturday. I'll explain later." I pulled away and raised my voice to a conversational level. I didn't know you were coming back so soon."

"I'd done everything I could in Dallas."

"When did you get in?"

"A couple of hours ago. I stopped at the grocery on the way home."

"Ye of little faith."

He laughed. "And much prior experience. After four days of coffee-shop dining I was hungry for something more than canned soup and a cheese sandwich."

"It smells divine," Faye said. Then to me, "Imagine, a man who can cook. Could I have a little more wine, Kate, while you're up?"

I refilled her glass and poured a large one for myself.

Libby waltzed through the kitchen on her way to the fridge. "Hi, Kate," she said, reaching for a Coke. "Didn't know you were home. I asked Mr. Melville about Judge Burton."

My confusion must have been evident in my expression. "You know, about whether Julie had mentioned him in connection with her term project. Mr. Melville said she hadn't told him anything about the assignment at all.''

Michael slipped the lasagna into the oven, then gave me a one-eyed squint. "Are you still working *that* angle?"

I shook my head. "Not after today."

Faye, Michael, and I took our wine into the living room and I told them about my meeting with Steve Burton. "You were right," I said to Michael when I'd finished. "None of it had anything to do with her death. The book of poems, the letters she got at Dennis Shepherd's, the news clippings and research on Judge Burton, none of it turned out to be important."

"That poor girl," Faye said sadly. "Imagine seeing 'father unknown' on your birth certificate."

Michael nodded. "It's fortunate that she found him, and that he seemed to welcome her into his life."

"Seemed?" I turned. "You sound like you don't believe him."

"Sorry, force of habit."

Faye sighed. "Too bad the reporter who wrote the article in today's paper didn't talk to you first."

"What article?"

"It's in the *Sun.*" She rustled through the papers on the coffee table and handed it to me.

"Susie Sullivan?" Michael asked.

I checked the byline. "The one and only. Here, you read it."

While Michael scanned the article, Faye continued to sigh. "Poor girl, so sad."

"Well?" I asked when he'd finished.

"It's kind of a jumble, but her information is accurate. To her credit, she hasn't jumped onto the Parkside Killer bandwagon either. Makes it clear there's no solid connection between Julie's death and the Purcell murder. There's even mention of some mysterious search Julie may have been conducting." He tossed the paper back on the table. "Your friend Susie's never going to get anywhere, however, until she learns to write a complete sentence. A lesson in correct usage wouldn't hurt either. Did that woman even make it past sixth grade?"

I laughed. "She's actually the graduate of a very expensive, though little known, college founded by one of her ancestors."

We ate dinner in the dining room with Anna chirping away happily about the upcoming Halloween parade and the cookies they were going to decorate in class. Libby seemed preoccupied and left the table as soon as she'd finished eating. After dinner, Faye also retired, somewhat bleary-eyed, to her room and Anna went off to watch TV.

While I was cleaning up the kitchen, Michael wrapped his arms around me and pulled me close. "I was counting on picking up where we left off last Saturday."

"Before your beeper went off, you mean?"

"Exactly." He kissed my ear. "So, what's the story with Faye? Why is she still here?"

I explained about her illness and the missed flight. "You must have been surprised when you found that she hadn't left."

He laughed. "Not as surprised as Faye to find a man she hadn't expected puttering around the kitchen. Good thing she has a strong heart."

"It must have been awkward. What did the two of you ever find to talk about?"

"Oh, a little of this, a little of that." He ran a hand

down my back. "Give her a glass of wine and she isn't half bad."

"Does that mean you're moving back home?"

"It's either that or a hotel. I already returned the key to Don's apartment."

"I'm glad." I nuzzled his neck with my nose, kissed the hollow of his throat, and was working my way to the warmth of his mouth when Anna skittered past on her way to get Max a doggie treat.

"Yuk," she said. "Do you have to do that mushy stuff in public?"

"It's not mushy, and the kitchen is hardly what I'd call a public place."

The phone rang and Anna grabbed it. "Libby," she yelled, loud enough to wake the dead. "It's Brian." Then she turned to me and made a face. "More mushy stuff, I bet."

"So tell me about Dallas," I said as we moved into the other room. "Is Frank Davis your man?"

"He doesn't appear to be. But the DA thinks we've got enough to get a court order giving us access to the computer in Cindy's apartment."

"But you already checked it."

"Only what was obvious. The roommate wouldn't let us take it, remember? Said she needed it for class. But there can be a lot of information stored on a hard drive, including files that have been deleted. We'll get an expert to go through the thing and see if we can't come up with names of more guys Cindy may have been in touch with."

"So you really think it was someone she met on-line?"

"Right now it's the only lead we've got. Everything else has been a dead end."

"Is Gates looking into this Internet stuff as well?"

Michael nodded. "I talked with him just yesterday, in fact. Maybe we'll be lucky enough to find the same name showing up in both places." Michael yawned. "You think if I leave the house by seven o'clock tomorrow morning, I'll be out before Faye gets up?"

I poked him in the ribs. "Chicken."

He flapped his arms at the elbows and squawked. And later, when the house was quiet, we got back to the mushy stuff.

As it turned out, Michael needn't have worried about crossing paths with Faye. She was still in bed when I left for work the next morning at nine.

Yvonne hailed me as I passed her classroom on the way to the faculty lounge. "Steve told me about your conversation yesterday." She lowered her voice. "I'd appreciate it if you didn't mention it to anyone around school."

"Of course not."

"But I'm glad you know the truth. It's been so hard dealing with this—first with Julie's sudden appearance in our lives and then with her death—and not having anyone I could talk with about it. I know it's been even harder on Steve."

"It must have been terrible."

"We'd initially decided not to say anything until after the election, and then when Julie was killed, there didn't seem to be a point in saying anything at all. But that only added to the strain."

"If I can help in any way, or if you want to talk it over—"

"It's a relief to know I can let down my guard with someone." She reached into the closet by the door. "I was just making myself a cup of coffee. You want one?"

"Coffee?"

"One of the advantages of having a science lab for a classroom. And it's far better than the stuff in the faculty room." She filled a Pyrex beaker with water and set it on the burner.

Brian Walker opened the door and peered into the room. "Sorry," he said. "I'm looking for Skye."

"She's in the library, I think." Yvonne spooned coffee into a cone filter and poured the water through.

"Thanks." Brian ducked out as quickly as he'd appeared.

"What's the story with Brian's father and Steve?" I asked. "Was it Brian's grandfather that Steve worked for years ago?"

She nodded. "As I understand it, Steve's former father-in-law and Brian's grandfather went to law school together. That's how Steve ended up with the firm in the first place. He and the senior Walker didn't get along, however, so it didn't last long."

"And what about Brian's father?" The coffee was hot and strong. Yvonne was right; it was much better than the stuff in the lounge.

"Walker senior didn't get along with him either. He wanted his son to be a lawyer, follow in the family footsteps. Thought he was wasting his life with music. And with Brian's mother, who had a history of psychological problems and substance abuse. She had a couple of brushes with the law. Walker senior turned his back on them; Steve tried to help. When Brian's father learned he was dying, he asked Steve to set up a trust and to act as trustee. He didn't have much respect for lawyers, but he trusted Steve."

"Poor Brian. Kids that age may think they don't need parents, but it must be terrible to know you're all alone."

Yvonne nodded. "I've taken to counting my blessings every day."

The bell rang and I hastily drained my cup. "Thanks for the coffee."

"Any time. Are you coming back for the faculty meeting this afternoon?"

"Do I have a choice?"

She grinned. "Depends on whether you want to keep your job."

Friday afternoon was a lousy time for faculty meetings to begin with, and with Combs at the helm, they seemed much longer than the hour or so they actually took. He rambled, he backtracked, he added anecdotes that were supposed to enliven the proceeding but ended up only drawing it out more than was necessary.

When we finally adjourned, Yvonne waved me over once again. "Can I bum a ride home?" she asked.

"Sure. What happened to your car?"

"Skye took it. She didn't want to wait around until after the meeting. She offered to come back and pick me up, but I told her I'd try to dig up a ride myself."

We stopped by the office to sign out, and ran into Marvin Melville toting two large boxes back to his classroom.

"You need some help?" I asked.

"No thanks, I can handle it. This is the paper that was supposed to come out today. Back from the printers a little late for that." He gave us an easy, boyish grin. "Guess Monday will do just as well."

"He seemed chipper enough," Yvonne said when we got into the car.

I nodded. "End of the workweek, who can blame him."

"I heard his girlfriend broke up with him recently."

"Cheri? The aerobics instructor?"

"I don't know the name. I overheard him talking in the faculty room."

"They seemed lovey-dovey enough last Saturday."

Yvonne shrugged. "Maybe it was just a lovers' quarrel."

As I turned onto Yvonne's street, she suddenly grabbed the dash. Before I had a chance to ask what the problem was, I saw for myself. There were two police cars parked in front of the Burtons' house.

30

Yvonne was out of the car and headed for the house even before I'd turned off the engine. I followed seconds later.

"You the lady of the house?" an officer asked as she rushed through the door.

Yvonne nodded, managing only a high-pitched mewing sound in place of words.

"Your daughter's fine," the officer said gently. "She wasn't even home when it happened."

Yvonne slumped against the wall. I could hear her sucking in her breath, the panic subsiding. "When what happened?"

Before he could answer, Skye appeared from down the hallway and rushed into her mother's arms. "Oh, Mama, somebody was here. He broke into our house." Her voice grew more breathless with each word.

"There was a burglary?" I asked, turning to the policeman. He was tall and thin, with downy soft skin that still bore traces of adolescent acne.

"Looks like it. A pane of glass at the back of the house was broken." He nodded to Yvonne. "We'll need your help to determine what's missing. The little lady here"— this time he looked at Skye—"handled the situation admirably. She called 911, then waited for us out front."

Yvonne smoothed her daughter's hair. "Thank God you're all right. But he might still have been in the house, honey. You should have gone next door to call."

"At first, I didn't even realize there'd been someone here. I mean, it's not like the whole house was torn apart. It wasn't until I saw the broken glass and the . . ." She hiccupped as a sob worked its way loose. "And then I saw Daddy's study. There were papers all over the floor." Her eyes welled with tears.

Skye had apparently managed the crisis with remarkable control, but now her emotions took hold. An understandable delayed reaction, but knowing Skye, I suspected she might have been dramatizing a bit. Given what she'd been through, I didn't necessarily fault her.

"Whatever he took," Yvonne murmured, "it doesn't matter as long as you're not hurt." She continued to stroke her daughter's head. "To think that you might have been home when he did this. That you might have been in the house and . . . well, it could have been much worse."

The officer cleared his throat. "When you're up to it, ma'am, I'd like you to walk through the house and tell me if anything's missing or isn't where you left it. You'll have time to do a complete inventory later, but your initial reaction would be helpful."

"Is there anything I can do?" I asked Yvonne.

"Thanks, but I don't think so."

I turned to Skye. "Would you like to come to our house for a while?"

She shook her head, still wiping away the tears. "I need to stay and help my mother," she said gravely.

I drove home with an unsettled feeling in my chest. I didn't see how the burglary could be connected to my conversation with Steve or to Julie's death. But I didn't see how it could be pure coincidence either.

Friday night was one of those awful times when there was too much going on and none of it seemed to mesh. Libby was going to a party where she was hoping to encounter Brian. The usual trying on of multiple outfits escalated to a full closet search for the perfect ensemble—if what she finally chose, black netting over a black leotard and latex leggings, qualified as an ensemble. Anna was trying mightily to train Max to speak, in English, and Faye had taken it into her head that she had to wash and iron everything in her suitcase before repacking it. Michael had called to say he'd be *a little late*—which meant he could show up any time between 8:00 P.M. and 8:00 the next morning. And to top it off, Andy had left a message that he'd stop by with pizza for a farewell meal. It had apparently dawned on him, rather late in the game, that he'd seen very little of Faye during her visit to California.

He arrived a little before seven, carrying a puny sized pizza box and a six-pack of beer. I was glad that Libby and Michael were eating elsewhere or the meal would never have stretched.

"Your friend Walton Shepherd pulled out of the deal," he said to me partway through dinner. We were eating in the dining room in honor of the occasion.

"The rod and gun shop?" I asked.

Andy took a swig of beer and nodded. "He's already signed the lease so technically we could hold him to it, but in an upscale shopping center the last thing you want is a deadbeat tenant. Or space that sits vacant for months on end."

"Did he say why?"

"Something about financing and capital." Andy rocked back on the rear legs of the chair, a habit that drives me crazy. He's a big man, and the chairs are already rickety from years of abuse. "This job is beginning to lose some of its appeal," Andy said after a moment.

"In what way?"

"It's the same old stuff, day after day."

So were most jobs. "Much of the appeal is in a steady paycheck, isn't it?"

He shrugged. "You and Anna won't starve, if that's what you're worried about."

I gritted my teeth. Although the money was certainly an issue, his attitude was what irked me. It was one of the wedges that had driven us apart from the start. Andy had some good points, but diligence wasn't one of them.

"Have you found something better?" Faye asked hopefully.

"Something will turn up. There's no point sticking with a job you don't enjoy."

They don't call it work for nothing, I muttered under my breath, but I didn't pursue the issue.

We'd just about finished eating when Michael arrived.

"Hey, Mike." Andy stood to shake hands. "Nice to see you again, buddy."

"Likewise," Michael said, not quite so fervently.

While there is no real animosity between the two of

them, there's a level of discomfort about these encoun-
ters that puts me on edge. I sometimes think it stems as
much from their disparate personalities as from the
nature of their relationship.

"Help yourself to a beer," Andy told him with hearty,
old-boy cheerfulness. "They're in the fridge."

Michael grabbed a bottle of beer and pulled a chair
up next to mine. After eyeing the empty pizza carton, he
reached for the crust that remained on my plate and
began nibbling.

"We weren't expecting you until later," I said by way
of apology.

"Not a problem. I'll find something in the kitchen."
Michael seemed distracted, and while he did his best to
be sociable for the remainder of the evening, I could tell
that his mind was elsewhere.

Finally, when we'd cleared the table and stuffed the
empty beer bottles and pizza box into the recycle bins,
Michael suggested a walk. As we left, Andy, Faye, and
Anna were scooping out bowls of ice cream, readying
themselves for an evening of television.

Although the day had been sunny and mild, the evening air held the nip of autumn. Michael's hand found
mine and I reveled in the warmth of his touch.

"The Burtons' house was broken into this afternoon,"
I told him.

He nodded. "I saw the report."

"Do you think it might be connected somehow with
the fact that Julie was Steve's daughter?"

"Can't say that the thought didn't cross my mind,
although for the life of me I can't see what the connection
is."

A cool breeze swept the fallen leaves along the pavement. I pulled my sweater tighter. "Do you know yet what was taken?"

"The preliminary inventory is fairly short. Cash from the kitchen drawer, a watch, a gun, and a couple of cameras. Not much of a haul. Looks like most of the activity took place at the front of the house. Maybe the guy was scared off before he had a chance to finish the job."

I thought of Skye's walking into the house alone. Maybe the intruder *had* been there when she arrived home. I shivered at the idea of what might have happened had he turned on Skye instead of fleeing.

Michael scratched his cheek. "Looks like we're finally making some progress on Cindy Purcell's murder."

"That's great."

He grunted. "Damn right it is. I feel like I've been chasing fireflies for the last month."

"Fireflies?"

"You know, you see a speck of light, you grab for it and it's gone. Didn't you chase fireflies as a kid?"

"Not growing up in California."

"Poor Kate, you led a deprived youth." He kicked through a mound of dried leaves.

"So tell me about your progress on the case."

"You'll never believe this newest development. Turns out it was Cindy's roommate who was sending all those suggestive messages on-line."

"Toby? That timid, mousy woman who stared at her hands and had trouble completing a sentence?"

He nodded. "Her imagination is anything but timid."

"Cindy didn't send any of them?"

"There was one night when they were both home and kind of horsing around. That's how it started. Cindy apparently had better things to do with her time, however. Toby didn't. She kept it up on a regular basis, communicating with a number of different men. Only she assumed an identity that wasn't hers.''

It was suddenly clear to me where this was going. "You mean she pretended to be Cindy?"

"More or less. Whenever Toby needed a personal detail, she drew on what she knew of Cindy. When she was supposedly describing herself, she gave a description of Cindy. She used Cindy's major, her background, her class schedule.''

"Oh, my God. Did she set Cindy up to be killed?''

"Not deliberately. At least, that's what she claims and I think she's telling the truth. But she'd arrange dates, like she did with Frank Davis, and then not show. Well, she actually would show up, but not as Cindy. Toby would sit and watch the guy, maybe even say a few words to him, but of course he was waiting for a tall, thin blonde named Cindy.''

Our walk had taken us on an L-shaped path. We crossed the street now and headed back. Twilight had given way to night. I stepped carefully to avoid tripping.

"We've got experts working on the hard drive,'' Michael continued. "Trying to retrieve old messages. Toby recalls a series of fairly erotic exchanges, some with talk about feet and shoes. For her part, she said, she'd mostly parrot back what Prince Charming had said in an earlier message.''

"Prince Charming?''

"That was his screen name.''

From Cinderella and the glass slipper, I thought. It was a macabre connotation. "So if you can retrieve one of these messages, you can locate this Prince Charming?''

"That's our hope. I just wish Toby had spoken up earlier. She claims she didn't remember until now, but to my mind that's a lame excuse. I think she was afraid to be implicated. I'm guessing the full impact of what she'd done didn't hit her until a couple of weeks ago when I asked to look at the computer. She panicked and erased whatever messages had been saved."

"Did Julie ever communicate with this Prince Charming?"

"There's no record of it. But that doesn't mean she didn't."

"What about Julie's murder? What does this do to the Parkside Killer theory?"

Michael laughed without humor. "The guy could have written poetry about feet for all we know. Gates is checking on it."

As we approached the corner, Michael slowed his pace. "What's the matter?" I asked.

He rubbed his chin. "I'm not any too anxious to get back to the house. Too many Austens there. I'm outnumbered."

"You do well at holding your own," I told him lightly.

Michael put an arm around my shoulder, suddenly serious. "I want our own house, Kate. One that isn't a hand-me-down from your marriage with Andy."

"I know." We'd talked about this before. But at the moment it wasn't practical financially. "Anyway Andy will never be completely out of the picture, because of Anna."

Michael nodded. "I understand that. And I admire the way the two of you have managed to stay on friendly terms. It's just that in some respects it will always be his house. It's awkward. I feel like the interloper."

I kissed him. "Well, you're not. But we'll think about it, okay?"

"I'd also like a household with fewer Austens."

"Faye's leaving in the morning."

The corners of his mouth angled up in a crooked smile. "I was talking about something different." He turned and waited expectantly. "Like having an Austen become a Stone."

The M-word again. It had been months since we'd last discussed marriage—and I wasn't any closer to a decision than I'd been then. I thought briefly of Luke Martin before pushing the image away. Was I really ready to be married again?

My hesitancy had nothing to do with my feelings for Michael, I was sure of that. But it was there nonetheless and I couldn't convince myself otherwise.

I bit my lip, wondered how to explain. "We were going to—"

Michael cut me off. "At least say you'll think about it," he said glumly.

"I will."

"Promise?"

I nodded and sealed it with a kiss.

31

Because of heavy traffic, we were late getting to the airport the next morning. Faye's plane was already boarding by the time we made it to the gate, but she seemed in no hurry to rush off. She set her bag on the chair and bent down to give Anna a long, hard hug.

"I'm going to miss you something terrible," she said.

"I'll miss you, too," Anna told her, and then added, without prompting, "and thank you again for my princess dress. It's really, really beautiful."

When she'd modeled the dress for her dad the previous evening, she had indeed assumed a princess-like air. It was a side to Anna I'd not seen before.

"Well you wear whatever you want for Halloween," Faye said reasonably, "but be sure to send me a picture." She turned to me. "Thank you, Kate, for having me. And for taking care of me this last week. I know it's not easy having a house guest."

"I'm glad you could come see us."

Faye hesitated, studying her hands. "I hope things

continue to go well with you and Michael. He seems like a nice man."

I knew how much the comment cost her and I felt a swell of gratitude.

"Thanks," I told her warmly. "He is."

"I love Andy with all my heart," she continued, "but I can see how it might be difficult to be married to him." She sighed then looked at me with a wan smile. "He's a lot like his father was."

There was another call for her flight. Faye picked up her bag and gave us each a peck on the cheek. "Come see me soon." She disappeared down the boarding ramp with a final wave at the gate.

The drive to the airport had been filled with Faye's and Anna's chatter and the urgency of getting there on time; the ride home was relatively quiet. I turned the radio to a classical station and hummed along to the strains of Schubert's *Trout* quintet. Free of company, I was feeling newly liberated and energized. But in the back of my mind was an uneasiness that would not rest. The burglary at the Burtons' and the mysterious *Prince Charming*—both had kept me awake a good part of the night.

When we'd left to take Faye to the airport, Libby had still been sound asleep. She'd managed to pull herself out of bed by the time we returned.

"Did you have a good time at the party last night?" I asked.

She nodded, dreamily.

"I take it Brian was there?"

Another nod, equally starry-eyed. "He's different from the other boys at school," Libby said.

I'd have pushed for a clarification if I thought she could give me one. Instead, I asked about Prince Charming.

"That's what he calls himself?" she asked in disgust. "The guy must be on a major ego trip."

If Michael was right, the guy was on the ultimate ego trip.

"Did Julie ever mention the name to you? It might have been someone she corresponded with over the Internet."

She shook her head. "Julie wasn't stupid."

When she'd finished breakfast, we moved Libby's things out of Anna's room and back into the room vacated by Faye. Then I made a quick trip to the grocery, did the laundry, and set about cleaning with the quiet satisfaction of knowing my house was once again my own.

Midafternoon I called to check on Yvonne. They were all still a little shaken, she said, but trying to put the break-in behind them. Nothing of much value had been taken and the house had not been trashed. All in all they'd been lucky—even if the police thought it unlikely they'd ever find the thief.

When the mail came, Anna dumped it on the table and began sorting it by name, a skill she'd only recently acquired.

"Libby has a letter," she announced. "Why don't I ever get letters?"

"You do. You got an invitation to Kyle's birthday party just last week."

"I mean a real letter, like this." She checked the stack again before scooting off toward the hallway. "I'll take it to Libby."

I continued to empty the dishwasher, the muted buzz of conversation from Libby's room barely discernable in the background. Suddenly a shriek pierced the afternoon calm. I hurried to see what the problem was, expecting nothing more serious than a thick-bodied spider or maybe a cornered mouse.

I was wrong.

Libby was standing, frozen in place, like a pillar of salt. The color had drained from her face and her eyes held a look of panic.

"What is it?" I asked, fear rising in my throat.

She pointed to the envelope lying on the floor at her feet. "It's . . . it's . . ."

I leaned over, picked up the envelope, and unfolded the sheet of blank paper inside, revealing a sizable lock of blond hair.

"It's hers, isn't it?" Libby said, her voice spiraling. "It's Julie's."

I swallowed the nausea that soured my mouth. "We don't know that." I tried to sound reassuring, but I found myself in the grip of the same sickening certainty.

"Just like the shoes," Libby added. "And the plastic skeleton. They all came from the man who killed Julie and Cindy Purcell." Libby was no longer frozen in place. She began to shake and sob.

I hugged her to my chest. "Honey, we don't know any of that for sure. But we're certainly going to take it seriously."

Michael took it seriously, too, which frightened me as much as anything. Michael is not one to overreact.

No one had answered the phone when I'd dialed the detective division directly, so I'd had to call the regular police exchange. The dispatcher on duty, a woman I'd met previously, finally got a message to Michael, who was holed up with his computer expert.

"Do you think it's really Julie's hair?" I asked when I'd explained what had happened.

"We can't know without running some tests. Can you bring the envelope in?"

"Sure. Right away."

"Handle it carefully, with a pair of tweezers, and put it in a plastic bag. I doubt there are any prints, but we'll test for that as well. I may not be here myself, but I'll alert whoever's on duty."

"Where will you be?" I'd been counting on the comfort of being with him.

"I'm not sure. Things are beginning to move on the Purcell case."

"You've found Prince Charming?"

"We've found a message from him. It's amazing what these computer whizzes can do. You think you've deleted a file but ninety-nine percent of the time you haven't. It's still there until it gets written over."

"Can you tell from the message if he's the guy you're after?"

"The note is definitely kinky," Michael said. "And he talks about meeting Cindy in person. We're hoping to find other messages from him as well. It will be a lot easier to make a case that we ought to have this guy's real name and address if we can show ongoing correspondence. Toby remembers half a dozen exchanges at least."

"Did she actually set up a meeting with him the way she did with Frank Davis?"

"I suspect so, although she claims not to remember. She's walking a fine line here between pretty heavy-duty guilt and self-serving denial."

Not an easy line to walk, I thought. "Do you know if he communicated with Julie Harmon as well?"

"Gates is handling that end. We're working together on this." There was a pause. "Have you asked Libby about him?"

"You mean, you think she might have received messages from this Prince Charming?"

"If he's the one sending her stuff, he has to have found her name somehow."

"But you said he might be doing all this to taunt you, because you're working the case."

"That's certainly a possibility," Michael agreed.

I had trouble imagining Libby writing kinky letters to strange men on the Internet. "I asked her about the name in connection with Julie. She didn't act like it was familiar."

Michael's tone grew softer. "I don't want to frighten you, but I think you should tell Libby to stay close to home this weekend. I'll have an officer drive by on a regular basis. I don't think she's in danger at the house. That's not the way this guy has operated in the past."

It was a sign of how scared Libby really was, that it took no effort at all to convince her to follow Michael's advice. She stayed in the house or at my side, and sometimes both, for the rest of the weekend. She didn't want to go to school on Monday, but I insisted and Michael backed me up. I promised to drive her there and back home. I even offered to accompany her to classes. It was an offer she didn't readily embrace.

Skye, I noticed, was not in school.

"She's not feeling well," Yvonne told me when I ran into her by the copy machine.

"My mother-in-law had the flu last week. It must be going around."

"I'm sure the anxiety of the weekend didn't help."

I nodded agreement. Skye tended toward emotional extremes under the best of circumstances.

I glanced across the breezeway toward Mr. Combs's office and caught sight of a familiar form stepping into the entryway. "What the heck—"

Yvonne raised her eyes.

"It's Michael," I explained. "What's he doing here?"

And then I had the disturbing thought that maybe he'd come to find me, come because something dreadful had happened. I sprinted across the open corridor and into the principal's office.

Michael was with another man from the department. He turned when he saw me. "Not now, Kate. I'm busy."

"But what—"

Just then Marvin Melville came through the doorway in the company of Mr. Combs. Michael held out his badge and addressed Marvin.

"We'd like to talk with you about the death of Cindy Purcell," he said.

Marvin stepped back as though he'd been slapped.

"Before we begin, I need to advise you that you have the right to remain silent . . ."

Marvin didn't protest. He didn't ask what in the hell was going on or what they wanted with him. He didn't even hear Michael out because he'd collapsed in a heap on the floor.

32

Marvin had revived almost immediately, but his mutterings were those of a person whose mind was still befuddled. Not that I'd had an opportunity to listen to them for very long. He'd been whisked into Combs's private office as soon as he was able to stand, and the door had been unceremoniously slammed shut.

When he'd emerged a short while later, he was no longer muttering. Hand-cuffed and sandwiched between Michael and the other officer, Marvin was forcefully escorted to the police car parked in front of the school.

They'd tried to handle the whole thing discreetly, waiting until classes had settled in before making the trek to the car. But I wasn't the only one gawking. Within the hour, rumors were spreading like wildfire. Marvin Melville had been arrested for murder.

I spent the afternoon pacing around the house, reluctant to step beyond arm's reach of the phone. I pounced on Michael the minute he came home.

"Is it true?" I asked, my voice charged with pent-up excitement. "Did Marvin kill Cindy Purcell?"

Michael loosened his tie, ran a hand through his hair, and dropped into the nearest available chair. "It's true," he said wearily. "The guy gave us a full confession."

As the reality of his words hit, my excitement drained away, leaving me feeling as empty as a helium balloon gone flat. Mild-mannered Marvin Melville, a man I'd talked and laughed with, a murderer.

"Julie, too?" I asked.

Michael shook his head, pressed his fingertips against his temples. "He says not. Swears he had nothing to do with that."

My stomach was churning. "What about the gifts to Libby?"

"Not that, either." Michael looked up. "You want some wine? I'm going to have a glass, and maybe some cheese or something. I'm starved." He started to stand.

"I'll get it," I told him. "You just sit and rest." I opened a bottle of zinfindel, then set out cheese and crackers and olives. "Marvin really confessed?" I asked, returning to sit across from Michael.

"I think he was glad to get it off his chest. Besides, the evidence against him is fairly strong."

"What evidence?"

"The e-mail messages he sent—"

"Marvin is Prince Charming?"

Michael nodded. "We were able to get his name and address through his on-line provider. When we showed Toby his picture, she recognized him as the man she'd set up a date with. The manager of the video store where Cindy worked recognized him, as well. Apparently Marvin had been in the store several times in the preceding week, chatting with Cindy."

I slumped back in my chair, hugged my arms to my chest. "Did Marvin say why he killed her?"

"It was an accident. At least that's the spin he's put on it." Michael cut a wedge of cheese. "The rest is pretty much the way we'd laid it out in theory. Toby, posturing as Cindy, connected with Marvin through an on-line bulletin board. They exchanged messages about sexual fantasies and preferences, as well as tidbits of personal background. Toby arranged a meeting and then didn't show."

"Just like with Frank Davis."

"And a few others. But Marvin didn't give up. From their earlier messages he knew where Cindy worked and he had a general description of her. He started going to the video store, joking around with her, thinking she was the same woman he'd been talking with on-line. But he never let on that he was the guy she'd been exchanging messages with. Got a real charge out of it because he knew things about her, he thought, that she didn't know he knew."

Michael paused to let me work through the forest of pronouns.

"Knowing her interest in acting, Marvin presented himself as a production scout, working on an assignment for an upcoming Kevin Costner film. He said he needed to take a quick look at a location out by the reservoir, but that his car was acting up. Cindy offered to drive him."

"She actually volunteered?"

Michael shrugged. "Maybe he asked. In either case, he was someone she'd seen in the store. They'd probably had a couple of brief conversations. And the chance to get a behind-the-scenes look at film production . . ." He held out his hands. "Her behavior doesn't strike me as unusual."

"I guess not, except in retrospect."

"According to Marvin, all he wanted was a chance to talk to Cindy, time to connect in person. But things didn't progress the way he expected."

"So he killed her?" I was still having trouble relating the *he* of our conversation to Marvin.

"That's where the guy's story becomes less clear. I'm not sure even he knows at this point what happened."

Michael paused to refill his glass. I'd barely touched mine. My stomach had a sour, queasy feeling that wine would only make worse.

"I gather that once they were at the reservoir, Marvin started coming on to Cindy," Michael continued. "Trying to play with her mind, among other things. All this stuff he supposedly knew about her, he thought it gave him the upper hand, but it was all wrong. She didn't respond the way he expected, denied half of what she'd supposedly told him earlier via e-mail. The thing that really did it, though, was when she called him a pervert for some of the very stuff they'd enjoyed talking about before. He got angry and grabbed her. She screamed, and in the melee that followed, he ended up choking her. He claims he was only trying to get her to stop screaming."

"And then?"

"And then, he panicked. He covered her body with leaves and walked away."

"What about all the ritual stuff?" I asked. "The shoes, the hair, the plastic skeleton."

"Melville took her shoes with him. He really does have a thing about feet, just as we surmised the killer did. That's apparently what started their fight. He wanted to paint her toenails. The thing with the hair is similar."

"And the skeleton?"

Michael rocked back in his chair. His laugh was clipped and humorless. "The skeleton was Cindy's. She'd picked it up that afternoon at a card shop near campus. One of those places that sells novelty items and balloons as well as greeting cards."

"Cindy's? So it wasn't a clue after all?"

"Right."

I drew in a breath. "What's going to happen to him now?"

"That depends on the lawyers." Michael stretched. "Guess we should start dinner."

We moved into the kitchen. Michael worked on the salad while I watched the pot of water work its way to a boil. "Do you believe him when he says he had nothing to do with Julie's death?" I asked.

"Hard to say. If he's telling the truth about what happened with Cindy Purcell, it's difficult to see why he'd go after another young woman, or why he'd try to scare Libby. But there are an uncanny number of similarities between the two murders."

"Could it be a copycat?"

"Could be. But the stuff about the skeleton wasn't ever made public. And don't forget that Melville knew both Julie and Libby."

"He knows Skye, too. Maybe she somehow found out and he broke into her house looking for the evidence she had."

"Maybe," Michael said with skepticism. "But things don't usually wrap up quite so tidily."

Libby came bounding through the front door just then and headed straight for the kitchen. "Is it true?" she asked Michael. "Was Mr. Melville arrested for murder?"

While he tore the lettuce into bite-sized pieces, Michael went through the whole story again, in abbreviated form, for Libby's benefit.

Over dinner we talked of other things, but it was a halfhearted attempt at normality. Michael was tired, I was thinking, and Libby was clearly upset. Even Anna was subdued.

When the phone rang after dinner, I picked it up. Silence greeted me on the other end. And after several seconds, a faint click.

"Who was it?" Michael asked.

I shook my head. "No one. Must have been the wrong number."

"That happened last night, too," Libby said. "Twice."

Michael and I exchanged glances. When we were alone, he said, "There's something I haven't had a chance to tell you."

"What's that?"

"The lock of hair Libby got in the mail—it's Julie's. The test results just came in this afternoon."

33

Tuesday, school was a buzz of rumor and gossip, some of it fairly outlandish. This despite the fact that the story of Marvin's arrest had run in the morning paper.

Because the morning was devoted to an all-school assembly, which was an attempt by Combs to allow students to "process the recent traumas," my art class didn't meet until after lunch. The students were pretty much talked out by then, so they drew silently. And the lesson for the day, a still-life sketch of bananas and apples, didn't do much to inspire conversation.

I was tidying up the room at the end of school when I discovered that Skye had left her math book in my classroom. I hurried down to the science lab to catch Yvonne, but she'd already left for the day.

When I got to my car, I dumped the math book on the back seat. I could ignore it and live with a guilty conscience (I knew there was a test the next day), or I could take it to her and feel deservedly peeved. I opted for peeved.

"You left your book in my classroom," I told her when she'd unfastened the chain and opened the door.

"Oh." Skye looked at the book and then at me. "Thanks."

"Is your mom here?"

"She had to run to the store. She should be back any minute." Skye tucked a strand of flyaway frizz behind her ear.

"Mind if I wait?" As long as I was already there, I figured I might as well talk about framing options for the lithograph she and Steve had purchased.

Skye shook her head. Her expression was tight, her coloring wan.

"Are you okay, Skye?"

"I'm fine."

I handed her the book and we moved to the rear of the house. She'd been unusually quiet during class, but then so had the others. Now I wondered if there wasn't something more troubling her.

"This has been a rough couple of weeks for you, hasn't it? A teacher arrested, a friend murdered."

She looked at me but didn't acknowledge the words.

"Are you worried that maybe there's some connection between those two events and the break-in at your house?"

Her eyes flickered to life. "That's absurd. Why would there be a connection?"

I shrugged. I didn't have an answer either.

"It's spooky, that's all. I mean, that it turned out to be someone I know." Skye bit her bottom lip. "You want a soda or something?"

"Sure, thanks."

She bolted for the kitchen. I heard the clatter of ice

cubes and glass. "It's diet," she said when she returned. She handed me a tumbler of cola.

"This stuff about Mr. Melville," I said sympathetically. "It's upsetting for all of us."

"Yeah. I guess."

The phone rang and Skye leapt to her feet, brushing awkwardly against the sofa table. Her math book and soda toppled to the floor.

Ignoring the phone, she raced for paper towels. I began picking up the ice cubes and loose math papers that had fallen from the book.

Math papers—and a pink slip of paper stamped CITY OF BERKELEY. A slip of paper similar to the one I'd been awarded for speeding.

"Looks like you got tagged by the Berkeley police too," I said.

I started to wipe it dry when the date and time on the citation caught my eye. October 13, 7:30 PM—the evening Julie was killed. Skye had been speeding on San Pablo Avenue.

"Did you go to Berkeley with Julie?" I asked.

Skye snatched the envelope from my hand. Her face was the color of waxed paper.

"Were you there that night? Do you know who Julie was meeting?"

I heard a car door slam out front. I glanced through the window and saw Yvonne hoisting a bag of groceries from the back seat of their dark green Cherokee. Like an unexpected punch in the chest, it hit me.

"You were the one who picked Julie up on San Pablo, weren't you?"

Yvonne came in through the side door and set the grocery sack on the counter. "Hi, Kate. I wasn't expecting you. Sorry I had to run out for a minute." She looked at the expression on Skye's face. "What's wrong? Was there another burglary?"

"Get out," Skye screamed, her cheeks suddenly flushed. I couldn't tell whether she was addressing me or her mother. Hysteria had taken hold and she looked at neither of us. "Just shut up and get out."

"Skye," Yvonne said sternly.

"She doesn't know what she's talking about," Skye said shrilly.

Yvonne tried again. "What is going on?"

"Skye was in Berkeley the Friday night Julie Harmon was killed," I explained. "It was Skye who picked Julie up on San Pablo." I turned to Skye. "Was it you who took her to Tilden Park?"

Skye's face froze in terror, like an animal caught in the lights of an oncoming car. "I had to," she said, in a voice so thin and high it sounded more like a yelp. "I had to. Julie would have ruined everything."

Yvonne's confusion gave way to horror. "Dear God, it's not true. Tell me Kate, tell me she didn't kill Julie." Yvonne looked at her daughter. "Tell me, Skye, tell me you didn't."

"I was going to have to share my house with her. My things. My, my family. She'd be his favorite, his real . . ." Her voice broke, "His real little girl."

Skye turned and ran for the stairs, charging up them like a frightened squirrel. We followed, several paces behind. She'd locked herself in the bathroom before we reached the top.

Yvonne pounded on the door. "Let me in, Skye. We need to talk. We'll talk about what to do."

From inside I heard the click of a cabinet, the groan of a drawer, and above all the sound of sobbing.

"You're not alone, honey. I love you and I'll help you." Yvonne pressed herself against the door, frantically jiggling the knob. The door remained locked.

"Skye?"

Nothing but the keening of hopeless despair. The sobs rose from low in her chest and caught unevenly in her throat.

"Honey, please open the door."

"Is there access from outside?" I asked.

"Just the window."

"Call 911."

"Skye? Honey?"

"Now," I barked.

I dashed into the master bedroom and looked sideways out the window toward the bathroom window to the right. About five feet below, where the first floor roof angled upward, was a narrow overhang. It would be a tight approach, but it was probably doable.

I opened the bedroom window and slipped through. The flat, stucco siding provided nothing for me to grab hold of. I held on to the exterior sill for as long as I could, then slowly inched toward the bathroom window, keeping my weight forward. As long as I didn't lose my balance, I'd be okay. As long as I could keep my eye on the window and not look down.

Finally, I reached around the drainpipe, caught hold of the window casing and pulled myself to it. The window was curtained and shut tight.

Inside, I could hear Yvonne, still pounding on the door. But nothing from inside the bathroom.

Flexing my knees, I lowered myself so that the gap at

the bottom of the curtain was eye level. Because of the reflection I had trouble seeing into the bathroom, but by shielding the light with my free hand, I was able to make out a form sprawled on the floor near the tub. I couldn't see Skye's face, but I didn't need to. The pool of blood near her wrists was enough.

"Skye!" I screamed her name and rapped hard on the window with my fist. Then I took off my shoe and rapped harder, beating at the glass until it shattered. Like shrapnel, small shards flew back and peppered my face and hands. My skin stung, and my right cheek felt as though it had been clawed by a tiger. But my mind had no room for pain.

I reached through the jagged frame and cranked the window open. Then I eased myself under and climbed through.

When I reached Skye she was unconscious, but breathing. I opened the bathroom door for Yvonne, then pressed towels hard against her wrists to stem the flow of blood.

In the distance I heard the wail of sirens. I hoped they made it in time.

34

I opened the door to a skeleton.

He was about three feet tall, with wisps of blond hair.

"Trick or treat," he said.

"Give us something good to eat," chimed the pirate at his side.

They both giggled.

Anna tugged at my shirt as I handed out the treats. "I thought you said it was too early, but *they're* going out already."

The day had been sunny, with an autumn breeze that sent leaves tumbling into colorful heaps. The evening brought with it added crispness, the pungent aroma of smoke, and a magnificent harvest moon. A picture-perfect Halloween.

But Anna was the only one of us in the holiday spirit.

"You can go out in a bit," I told her. "Libby's not even home yet."

"But what if everyone runs out of candy before I get there?"

"They won't." I gave Anna a hug, which she endured impatiently, and then I watched as she trotted off to admire the cookies she'd decorated that afternoon at school.

What I wanted, really, was to hug her tight and never let go. To build a cocoon where the world was forever safe and happy. What I wanted was to wipe from my mind the layers of sorrow that had built over the past few weeks.

When Michael arrived home not long after I gave him the heartfelt hug I'd longed to give Anna. I nestled against his chest and took comfort in the familiar curves and textures of his embrace.

"You'd think I'd be happy to have these murders solved," I told him. "Instead, I feel sad and empty, like there's a gray cloud over everything."

He stroked the back of my head. "I know, sweetheart. But it isn't often that life wraps up the way we want it to."

"But the way it turned out is awful. I feel so sorry for Yvonne and Steve."

He nodded. "It has certainly got to be high on the list of every parent's nightmare."

Yesterday I'd stopped by Yvonne's to drop off a meal and see if there was anything I could do. It was a brief, uncomfortable visit, weighted with tears and a stiff formality. Skye would live, Yvonne informed me. She was under suicide watch in a locked facility. Beyond that, was anyone's guess.

She'd thanked me for reaching Skye in time. And she didn't blame me, she said, for uncovering the truth. But she'd rather I didn't visit again. Not for a while anyway. It was simply too painful.

"I hear that Steve Burton is really beside himself,"

Michael said, tossing his jacket on the living room sofa. "His daughter, dead. His stepdaughter, a killer. His gun, the murder weapon. And as I understand it, rivalry over his affections was what was at the heart of it all."

We moved into the kitchen. "You found the gun?" I asked.

Michael nodded. "When Skye read Susie Sullivan's article and realized the police weren't convinced it was a serial killer, she panicked. She figured that if we were looking into Julie's recent activities, we'd eventually discover her relationship to Steve. And she knew that if we searched their house, we'd find the gun. But she couldn't just get rid of it or Steve would notice. So she staged the burglary. The problem was, she hadn't yet had time to dispose of it."

I was still having trouble believing Skye had committed murder. Not only committed, but planned it. "Did you talk to her today? How is she?"

"Like the walking dead. It's as though she's withdrawn from the world. It may be the medicine they have her on. Or maybe she's finally faced up to what she did. I talked to the doctor briefly. He says it's too early to tell what her mental state really is."

"But she admitted killing Julie?"

Another nod. "She was behind the doll shoes and lock of hair Libby got, as well."

"What about the skeleton in our mailbox?" I asked.

"That, too."

I took the glass of wine Michael had poured. "But why? What did she have against Libby?"

"It wasn't Libby. Skye wanted us, the detectives on the case, to stay focused on the idea of a serial killer. She thought it would help cover her tracks."

"You mean if you were looking for a serial killer, you wouldn't look at anyone who was a friend?"

"Right. Skye didn't even know Cindy Purcell. But the case was big news. Skye saw it as an opportunity. One she seized and ran with. She was in a good position to do so, too. Skye knew things about the case that weren't public, like the skeleton found by the body and the painted toenails."

"How?" I asked. And then my heart sank. "Was it something I said?"

"It might have been. Or Libby. But Steve Burton also knew the details of the case. He has close ties with the DA's office, and he was the judge who issued the first search warrant on the case. Besides, we hadn't necessarily tried to keep the information confidential."

I felt the wash of guilt anyway. I dropped down into the chair nearest the counter. "Me and my big mouth."

"Kate, don't go around beating yourself up over it. You were the one who figured it out, after all."

His words were kind, but I took little comfort. The whole situation left me with an odd assortment of emotions, none of them pleasant.

"About the only people who might conceivably feel good about any of this," I said, "are the Shepherds. Julie's killer has been found, they're no longer burdened with her presence, and they've come out well financially."

"Not so," Michael said. "At least the financial part. I think Walton Shepherd was probably skimming off some of Julie's trust money while she was alive, which is how he hoped to finance his gun shop. But now that she's dead, the money goes to charity. That's why he pulled out of the deal."

Our conversation was cut short because Libby and

Brian came in then. Both had black noses, painted whisk-ers, floppy felt ears, and tails.

"Hi, Kate," Libby said, dragging an obviously reluctant Brian. "You think Max would mind if we borrowed a few of his dog bones?"

"I feel like a fool," Brian grumbled.

"Well, you look like a dog. Sort of." Libby adjusted one of his furry brown ears. "It would have been better if you'd agreed to be the hind end. We'd look more like a dog in tandem."

"Not better for me."

It was nice to see Libby in a lighthearted mood for a change. It had been a difficult couple of weeks. And Skye's guilt had hit her almost as hard as Julie's death.

"Well, we can't take Anna out if we're not in the spirit of things," she said. "It isn't fair."

At that moment, Anna appeared.

After a moment's silence, Michael and I spoke in uni-son. "What are you supposed to be?"

"Can't you tell?" she asked with an air that was defi-nitely regal.

But a princess she was not. Not in my book, anyway.

Anna was wearing the gold taffeta dress Faye had made, along with the black cape and a wicked looking set of vampire teeth. Her mouth was bright pink, her hair dripped silver glitter, and she had a tattoo (one of Libby's press-on ones, I hoped) on her cheek. On her feet she wore a pair of black high-top sneakers, and around her neck, Max's studded dog collar.

She beamed pleasure.

I swallowed. "A vampire princess," I said at last, hoping my tone sounded more blithe than critical. My daughter looked as though she belonged on the album cover of a punk rock band.

"The Princess Vampire," Anna corrected. "There's a difference." She looked to Libby. "Right?"

Libby nodded solemnly. "Absolutely."

"Well, I guess we'd better get a picture for Grandma," I said. Although I wasn't at all sure I'd have the nerve to send it.

"She wanted to wear both the dress and the cape," Libby explained when Anna went to get her candy bag.

"Did she need all the other stuff as well?"

Libby crossed her arms. "She didn't want to be a plain old vampire princess."

"What do you mean 'a plain old—' "

"Especially," Libby added, "since you'd been the one to suggest it."

When they'd gone, Michael shook his head and burst out laughing. "The funny thing is, she looked cute as a button in that getup."

"Maybe she's on to something. Princess and vampire. The yin and yang of life. It's the balance that's essential."

"Do you think Faye will understand?"

"She just might. Speaking of which, we got a nice note from her."

"We?"

"I think you really wowed her with your charm."

"Hey, I'm a charming guy."

I wrapped my arms around him. "Yes," I said, "you are."